Murder on the Toy Town Express

Also by Barbara Early

Vintage Toyshop Mysteries

Death of a Toy Soldier

**Bridal Bouquet Shop Mysteries
(writing as Beverly Allen)**

Floral Depravity

For Whom the Bluebell Tolls

Bloom and Doom

Murder on the Toy Town Express

A Vintage Toyshop Mystery

Barbara Early

CROOKED
LANE

NEW YORK

Copyright © 2017 by Barbara Early

Published in the United States by Crooked Lane Books, an imprint of The Quick Brown Fox & Company LLC.

Crooked Lane Books and its logo are trademarks of The Quick Brown Fox & Company LLC.

Library of Congress Catalog-in-Publication data available upon request.

ISBN (hardcover): 978-1-68331-309-0
ISBN (ePub): 978-1-68331-310-6
ISBN (ePDF): 978-1-68331-312-0

Cover illustration by Hiro Kimura
Book design by Jennifer Canzone

Printed in the United States.

www.crookedlanebooks.com

Crooked Lane Books
34 West 27th St., 10th Floor
New York, NY 10001

First edition: October 2017

10 9 8 7 6 5 4 3 2 1

Dedicated to the parents, teachers, librarians, and booksellers who spend their hours getting good books into the arms (and minds) of children. You are changing the world!

Chapter 1

"I swear the My Little Ponies reproduce when we're not looking." I stretched my back and glanced around the toyshop. After four hours of carefully weeding out inventory and loading it into our cars, our shelves still looked fully stocked.

"Naughty little ponies," said Cathy, my sister-in-law and our self-appointed doll czar. "Too bad they don't, Liz. What a cost-effective way of increasing inventory." She blew out a breath that ruffled her bangs. "Why is it so hot in here?" she asked loudly, looking over to where my father was sorting through our selection of train engines and cars.

This November had brought unseasonably warm temperatures, and heat rippled from the brick street as bright sunlight beat through the display windows of Well Played. Our vintage toyshop felt like it could be in Florida instead of Western New York, especially at a time of year when we're accustomed to seeing snow swirling in the streets.

"Fine," Dad said, mopping his own sweaty brow. "Turn on the air. Let's just hope we make enough at the toy show to pay for it." My father, Hank McCall, had always talked about starting a toyshop when he retired as East Aurora's chief of police. When that retirement came earlier than expected, courtesy of a bullet wound and the lengthy recovery that followed, he'd made good on that threat. After several lean years, we were almost solvent.

Cathy was at the thermostat like a shot, and soon cool air blasted around the shop. She stood directly under a vent and threw her head back, letting the coolness fall down on her as if she were taking a shower.

Othello, the tuxedo cat who shared our shop and apartment above it, was the only one who didn't appreciate the drop in temperature. He hopped down from the wall-mounted train tracks, sent Cathy a sour look, then curled up in a sunny spot in the window next to the stuffed Scottie dog pull toy that had become his best friend.

I found my own comfortable spot by the board games—I'm a self-proclaimed board-game junkie—and continued loading a selection into a large cardboard box, choosing a couple of the rarer titles that savvy collectors might be looking for—The Addams Family Card Game and The Beatles: Flip Your Wig game, a recently found gem from 1964. I augmented these with all the classic favorites such as vintage Candy Land and Life.

"How about we take the Santa?" Dad said, holding up the box innocently marked "Happy Santa, With Lighted Eyes." Dad had picked up the toy—a battery-operated Santa sitting at a drum set—at an estate sale he'd attended without me. It was made in postwar occupied Japan, when factories that once turned out guns and bombs and planes were retooled for more peaceful purposes, like cheesy holiday decorations. This little guy was adorable . . . at least until you turned it on.

"You know people will be thinking Christmas," he said.

"It's not even Thanksgiving yet," Cathy whined.

"Besides," I said, "that thing is seriously creepy. You can't tell me those red eyes are original." Light up that thing in a dark room, and it'd make Krampus look like Lamb Chop.

"Maybe," Dad said, "but if we sell it at the show, you won't have to look at it anymore."

"Bring it!" I said.

The annual train and toy show—and sale—had moved to a conference center only a stone's throw from the shop this year, and we crossed our fingers that the onslaught of collectors heading into our territory would be good for business.

Cathy sealed up a box and brought me a piece of paper. "Here, I made a list of the dolls I packed. I color-coded everything to match the color of the dress so you don't have to look them in the eye, since I know dolls aren't your thing." An understatement. I'd been assured pediophobia, fear of dolls, was fairly common, but it was certainly a drawback when you worked with toys all day. Barbies were okay, but those creepy, old porcelain dolls with eyelids half-open and those chipped smiling faces . . . I was thankful for Cathy's willingness to work the doll room.

I looked at the page. "What are all these numbers?"

Her zebra-print manicured fingernail pointed to the top row of figures. "This is the first price you give them when they ask the cost—that is, if you like an occasional steak. Maybe not filet, but a nice sirloin now and then. The one underneath it will get you a good burger at most places in town. The third? That's living on ramen."

"And the fourth?"

"It's what we paid for it. Make a habit of selling at cost, Mother Hubbard, and you'll quickly lose those twenty pounds."

"Gotcha. You're sure you'll be okay running the shop all by yourself?"

Cathy rolled her eyes. "It's only for the weekend. It's not like you'll be in Spain or anything. I'll call you or Dad if something comes up."

"Spain might be easier. The food's certainly better. Cell reception at the conference center is a little spotty, and it's so loud you can't always hear the phone."

"Stop worrying! It's a toyshop, after all. What could happen?"

I squinted at her. Truth was, bad things could happen in a toyshop.

Cathy caught my meaning, and her expression sobered. "I have the police on speed dial." She paused and bit her lip. "Which reminds me, what should I do if one of the men in your life stops by and asks for you?"

"The men in my life? You make me sound like some debutante, with guys throwing themselves at my feet."

"Hey, there are two eligible bachelors expressing interest . . . and let's face it, you're not getting any younger. It might be time to stop hitting the snooze button on that biological clock."

"Well, none of us are getting any younger," I hedged. I was often guilty of saying that I wasn't ready to settle down.

That wasn't exactly true. I could certainly see myself establishing my own home, maybe having a couple of kids while biology still allowed—not that I was unhappy or in a panic to make a change. I'd seen enough of bad relationships to know that I'd only want to pull that matrimonial trigger if I was sure of the proper partner. Maybe it's because it's impossible to be 100 percent sure of anyone that I hadn't been willing to narrow the field. Or maybe it was because I had genuine affection for both Ken and Jack that I didn't want to lose either from my life. Whatever the reason, I'd been avoiding what should be an inevitable decision. Maybe "snooze button" was an apt analogy.

Dad came up behind Cathy and put his arm around her shoulder. "If I'm hearing talk of grandchildren, I should remind you that you and Parker have a head start. I'm still waiting for news on that front."

Her cheeks colored. "As soon as I have news to share, I'll let you know."

That seemed to satisfy Dad, who went back to his trains, but something in the way she phrased her answer made me study her face. In a moment of telepathy more befitting sisters than sisters-in-law, I knew. My jaw dropped, and I wanted to rush over and hug her.

She put a finger to her lips, checked that Dad was still distracted with his trains, then mouthed, "Parker doesn't know."

I spun toward the front of the store so Dad wouldn't be able to see my broad smile. It'd be nice to have kids running around the shop one day.

Cathy cleared her throat. "About Ken and Jack?"

"We're just friends." Again, my phrasing wasn't *quite* accurate. But since I was still seeing both—occasionally and nonexclusively—neither one could really be considered a boyfriend. So *friends* it was. And no benefits involved, except for maybe a little hand-holding and an occasional kiss.

"Still, you're dating. More exciting than my life, which consists mainly of cleaning animal dung off of Parker's trouser cuffs." She winked at me. "Good thing I have my writing to sustain me."

Cathy had switched from her first love of poetry and claimed to be writing a novel inspired by a murder that occurred in our shop last year—when a man who'd come for an estimate on a box of old toys was found dead in aisle three, impaled by a lawn dart. My father was briefly a suspect, and the whispers, especially in a town as small as East Aurora, nearly sounded the death knell for our business. That string of events, during which Dad did his best to embroil both of us in solving the case, was enough excitement to last me for a lifetime. Cathy's fictional version was a little more embellished, containing spear guns, spies, bikinis, an occasional zombie, and a whole lot of steamy embraces. She insisted readers would need something spicier.

I wagged a finger at her. "And don't go trying to spice up my love life, either. If Jack or Ken stop by, just tell them I'm at the train show."

"Okay." But her eyes lit up like a Lite-Brite.

"Cathy?" I warned.

She held a hand up. "I promise. If they stop by, I'll tell them you're at the train show. But I never said *how* I'd tell them. Look, have you considered that it's not fair to string both of them along?"

"Someone's not listening. I just said we were friends. Last time I checked, people were allowed to have more than one friend."

"Sometimes friends become more."

I eyed her warily.

"Sometimes they need a little push." She sent me an impish look.

Spain was sounding better by the minute.

# # #

Dad and I were on our own at the conference center the next morning. I sipped my coffee and stared at the mountains of boxes piled in our trunks. Somehow we needed to get all that stuff from the cars to our designated tables, unpack, and then try to attractively arrange our inventory. We needed either twelve more people or way more caffeine.

Dad was looking chipper, though, barely using his cane today. "How about we each grab one small box and check out our space?"

I tucked a small selection of loose board games under my arm, and we made our way into the center. The voices of vendors setting up their tables and booths already echoed from the high ceilings. We showed our passes to a harried-looking conference worker who was trying to arrange a table outside the main doors. Then we waved or stopped to exchange brief pleasantries with a few familiar vendors while we looked for tables thirty-two and thirty-three.

After traversing an aisle or two, we figured out the theme. The toys and other items were arranged along the outskirts, with the large displays of tracks and tiny buildings—or lay-outs, as Dad said they were properly called—clustered in the center of the conference space. We even passed a full-size Santa's Village, decorated in glittery snow and capped with a plush, but now empty, red velvet throne. Barrels were set up for toy donations to go to deserving kids. A sign speci-fied new toys; otherwise, that demon-eyed Santa might have "accidentally" ended up in one of the barrels. A table next to the village conveniently sold new toys for that purpose.

We finally found our spot near a corner, right next to a booth that already sported a banner from another familiar East Aurora business: Craig's Comics.

I swallowed hard. It was going to be a long two days.

One might think that a toyshop and a comic store in the same small town would get along. Only a small selection of our inventory competed with theirs—namely, superhero and other action figures. But it wasn't the competition that was the problem.

It was Craig.

Craig, who in kindergarten dumped my full carton of chocolate milk down the front of my favorite dress. We let that one pass. Accidents happen.

Craig, who in the third grade decided he preferred my lunch to his own. Repeatedly. Until I finally fessed up to Dad about what was happening, and he had a talk with Craig's foster family.

Craig, who in the fifth grade flipped my science project into a mud puddle and shook my report folder until all my neatly handwritten pages—well, maybe not so neat, but I tried hard—fell out and blew away in the wind. Dad had a talk with his new foster family.

And Craig, who in the eighth grade decided to see if I could fit in my locker. I couldn't but ended up with broken glasses, three cut and sprained fingers, and assorted bruises all over my body from the attempt. Follow this up with the humiliation I felt when Dad insisted every single bruise needed to be photographed. Shortly after, Craig disappeared, rumored to be in some juvie facility.

I didn't see him again until I ran into him several years ago at the grocery store after I'd moved home to East Aurora. I barely recognized the pudgy man in the too-small light-gray sweats, but he certainly knew me. While the fat on the rest of his body jiggled—tight sweats were not this man's friend—his face was hard and his eyes cold. He said nothing but glared at me. It unnerved me so much I ended up putting four boxes of Cocoa Puffs into my cart. And I'm not all that cuckoo for Cocoa Puffs. I'm more of a Froot Loops kind of girl.

We never figured out what the man had been doing all these years, but Dad got one of his friends on the force to check for prior offences. Nothing—not as much as a parking violation—came up, so apparently he'd changed his ways. Still, that glare warned me to keep my distance, and Dad promised to keep his eyes open as well. We watched as the former bully joined the chamber of commerce and, embarrassing to admit, had a slightly better rating on Yelp than we did. Maybe I needed to give him a chance to prove he'd changed.

This new close proximity might allow, or rather force, that to happen.

Or maybe not. Because he was nowhere to be seen, unless he'd shown up in drag. His tables were being organized by a rather portly older woman with graying curly hair and glasses. Unlike Craig, she had a friendly smile. She waved as we approached.

"Howdy, neighbor," she said, holding out a hand. "Name's Maxine."

"Liz McCall," I said. "And my father, Hank."

She shook his hand. "Looks like it's going to be a great little show, huh?"

"Not much little about it," I said, eying the venue. There had to be at least an acre of trains, toys, and collectibles, not to mention the ubiquitous but seemingly unrelated direct sales items—jewelry, tools, and household cleaners—that always seem to find a spot at a show of any kind.

She laughed. "Just a figure of speech. I'd help you unload if I could, but I still have more to set up. Feel free to use our cart, though." She pushed over a gray industrial cart.

"Oh, I like you," I said. "That would be fantastic."

And it was fantastic, at least for the first three trips. But on the last one, I heard shouting as we neared the table. Maxine was being harassed by a large man wearing a yellow cape with red and orange flames appliquéd to the bottom. When he turned around, it was even worse. I immediately recognized Craig's hard face under that bright-orange cowl. I tried hard not to look any lower. Ninety-nine percent of American men can't pull off spandex and tights, and Craig certainly was no exception. The fake six-pack sat above his natural keg, making him puffy all over. I'd never seen anything like it, and if I lived right, I'd hoped to never see anything like it again.

"Finally!" He said it with so much force I took a step backward. "I need our cart." Without allowing us time to unload, he started pulling off our items and flinging them onto our table. Both Dad and I had to hustle to unload to minimize any potential damage. Dad went for the antique tin toys on the bottom, while I rescued Cathy's box of fragile dolls.

Once everything was off the cart, he took off without another word, his cape waving in his wake.

Maxine bustled over. "I apologize for that. Craig's a good kid, but sometimes he's just so focused that he forgets his manners."

I nodded, mainly for her benefit, not because I believed her excuse.

Dad stepped up. "How long have you known Craig?"

"Since I started working for him three years ago."

"He can't be an easy man to work for," I said, noticing he'd stopped the cart a few rows down to chat with another vendor. Somehow, he didn't seem to be in such a hurry anymore.

"He's okay once you get to know his moods," she said, following my gaze. Her smile drooped a little. "And I like the work. At first I thought I was daft to apply for a job in a comic book store. I mean, what did I know about them? And Craig was probably just as daft to hire me, but they're more interesting than I thought. Soon I was reading them on my breaks and borrowing them to take home. Anything that can get teen and preteen boys to read can't be all bad, right?"

All I could think was, *That poor woman.* But since that was inappropriate to say aloud, I didn't.

"I think of all those boys who hang around the shop as my own." She looked down at the stack of comic books still in her hand. "Sounds silly, I bet."

"No," I said. "I'm sure they all appreciate you." My next slightly snarky thought was that Craig probably didn't, but I felt guilty for jumping to that conclusion. I was determined to do my best to extend the proverbial olive branch, even if I still thought the hulking boy I knew from school was a total jerk-face and would probably grab the branch out of my hand and end up hitting me with it.

But Maxine seemed nice, so when she struggled to unroll some of her signage, I rushed over to help. Once the balky banner was set up, I found myself staring at a full-size image of Lexi Wolf.

"Are you selling this?" It might make me a nerd or a geek, but I was a major fan of Commander Lexi Wolf. *Earthship Feronia* only ran for six episodes (fewer even than *Firefly*), but I'd seen each of them about twenty times when I was in college, and at least once a year since. I could picture this banner in my bedroom—as long as nobody knew about it.

"No, sorry," she said. "Well, maybe after the show. Right now it's just advertisement. She'll be here at ten."

"Lexi Wolf is coming *here*?" I tried to keep my voice cool as Maxine nodded. After all, it was probably just some look-alike cosplaying as Lexi Wolf. The real actress, Tippi Hillman, was likely wowing the crowds at Comic-Con somewhere.

"Who is Craig dressed up as, anyway?" Dad asked. "I thought I was up to date on all my superheroes, but I don't recognize the costume."

Maxine's lips drew into a mischievous smile. "You can't guess?"

Dad turned to me. "Have you seen it before?"

"You know more about superheroes than I do," I said.

"The old ones, maybe," he said. "But you get out to the movies more than I do, with your fellas."

"Fellas?" Maxine asked, her emphasis on the plural.

I punched him playfully in the shoulder. "Quit making me sound like a flirt. They're friends."

"Oh, so you're not engaged or steady with anyone?" Maxine asked.

I shook my head and was momentarily confused when Dad sent me a warning look.

"You know, Craig *is* on the market," Maxine said airily.

"Oh, I . . . uh . . . I should probably make up my mind soon," I said, spewing Cathy's words. "It's not right to string two men along. Besides, I'm not getting any younger."

Dad came to my rescue yet again. "So, what superhero is he?"

"That," Maxine said, "is Mr. Inferno."

No hint of recognition lit Dad's face, and I'd never heard of him either. "Is he new?" I asked.

She nodded.

"What universe?" Dad asked. "DC? Marvel?"

She shook her head, then ran an imaginary zipper across her lips. "Be around at ten for the big announcement, and you'll learn everything!"

Chapter 2

Dad checked his watch. "Since the public won't be in for another half hour, how about I look at the trains?" He wasn't exactly asking permission, because he was already walking toward the train layouts as if hypnotized.

I smiled, my natural expression when gritting my teeth. "How about I go with you?" Allowing Dad to roam these aisles freely could very well put us on the fast track—no pun intended—to bankruptcy.

The model trains were already chugging away. Some put out little puffs of smoke. Others clanged and blew whistles. They pulled coal cars, sleeper cars, diners, and cabooses through tunnels, across bridges, and past stations and towns and farm dwellings, some with fine details, moving parts, internal lights, and tiny people in various tableaus, all to scale and all for sale. We'd come out better if someone picked Dad's pocket right now.

"Well, well, well, if it isn't my old chief."

Dad spun around slowly. I didn't recognize the man in the stiffly pressed security guard uniform, but Dad did. I could see it in my father's polite but not-quite-genuine smile.

"Lionel," Dad said, offering a tentative hand. "I didn't know you were working here."

The guard looked at Dad's hand for a moment, as if he were considering not shaking it, but then took it briefly. "Head of security," he said. "Been working here since . . . but that's water under the bridge. No hard feelings."

Dad nodded, his solemn expression telling me something serious had gone down between these two. He didn't introduce me, but the guard's full name was on his badge: Lionel Kelley.

"I actually like this kind of work," he said. "The hours are great, and there's something different all the time coming through here. One week it's livestock. The next, gardening. The gem, fossil, and mineral show was a real hoot. Rock on!"

I couldn't tell if he was being sarcastic, but Dad seemed to take him at face value. His expression became less pained and his smile more genuine. "Good to hear it."

"This is the first time we've had the train and toy show." He stuck his thumbs in his belt. "I'd like to think our ramped-up security proposal had something to do with it. Can't be too careful these days."

"Scary times," Dad said.

"Speaking of which," Kelley said, gesturing to the cavernous space, "I should get back to checking the vendors before we open the doors. I take it all your tax info is in order. Nothing . . . illegal . . . in your inventory?" He stressed the last question, probably referring to that unfortunate lawn dart incident.

"Nope. We're good to go," Dad said.

"Good," Kelley said. "I wish that was the case with all the vendors. I'll be back to double-check with you, but I think we both know who our troublemakers are going to be this year." He gave a nod in the direction of Craig's Comics. "Don't worry. I got it under control."

As he walked away, Dad took my arm. "Somehow that doesn't fill me with confidence."

"Who was that?" I asked.

"He was briefly in my employ, right after he graduated from the police academy."

"I'm afraid to ask why you parted company."

Dad wiped his mouth with the back of his hand, one of his favorite stalling tactics. I'd seen it often when growing up, whenever I'd asked for an advance on my allowance or an extension on curfew.

"That bad?"

"Lionel was a nice enough young man. Took his job seriously. Was responsible to a fault. He just tended to be a bit . . . overly exuberant, that's all."

"Out to save the world, was he?"

"And by the book," Dad said. "Every page he could muster, even the parts that were contradictory or obsolete. No common sense required. I don't think a day went by without a complaint about him."

I glanced over to Craig's Comics, where Lionel was thumbing through their selection. "Any chance he mellowed out over time? See, he's just looking at the comics."

While Dad hesitated to answer, Lionel pulled out a comic book and thrust it up to show Maxine. I couldn't hear what they were saying, but the discussion appeared heated, with

Lionel gesturing forcefully to the book and Maxine's cheeks flaring pink.

While they were talking, Craig swooped in on the conversation. Lionel took a step back, maybe recoiling from the look of Craig's costume or perhaps the volume of Craig's words, which I could hear. The background noise had subsided a bit since many nearby had stopped talking and were also watching the argument.

"That's absurd." Craig paced like a lawyer making his case, except with that cape swirling behind him. "Has anyone complained? Who would have a problem with that?" He may have included an expletive or two in the diatribe that followed, thrown among terms like "First Amendment" and "censorship."

"Just fix it." Lionel tossed the book to Maxine and turned on his heels. The look on his face as he walked away wasn't one of anger, but smugness.

Craig's red face and flashing eyes suggested he had surpassed anger and bordered on wrath. He exercised his First Amendment rights once again to send an epithet or two in Lionel's direction, then stormed off.

Maxine looked ready to break. I rushed over.

"What happened?" I asked.

"Let me catch my breath first." Maxine put a hand on her chest and forced a few breaths in and out. "That's never happened before. Apparently some of our stock violates some old decency law, which is weird because we've sold the same things in the shop all the time and never had a problem. Why would it be legal there and not here?" She held up the comic Lionel had tossed out. It showed quite a bit of cleavage, midriff, and thigh of a busty female superhero. The outfit wasn't something I would wear, even to a costume party, but I wasn't sure I'd consider it pornographic, either.

Maxine looked at her fully stocked table. "Now we have to pull out any 'similar images' before I can open. I'd hate to know how many of them there are." She blanched and pointed.

I trailed her gaze to the Lexi Wolf banner.

"What are we going to do about that?"

The banner was positioned to get attention from the aisle, and Kelley probably hadn't seen it at all. "Well, he didn't mention it directly . . ." I hedged. After all, the buxom commander of the *Earthship Feronia*, with those fishnet stockings and absurd cleavage peeking from the leather corset, was perhaps the epitome of what Lionel Kelley was just raving about. "How long is she going to be here?"

"Just an hour. Shaking hands and signing pictures and comic books." She pulled out one of the tie-in comics with Lexi on the cover. "I don't know if we have any *Earthship Feronia* without Lexi on the cover." She chewed a cuticle. "Maybe we could brown-bag them like the convenience stores do to *Playboy*."

"I don't know about that, but . . ." Since the banner was adjustable, I rolled up part of the poster, leaving only Lexi's shoulders and that amazing head of curls exposed.

Maxine raised thankful hands to the heavens. "That's a start!"

"I can give you a hand sorting through the books too." I bent over a stack of comics and started pulling out all the busty superheroes—and villains and victims—I could find, about one in every three or four of their books in stock. Dad joined in, and we placed all the "offending" comics in the boxes stored under the table skirt. We'd gone through all but the last two bins when the doors opened.

Maxine lifted the remaining displays off the table—strong woman—and shoved them underneath. "I'll go through them during the lulls," she said. "Thanks so much for all your help!"

Dad and I went back to our booth. With the doors open, the sound of the crowd still waiting for tickets was a roar, amplified by the hard floors and walls and high ceilings. But the show started with a whimper rather than a bang, since even preticketed attendees all had to show their tickets and get their hands stamped upon entering. As the public trickled in, they made their way first to the large central train layouts, which would soon be so congested that only the persistent and the extremely tall would be able to see. Only when they were three deep would we likely see a customer.

"Mind if I grab a coffee," I asked Dad, "before it gets busy?"

"Get me one?"

"You got it." I pulled a few bills from my purse and made my way, against traffic, toward the concessions area. I didn't get that far.

"Liz!" Jack Wallace headed straight toward me. He was dressed casually in jeans and a crisp navy polo, visible under his open jacket.

"Hey, Jack. What are you doing here?"

"I stopped by the shop, and Cathy told me about the show. I decided to check it out."

Interesting, since I'd mentioned the show to him. And it stuck in my craw, just a little, that he hadn't remembered. Not that I was sure what a craw was or where one might find one in the human anatomy.

"We got trains and we got toys. What's your poison?" I'd known Jack since high school, and I can't say I'd ever seen him obsessing over either. Except for that unfortunate hacky sack fad.

"Well, we could look at comic books," he said. "If anyone here has them."

"We?"

He glanced toward the men's room, where another man, bearing more than a little resemblance to Jack, was heading in our direction.

Jack and his older brother could've been twins. But where Jack's expression was congenial and he looked a bit outdoorsy—even though he barely got a chance to venture out of his restaurant—his brother's face was harder and his complexion paler. Then again, I've heard that prison can do that to a man.

I smiled and offered my hand as he approached. "Terry. Good to see you."

He took my hand but pumped it weakly. "Good to be seen."

"Liz was just saying there are comics here too," Jack said.

"Right next to our booth." I glanced at the growing concession line. "I was about to grab a coffee. Care to walk with me?"

"Sounds good." Jack shrugged off his light jacket and tucked it under his arm. "They're going to have to turn on the air today, I think."

"I hope," Terry said, falling in behind us.

"Maybe we could all grab dinner after you're done for the day," Jack said.

"Uh, the show closes at six, and I have a feeling I'm going to be dead on my feet by then."

"Bite of lunch, then?"

"Lunch is our busiest time. I couldn't leave Dad alone. We usually just grab fries or something during the lulls."

"Well, if you don't have time for me . . ." Jack stuck out his lip like a four-year-old who just missed the ice-cream truck. A little annoying, but there was something endearing about it at the same time. I wiped the phony pout away with a brief kiss.

"Get a room, people," Terry said.

When Jack glared at him, Terry just put his hands up. "Or get me a girl too. I'd be happy either way. Just don't want to be a fifth wheel here."

"This looks like a great show," Jack said as we joined the end of the queue of the concession stand. "I'm surprised you didn't mention it."

"I did. If I recall correctly, you responded by telling me you thought you needed a new seafood distributor."

He stuck his hands in his pockets. "I guess I've been a little distracted lately. That new seafood restaurant that's opening next week is getting great press."

"The reporter from the *Advertiser* apparently likes those sea bugs," Terry said, scrunching his nose.

"Sea bugs?" I asked.

"They're putting in a three-hundred-gallon lobster tank," Jack explained, "right near the entrance, so people can pick their own lobster while they're waiting for a table. It could really eat into my business. Now that Mom retired to Florida and the restaurant is solely under my management . . ."

Terry let out a loud, staged sigh.

"Well, Terry's helping, of course," Jack said.

"I have the crucial job of bussing tables," Terry deadpanned.

"It's where *I* started," Jack said.

"When you were sixteen," Terry said.

"Part of me wishes I were still bussing tables," Jack said, flashing his best disarming smile. "Now, all the bucks get passed to me. I only wish that meant dollars. I had to turn my cell phone off to ensure I wouldn't get called in. First time in three weeks."

"Trust me. I know about the challenges of running your own business." I shrugged. I may have been a bit distracted myself. I remembered Jack saying something about Terry returning to East Aurora when he came up for parole again, but I hadn't thought it would be this soon. Since Terry had already been sent back for parole violations once, for failure to check in, Jack had encouraged his brother to move to the village where he'd have more support.

"Just enjoy the day, you two," I said. "There's a lot to see, and if you're around during a lull, maybe we can grab a sandwich or something." I reached up to straighten Jack's collar.

As I did, Terry sighed, then the people behind us in line got frustrated with the snail's pace and left. Maxine moved up.

"How did you get sprung?" I asked, then introduced her to Jack and Terry.

"A lot of people are stopping to talk to Craig—excuse me, *Mr. Inferno*. He's already hoarse, so I said I'd pick him up something to drink." Her face brightened. "I got a peek at your tables on the way over—you have some lovely things. Not that glowy Santa, though. That looks like a bad Christmas Eve over Chernobyl." She leaned toward me. "I think you underpriced the 1986 Plastic Man. You could get double for it, especially mint in box like that."

"Double?" I'd thought it was pretty pricy to begin with. "I'll let Dad know."

"And if someone else should get there first?" Terry asked. "Like maybe a lowly busboy looking for a discount?"

"Terry . . ." Jack warned.

I chuckled. "The lowly busboy can have it at the price it's marked. It's still fair, and, frankly, that long-necked freak gives me the willies. I wouldn't mind taking a loss if that meant it went away." I faced Maxine. "I guess you know the superhero figures from working in the comic shop."

She pulled several folded bills from her apron. "We sell a few. Mainly the memorabilia just brightens the place up a bit. I imagine it must be fun to work with toys all the time."

I inched forward in line. "Some days more than others. If you're ever looking to pick up a few hours here and there . . . not that I'm trying to steal you away from Craig or anything. I just meant near the holidays or whatever." Yeah, smooth. But from what I'd seen, she was a loyal and diligent worker, and Craig treated her like garbage, so why not?

"Funny you should mention that," she said. "I could use a little more money around Christmas. Not that I have a lot of people to buy for, but utility bills are higher."

By this time we were at the front of the line, so I placed my order for Dad and myself. Jack added his and Terry's and

BARBARA EARLY

then paid for all of them. Maxine was waited on by a different clerk at the counter, and we ended up finishing about the same time.

"Here," I said to Maxine, setting my drinks down on a tall pedestal table a few feet from the counter. "Let me give you my card now. Call me after the show is over. We can arrange a time for you to come in, learn your way around the place, sign papers and all that."

Maxine looked around briefly, as if she were afraid of being spotted in cahoots with the enemy, but then she set her cups down and shoved the card in her apron pocket. "Thanks. You'll be hearing from me."

"Well, hey!" The new greeting startled Maxine, but it wasn't Craig spying on her. Ken Young, dressed very much like a civilian and not the current chief of police, sauntered up to the table.

"Looks like everyone has a day off today," I said.

Ken eyed Jack. The two were friends, of a sort, but that friendship was strained a little by the fact that I was casually seeing both of them. Moments like this could feel a tad awkward.

After they shook hands, Jack gestured to Terry. "Have you met my brother?"

Ken reached over to shake Terry's hand. "I don't think we've met, but you seem familiar."

"Give it time," Terry said. "It'll come to you."

As Ken stepped back, he jarred the table with an errant elbow. It wobbled, and a couple of cups tipped, and we rushed to right them. Only a few drops escaped through the lids, so crisis averted.

26

"I should get back," Maxine said, shaking a few drops of coffee from her hands before rushing off.

While Jack went to retrieve napkins, I asked Ken, "What brings you here?"

"You mentioned the show. It sounded like fun."

Only he didn't meet my eyes. Funny how a police chief trained in interrogation, in detecting those minute facial expressions that give away lies, could be so lousy when on the other end. He was trying to hide something.

"Why else?" I asked.

He took in a slow breath. "Your dad called."

"Called you? If it was about those comic books, I don't think they were illegal in the first place."

"Comic books?"

"That wasn't why he called?"

Jack returned with napkins to mop up our small caffeine puddle.

Ken didn't answer, just sent me a tight smile that was far from reassuring.

My retired father still liked to dabble in police investigations. For him to call in the chief meant two things: one, Dad had finally come to his senses and was going to let the actual police do the police work, and two, he felt he was onto some kind of major crime taking place, here, at the train show.

Whatever track Dad was on, my plans for a simple weekend selling toys just derailed.

Chapter 3

There were no lulls. A couple of hours into the show, my feet were tired from standing on the concrete, my throat was sore from all the dickering, and my brain was swimming from trying to figure out the lowest offer I could accept from the bargain hunters without taking a bath in red ink. Although a nice hot bath was sounding pretty good.

While busy, we were nowhere near as swamped as Maxine, who was moving from customer to customer as if she were the Flash. I secretly congratulated myself on offering her hours at the shop. If energy like that couldn't be bottled, at least it could be contracted.

But as my most recent customer walked away happy with his Fisher-Price castle, I looked up again to see Maxine thumbing through the comics. Her expression was anything but cheerful.

"I don't understand," she told a man standing in front of her table. "I packed them to bring to the show."

I stepped out from behind my table. "Is something wrong?" I asked.

She shook her head. "They have to be here somewhere." She turned to her customer and smiled. "Could you stop back? We had to do some last-minute rearranging, but I know we have them."

As he walked away, her expression grew more worried as her hands flew through the comic book selection.

"If you tell me what you're looking for, maybe I can help you find it," I offered.

"There was a special collection of comics." Her voice quavered slightly. "They weren't even supposed to go in the regular boxes. I packed and unpacked them myself." She pointed to the display shelf behind their sales tables. "The ones there now aren't the ones I put there." She stopped for a moment. "When you helped me unpack, did you move any? They would've been in rigid plastic cases."

"Of course not!" I said. Although the toy market was down in general, I still knew never to open boxes.

"Never mind." She started to rake a hand through her hair but then grasped a handful of curls. "I don't know what to do. Craig and I were here most of the morning, and I don't see how anyone could have gotten at them without one of us seeing."

"Could he have sold them while you were busy with another customer?"

"It's possible, I suppose. But he would've told me. If he sold everything that was on that shelf, we're talking thousands of dollars. He probably would have sent me to the bank. The ones there now are only worth hundreds." She closed her eyes. "If they've gone missing when I was in charge, Craig is going to kill me."

My mouth got dry just thinking about that kind of loss and what a quick-tempered bully like Craig might do if he found out. I made a mental note to stay focused on their booth, just in case Craig reappeared.

"Dad," I said as I returned to our booth, "keep an eye on Craig's booth, okay?"

"I have been," he said. "All day. What's up now?"

"A boatload of pricy comics is missing from their display. Is that why you called Ken in?"

He shook his head, then went to greet a new customer. They chatted for a few minutes, and Dad made the sale, tucking the cash in his apron. He picked up our conversation right where we'd left off. "It's an interesting development, but that's not why I called Ken."

I cocked my head and waited.

"Fine," he said. "I saw a couple suspicious characters wandering around."

"Shoplifters?" As soon as I said it, I wondered if he'd meant Terry, who'd spent a good hour poring over the comics. He'd been sent up for burglary, though, and not shoplifting. In fact, it was my dad who caught him in the act and testified at his trial, which had ended up triggering yet another breakup between Jack and me. It also had given his mother yet another reason to decide I was unsuitable for her son.

"No," Dad said. "These were faces I thought I remembered from old FBI posters. Organized crime types. And more than one wandering through the show."

"The mob? Dad, you can't be serious. What would the mafia be doing at a train and toy show in East Aurora?"

He shushed me. "*That's* why I called Ken."

"Thank you for not trying to take down the whole syndicate by yourself. Are they still here?" I hazarded a glance around. "Can you point them out?"

"Lizzie, you don't need to be involved in this. I managed to get pictures and e-mailed them to Ken. I mean, I might be wrong, and these guys could just be look-alikes. My eyes are getting older, and my memory isn't what it used to be."

"You have a mind like an elephant's."

"Yeah, wrinkled, gray, and way too much junk in the trunk. But that's totally irrelephant."

I rolled my eyes and glared at him. Otherwise, he'd be making elephant jokes all day.

His face instantly sobered. "Ken is checking for outstanding warrants and seeing if he can confirm their identities. Meanwhile, you just stay away from them."

"How will I know who to stay away from unless I know who they are?"

"Fine." He then casually began to scan the crowd. "Bolo tie and cowboy boots at three o'clock."

I glanced to Dad's right and saw a jovial older man who looked more grandfather than godfather.

"Batman T-shirt at seven o'clock. My seven."

The second guy took a little while to locate, but my eyes eventually found a younger man wearing black jeans and a weathered black tee with a bright-yellow Batman logo on it. He was heading in our direction. The suspected mobster's eyes were sweeping the comic book table, and I accidentally made eye contact with him. I kept my gaze traveling, hoping he'd assume I was looking for someone else. "Shoot."

"You made eye contact, didn't you?"

"Sorry."

"This is why I didn't want to point them out."

But as the man approached the table, I pushed past Dad and deliberately made eye contact again. "Great shirt," I said. "Can I interest you in our Batman collectibles? We've got some nice Mego figures, trading cards, and I think we still have a 1960s lunchbox."

The man's eyes narrowed ever so slightly, so I made sure my smile never faltered.

"Yeah. I'd like to see those," he said. His expression relaxed. I must have passed muster as an overzealous vendor out to capitalize on his shirt.

I directed him over to our superhero section. "Let me know if you have any questions." And then I left him alone to peruse.

I faced Dad. "What's he doing?"

Dad continued to face me, but his eyes darted, just for microseconds, to take in the man behind me. "He looks like he's studying the case, but he's really keeping an eye on the comic book booth."

"Because he already robbed it? Could he have taken those missing comic books?"

"*Rob* means to take something by force from a person. If that had happened, we'd know it. Listen, Lizzie, if I tell you to hit the deck, you do it, okay? Don't argue with me or ask why." The last part wasn't a question.

I swallowed hard. "Yes, sir."

"I think you made a sale, anyway." He gestured toward the man. "Keep it casual. Like any other customer."

I spun around with a smile and checked out the man's purchase. He handed me a credit card and several Batman items and asked if I could wrap them up.

"Be right back," I said.

"Take your time," he said. "I'll keep looking."

By looking, he clearly meant absent-mindedly picking up every piece of merchandise on our tables while watching Craig's place.

I let Dad run the credit card, in case he wanted to check out anything about it while the authorization went through on our slow portable machine. Meanwhile, I wrapped the man's purchases while also watching him and Craig's place.

Maxine was still doing a booming business, although she didn't look nearly as happy as she had this morning. Those missing comics must be wearing on her. And Craig was nowhere to be seen.

She was so busy, in fact, that I don't think she noticed Lionel Kelley steal up to the corner of her booth. He quickly paged through the comic books, probably looking for more offending covers.

The appearance of the uniformed guard at the comic booth seemed to make Batman-man shrink back. He put on sunglasses, which seemed a little odd. Then I plumbed the depths of my high school geometry, estimated angle of incidence and angle of reflection, and theorized that the glasses were also mirrored on the inside and that he was using them to watch the goings-on behind him.

It didn't take long for the overzealous guard to find something he considered offensive, and soon he was in Maxine's face, shaking the book.

I gave up pretending to focus on my work and watched them openly. I wasn't alone.

At first Maxine took it. Then she tried to reason with Kelley. Apparently that didn't work. Moments later, she began draping fabric over her tables, her face red and jaw clenched.

At this inopportune moment, Lexi Wolf showed up. Whoever Craig hired to play the part was fantastic. Her legs in those fishnet stockings and stiletto boots looked like they were three miles long, and she even had the wolf makeup down perfectly. She was Comic-Con worthy. She was also far from modest, especially when she flicked her long cloak aside to expose the leather corset.

I was still staring when Dad nudged me and handed me Batman-man's credit card. I glanced at it. Edward Millroy. Was that his real name?

I held it out to the customer, who took several moments to notice, giving credence to my theory about the mirrored lenses. I had just offered him his gift bag when things heated up between Lexi Wolf and Lionel Kelley. Here's where the fake Lexi showed her true colors: she was slipping in and out of her trademark Aussie accent.

Maxine was caught between the lanky guard and faux sci-fi icon, and for a while, it seemed as if poor Maxine was getting it from both sides. Finally, she ducked out of the conflict and finished covering the tables. While gathering her purse and coat, she surreptitiously wiped a tear from the corner of her eye. I could understand her frustration. She kept her head down as she rushed away from the booth, pushing past Lexi, who was still engaged with the security chief.

It was one of those train wrecks. Too terrible to watch. Too compelling to turn away. But after several minutes of this, the crowd noise changed abruptly. Conversations stopped mid-sentence, and I heard more than one gasp. Several attend-ees pointed up, and I followed the line to the catwalks that crossed the area near the high ceiling. My eyes found the bright reds and oranges of Craig's costume.

"It's a bird. It's a plane," a nearby attendee said. "It's a cheap publicity stunt."

That got several titters of laughter from the crowd, but necks craned and visitors watched to see what kind of antics Craig would perform on the narrow catwalk.

I glanced at the large digital wall clock. Just a few minutes before ten o'clock. Maxine had said something about every-thing being revealed at ten.

Craig climbed over the catwalk railing, his heels still on the metal grating, but the rest of his feet dangling over thin air. That quieted the crowd even more, all except the wail of a nearby toddler.

Or maybe that was part of the stunt too. A lost helium balloon rested against the ceiling near Craig, the string dan-gling just out of his reach. He made a sudden grasp for it and overextended. His feet slipped. He managed to hold onto the railing with one hand, but his feet were kicking in the air.

A gasp went up from the crowd.

I squinted to see if I could make out the safety wires. Surely Craig wouldn't have been stupid enough to attempt such a stunt without some kind of restraint. But I figured they must have been well hidden, because it really did look like he was just dangling there, hanging on for dear life.

Seconds later, he lost his grip and plummeted, his super-hero cape rippling behind him.

Chapter 4

Screams ensued. Parents pulled their children closer and hid their eyes. Some attendees rushed toward the central train layout where Craig must have landed. Others hurried away.

Batman-man, a.k.a. Edward Millroy, grabbed his bag from my hands, said, "Thanks!" and started making his way to the door. Kelley had disappeared, and Lexi Wolf leaned against a pillar, her cloak pulled tightly against her.

Minutes later, the lights flickered, and Lionel Kelley's voice came over the loudspeaker. "Please remain where you are. The building is in lockdown. You will not be allowed to leave. Shelter in place."

Whispers went up, but nothing near the normal roar of the center. Shortly after that, a brief siren was heard in the main aisle, and the crowd started to shift to allow a golf cart through. Lionel drove the cart, lights flashing, as he spoke something unintelligible into a bullhorn. His cart was followed by a team of paramedics, on foot and wheeling a gurney piled with equipment.

I looked for Dad, but he had disappeared from our booth.

It was here that I experienced a personal revelation. Yes, I was miffed at Dad for running off to investigate. That aspect was pretty typical. I had often reminded him that he was retired and that butting into police work was dangerous for him. But now I was confronted with the uncomfortable truth that my attitude had somehow shifted. Instead of being angry at Dad for running off to investigate, I was sulking because he had run off to investigate *without me*. Curse that man. He was pulling me into another one of his escapades.

I found a few extra tablecloths and draped them over our inventory before cutting through the crowd. Even Santa was mingling with the rubberneckers near the spot where Craig landed.

Ground zero turned out to be an elaborate HO train layout. As a dutiful toy store manager, I could, in my sleep, recite the odd ratio between metric scale measurements and English real measurements: in HO scale, 3.5 mm equals 1 real foot. Now perhaps the most common size in production, the models were scaled to 1:87 (Dad could add a couple more decimal points there), a little less than half the size of the O-gauge trains made popular in the 1930s.

That was when they left the factory. These particular train cars had been compacted a little more by the meteor that was Craig. He'd landed on a hillside and had demolished it, exposing chicken wire and papier-mâché underneath. He'd also taken out a bridge, part of a river, and a considerable amount of track. The train had derailed and lay in a wreck on the floor near where Craig lay motionless, dwarfing the wrecked tableau around him, like Gulliver. Or Godzilla.

Craig wasn't completely motionless, however. As I elbowed my way passed the spectators, I could see his chest rise and fall slightly and his eyelids flutter.

Dad pushed himself up on his cane from where he'd been crouched next to Craig. He filled in the responders and then made his way to me. "He's alive," he said.

I continued to watch while the paramedics made their own assessments and then braced Craig's spine and neck for transport. It was at that point that Lionel started doing his best to disperse the crowd.

Dad took my elbow. "We should get back to the booth."

We snaked through the onlookers, right behind Santa on his way back to his throne. We had just reached our booth when the all-clear sounded.

"Business as usual?" I asked.

"Lockdown was a bit of an overkill." Dad quirked his head. "Still, I'd like to talk to Ken. See what his take is on this."

"It was an accidental fall, right?" I said. "We all saw him. He was up on that catwalk all by himself. Some kind of publicity stunt gone wrong. Tragic, but what else could it be?" I glanced up half expecting to see frayed wires dangling from the ceiling. But nothing up there suggested that Craig had been restrained in any way. The lost balloon was still there, though, bobbing in the air currents.

Dad inhaled and held his breath but didn't answer.

This was my cue to reexamine the situation. I had missed something.

Craig, dressed as a superhero, had climbed the catwalks, possibly as some kind of publicity stunt. He overreached, lost his balance, and fell.

But Dad had just given me the same look he used when he'd tried to help me with my homework in high school and I just wasn't getting it. I had made a mistake.

I started going through my original assessment point by point. Craig *was* dressed as a superhero. Fact. Even with the mask, that body shape forced into spandex was recognizable, and not in a good way.

He *was* up in the catwalks. Fact. Alone? *That* was an assumption. I hadn't seen anyone, but I suppose someone else could have hidden up there, perhaps behind a light or panel or in a dark recess. That warranted investigation.

"Was he really alone?" I asked.

Dad nodded, but grimly. I'd only solved part of the puzzle.

"And was it a publicity stunt?" That was also an assumption, based on the timing, when Maxine had told me all would be revealed. "We need to talk to Maxine."

A smile tickled the corner of Dad's mouth, his tell whenever I was close.

"And then there's the question of why the mob was watching his booth," I said. "It seems unlikely that the timing is coincidental."

"Bingo," he said. "I hate coincidences."

Dad didn't have to search for Ken. Maybe half an hour after Craig was whisked off to the hospital, the chief approached our booth, notebook in hand.

"How's it looking?" Dad asked him.

Ken paused for a minute, as if considering his words. Or perhaps how much he was willing to share with Dad. At times the new chief and former chief seemed like, if not best friends, at least the wise old mentor and his prized student.

"So far nobody has come forward claiming to see anything suspicious," Ken said, hazarding a glance up to the catwalk, "including our two bogeys."

"You interviewed them?" Dad asked.

"Casually and briefly. No more than any of the other nearby witnesses. Nothing to hold them on so I didn't want to spook them. Just the same general questions."

"I had my eyes on one of them while Craig was up there," Dad said. "He seemed as surprised as we were to see Craig try to pull a Wallenda. But they were definitely interested in him—or at least something at his stand."

"Still are," I said, discretely nodding toward the crowd where both Grandpa and Edward Millroy were hovering nearby, pretending not to know each other.

"Is that why it's closed?" Ken gestured toward the covered booth.

"That was Lionel Kelley's doing," I said. "He took objection to some of the comic books—and their special guest. Poor Maxine practically left in tears." Lexi Wolf was nowhere to be seen now, either.

Ken rubbed his bristly chin. "Wish I had a clue as to what was going on. I don't see anything to connect the mob to Craig McFadden, and I have no idea what that man was doing up there. Could he have been suicidal?"

"Craig?" I said. "I think he liked inflicting pain on others too much to let go of life just yet. Besides, Maxine said he had some kind of big announcement at ten."

"Do you know where she went?" Ken said.

"Not sure," I said.

"Took off a little before Craig's dive," Dad added.

"Is there some kind of conference nobody bothered to tell me about?" Lionel Kelley stood glaring, hands on hips, looking at where we were huddled behind the sales tables.

"I'm just interviewing the witnesses," Ken said defensively.

"I was thinking," Dad said, "that maybe we should ask the hospital to make sure someone thinks to run a tox screen. Maybe Craig wasn't in his right mind when he climbed up there."

"Good idea," Ken said, pulling out his phone.

"You're acting like this is some kind of criminal investigation," Kelley said.

Ken eyed him. "Yup."

"But it was an accident," Kelley said. "I mean, yeah, McFadden must have gotten by the safeties somehow to gain access to the catwalks. They're normally locked off. Only licensed tradesmen use them to access the HVAC and replace light bulbs."

"You check them regularly?" Dad asked.

Kelley spat out the next words. "Weekly, with additional checks after every scheduled maintenance and then again before events. I checked this morning, in fact. Everything was locked up tight."

"You should get a print kit out here," Dad told Ken. "Check for Craig's or any additional prints on the railings and ladder."

"Another good idea," Ken said.

"For an accident?" Kelley said. "Everyone saw him, up there, all by himself. He wasn't pushed. He didn't jump. It was a freak accident."

"Maybe," Ken said.

"I don't like where this is going," Kelley said. "I am head of security here. Don't I get a say?"

"Then you're just the man I need to talk to," Ken said. "I hope we can trust you to cooperate?"

Kelley didn't answer for a moment, then gave a reluctant nod.

"How soon can we get Craig's booth reopened? We were surveilling it, you see."

"Why?" Kelley asked. "We?"

"That's . . . uh . . . kind of need to know."

Our little group was forced in tighter when two older men I didn't know slid in behind our booth. One wore an old-timey conductor's uniform, right down to the hat and gold pocket watch. The other was dressed in a white shirt and tie.

Dad made introductions. The conductor was the head of the show and went by the title Chief Conductor Frank. I called him "Chief" when I shook his hand, and I think he liked it. He tipped his hat, anyway. "No need to be that formal."

"Thanks, Frank," I said.

"*Conductor* Frank."

The other man was Bruce Palmer, the events manager for the facility.

Bruce reached a hand to Ken and offered his full cooperation in any investigation.

"I was just asking your head of security here how soon the Craig's Comics booth could reopen," Ken said.

"As soon as you'd like," Palmer said.

"I didn't know they were closed," the conductor said. "Do they need help now that Craig is incapacitated? I could probably rustle up a volunteer or two."

"Wait," Kelley protested. "You want to give them volunteers? *I* shut them down. They were selling lurid comics."

Conductor Frank almost dropped his pocket watch. "Porn?"

Dad and I shook our heads.

Kelley rolled his eyes and continued in his most pedantic manner. "*Lurid* as defined in New York State law as, and I quote, 'devoted to or principally made up of pictures or accounts of methods of crime, or illicit sex, horror, terror, physical torture, brutality, or physical violence.'"

"That pretty much defines a comic book, all right," I said.

"I'm pretty sure that old law is off the books," Dad said.

"Even so," Kelley said, "decency is still subject to local ordinance, and even further restrictions here at the center, since we have the welfare of our patrons under the age of twenty-one to think about. I consider it my job—and more than that, my moral duty—to see to it that the material presented here is legal and safe for our patrons. This ought to be going through me."

"So, in other words," Palmer said, "you just didn't like what he was selling."

Ken snorted, then tried to control his face.

My dad's Adam's apple was bobbing up and down; he was going to crack up any moment.

The conductor cleared his throat. "I'm no judge, but if the police don't have a problem with what Craig was selling, let them reopen."

Palmer nodded.

Kelley's complexion reddened. He crossed his arms. "And if I don't agree?"

Ken took a step toward Lionel Kelley, towering over him by at least five inches. He raised an eyebrow. "If you want to play this game, chief of police trumps rent-a-cop. Every time."

Kelley glared at him for a moment, then without saying a word slapped his two-way radio down on the table, followed by a heavy duty flashlight, pepper spray, and his ID in his lanyard. Then apparently he thought twice about it, because he clumsily fished his security ID out of the lanyard and slammed just the card down on his table. "I paid for the lanyard." He crammed it into his pocket. "Good luck without me." He stormed off.

Palmer pinched the top of his nose. "I should have figured that would happen."

"Do you have a replacement in the wings?" Ken asked. "I'd like to have someone in security here that I can work with."

Palmer shook his head. "The rest of the staff is pretty green. A couple of guys quit when I promoted Kelley. I guess I should have seen the writing on the wall."

"We can't keep the show going without adequate security," Conductor Frank said. "Am I going to have to shut her down?"

Palmer's look grew more somber, then his head jerked toward my father. "Hank?"

"Oh, no," I said, putting up my hands in protest. "He's retired."

"Works for me," Ken said.

I closed my eyes. I'd already lost this one, but I figured I'd better at least make a formal protest. "He has a booth to run. And I don't want him up on those catwalks with a cane."

"I didn't say he'd need to climb anything," Ken said. "I'll bring in my men to check prints and investigate the catwalks."

"And I suppose, as temporary head of security, I'd have access to all records, such as security camera footage." Dad gestured up toward the cameras that I hadn't even seen.

"Sounds like the perfect solution!" the conductor said.

"Yeah, just ducky," I said under my breath. But I doubt anyone heard since they were so caught up in their plans.

"I'll get you a badge and uniform and introduce you to the guys. You can start right away," Palmer said. "I'll get moving on the paperwork." He rushed off toward the front offices.

Conductor Frank shook my dad's hand. "Thanks so much. You're a great help. Now I have to figure out how to fix this mess." Then he wandered off, hands clasped behind his back.

Only then did Ken seem to catch my expression of disapproval. I crossed my arms to emphasize it.

"Now, Liz," Ken said, "it's only temporary. And you have to admit it's the best solution."

Dad held up his hand as if taking an oath. "And I promise: no catwalks and I'll call in the police at the first sign of danger."

At this point, Ken checked his phone. "I gotta go. Craig just regained consciousness. Now maybe we'll get some answers as to what he was doing up there."

Chapter 5

To no one's surprise, I got stuck manning the booth. Once again, I tried to convince myself I was upset at being left all alone. Or worried about my father being pulled into an investigation that might involve my old school bully and the mob. Truth was, I resented that they left me out of all the fun.

Since when was investigating fun? Well, it was for Dad. And I wasn't entirely convinced he didn't latch onto this non-case while trying to shirk his work. What was there really to investigate? This was simply a matter of an idiot—okay, I winced when I thought of him as that, especially since he was still lying in a hospital bed—rather, *a man* overestimating his high-wire skills and almost getting himself killed. It was a good sign that he had regained consciousness. With proper care and time to heal, Craig would soon be back to his annoying self. At that I found myself breathing a surprising sigh of relief.

Why two mobsters were roaming the facility, showing an interest in Craig's booth, was another niggling question. But since I couldn't move about freely like Dad, with his spiffy new uniform and two-way radio, I could at least—in between customers, that is—keep an eye on the still-closed comic booth and the two now ubiquitous men who seemed to be hovering nearby in shifts.

"Think you can sneak away for lunch?" Jack asked, leaning across the table, upsetting one of Cathy's precious dolls in the process. "Oh, sorry."

I got her back on her metal stand without making eye contact. With the doll, that is. I had no problem making eye contact with Jack, who had the dreamiest eyes. "Not sure I can manage lunch," I said. "Dad's been pressed into service, and I'm all alone here."

"Pressed into . . . ? Does it have anything to do with the accident?"

"Long story, but he's now temporary head of security. And yeah, they're investigating what happened." I left out the part about the mobsters since there were too many people nearby who might overhear. I didn't want to create a general panic. Or get myself launched into Lake Erie wearing cement shoes.

"Can I help?" he asked.

"Aren't you busy with Terry?" I glanced around, expecting to see him. "Or did he go home?"

"Am I my brother's keeper?" Jack quipped, but I found the joke far from reassuring. It must've shown on my face. "Yeah, he went home. Why?"

"No reason. I just wondered if he, uh, enjoyed the show this morning."

"I guess."

"You weren't together?"

"No, we weren't together the whole time this morning. Why do I have a feeling I missed more than an accidental fall? Do you suspect him of something?"

"No! I just asked if he had a good time. Don't read anything into it."

Jack took a breath and then held it. "Sorry," he finally said. "Didn't mean to get overly defensive. I'm trying to find the line myself. He's my brother and I love him, but he's also an ex-con. I don't know how much to trust him and how much to check on him. And now that my big brother is working for me, our whole relationship is in flux." Jack wasn't a crier, but he couldn't hide the huskiness creeping into his voice.

"Family is tough sometimes," I said. "Always hard to find that balance. Like Dad—I don't know whether to tie him to his chair or enlist in his cause. Tell you what, though. I feel helpless just standing here. If that offer of help is still good, could you spot me for a quick . . . potty break?"

He saluted playfully, moved behind the table, and then stowed his coat underneath it. "Any instructions?"

I thought of all the carefully prepared charts with various prices, but those would be too complicated for a noob. "Don't take any lowball offers. Tell them anything less than ninety percent of the marked price will have to be approved by your boss."

"Yes, boss."

I kissed him on the cheek and grabbed my purse. "Thank you!"

Despite the fact that I really did need a potty break, I yielded to my curiosity and took the long way around to the restrooms, passing by the spot where Craig landed. The wrecked train layout was roped off but still drew a crowd. I inched forward and craned my neck to get a view over the shoulder of a white-haired man wearing a plaid shirt and suspenders.

"Here." The man stepped aside so I could get a look. "Such a tragedy. That kind of loss is hard to recover from."

"It'll be weeks. Maybe months," another man said. "Poor Frank."

"His name was Craig," I said. "Craig McFadden."

The man shook his head. "Nah. That's the idiot that wrecked it. Frank's the guy that worked for years on this lay-out and now has to fix it." He pointed to a man inside the railing.

"Oh," I said, recognizing his uniform. "You mean Conductor Frank."

Their smirks led me to believe that I was the only one who had to call him that. I mentally dropped the honorary title, especially since he'd removed his hat and rolled up his sleeves.

Frank was sorting through a box of what looked like, from a distance, herbs and spices. I'd learned my lesson earlier in the day when, hoping to score a good deal on oregano, I dis-covered vendors were using the same containers to hold rocks, sand, gravel, moss, and grass used to create realistic landscap-ing in the train layouts. He was readying his repair supplies.

"Years," said the other man. "He's been bringing that same layout to the shows for almost ten years now. Adds a little bit more real estate every year. This will never be the same."

I looked at the complicated layout. As Dad might say, Craig had left quite a first impression: half of a mountain had caved in. Train cars still lay in a twisted wreck on the floor. The bridge looked like the resistance had taken it out.

Frank drew closer and scrutinized the wreckage. He pulled out a tape measure and jotted numbers on a scrap of paper he fished from his shirt pocket.

"How are you gonna fix it?" the man next to me asked.

Frank rubbed his chin. "Don't think I'm going to. It would never be the same."

"How many cars did you lose?" someone asked.

"Eight."

Even over the crowd noise, I could hear the concerned gasp.

"Weird thing is," Frank continued, "the engine pulling them is just scratched up a bit. But another engine went missing."

"Valuable?" I asked.

"Sentimental, mainly," he said. "Belonged to my father-in-law. Good thing I insured it. Oh, well, you know what they say. When life gives you lemons . . ."

"If you're not going to fix it, whatcha gonna do with it?" someone nearby asked.

"Well, the police want me to leave it like this until they take some pictures. But then I was thinking about turning it into some kind of natural disaster. Like a meteor strike. Or maybe stage it like *Sharknado* or even *Mars Attacks*. Do you think folks would believe aliens did this? Crash landed, right about . . . there?" He pointed to the exposed chicken wire.

"I have some old flying saucers at our booth," I said, thinking about a weathered 1950s-era tin model that just might look great embedded into that ravaged hillside.

"To scale?" one of the spectators asked.

Frank put his hands on his hips and smiled. "That's the silver lining. Who's to say how big them aliens are supposed to be?" He looked around to see who might be listening. "Now don't go telling nobody. You know how some folks like to copy. I don't want anyone beating me to the punch."

# # #

After pointing Frank in the direction of our booth, my more pressing needs became urgent, so I headed up the aisle toward the ladies' room. The first stall was occupied, so I made my way to the next.

I'll admit to tarrying a little. So much had happened that morning, and I'd already spent so many hours on my feet, that the cool, quiet, and calm of the ladies' room was actually appealing. After washing my hands, I did my best to tame my hair and ran a cool, damp paper towel along the back of my neck.

I had just pushed on the door to leave when I stopped and glanced around. The occupant of the first stall hadn't budged, and faint sniffles were coming from behind the door.

I took a guess. "Maxine? Is that you?"

After a few more seconds with no response, a toilet flushed and the door opened. Maxine, her eyes red and puffy, barely made eye contact with me as she made her way to the sink. She washed her hands, then splashed cold water on her face.

I gathered several towels from the dispenser and handed them to her.

"Thanks." She pressed the towels to her face for several moments before taking a deep breath and looking up at my reflection in the mirror. "How bad is it?"

I wasn't sure if she was talking about her face or her boss's fall from grace, so I just smiled and lied. "I'm sure everything will be fine."

She ran more water over the towels and pressed them to her eyes. "He's not . . . ?"

"Craig's alive," I said. "In fact, I heard he regained consciousness. The police were headed to the hospital to try to interview him." I gestured to a couple of armchairs opposite the sink, probably designed for nursing mothers or train show widows.

After she collapsed into a chair, I angled the other chair so I could better see her as we talked. "I take it things didn't go as Craig had planned."

"That's the understatement of the year." Her voice grew husky. "I don't know exactly what he had planned. He'd kept it a secret, even from me. It was his big surprise."

"And it had something to do with that outfit?"

She nodded, then shut her eyes tight. "He was so proud of that thing. Had it custom made from his drawing."

"*His* drawing?" Ah, that was why I hadn't recognized the costume.

"That was the big announcement. Craig was about to launch his own line of comic books."

"I didn't know Craig could draw. Although I guess he was always a doodler in school." In his books and on the desks and on the bus seats. In ink. And later moved on to spray-painting bridges and railroad cars and industrial buildings. Many of his doodles probably should have carried a warning that they were intended for mature audiences.

"You went to school with Craig?"

"Briefly. Years ago. Before he . . . moved away." I wasn't sure how much she knew about his background.

She nodded gravely, as if she understood my euphemism perfectly. "He studied art from one of those correspondence schools. I know most of them are scams, but he learned something. His sketches were amazing. But it's a hard business to break into. So much competition. I know he was frustrated with the rejections."

"But apparently he did? Break through, that is."

"Well, let's just say that he found an alternate path. He was in the process of working with a local publishing company to put them into print."

"And that was the character he was dressed up as?" I asked.

She nodded. "Mr. Inferno. Or Doctor Inferno. Something like that. He had trouble finding titles that weren't being used. I've never actually seen his new series. He was very protective of it. But it was all about a superhero who could summon flames at will to fight the bad guys. Very novel approach, and he had such a tragic backstory."

I smiled politely. It didn't feel novel. I was pretty sure that just about every comic universe had at least one character who could perform such a feat. Dad could probably name a dozen. On the other hand, we could all probably count our blessings that Craig didn't descend from the rafters in a giant ball of flames.

"I suppose I should check on Craig," she said. "Then try to figure out where to go from here. I was so frustrated at being shut down and furious at Craig for not being there to handle things. It just got to be too much. I took off to look for him, to give him a piece of my mind. Then everybody was looking up and pointing, and I saw him . . ." She brushed a tear away.

"But he's alive. And some more good news," I said. "Because of a . . . staffing change in security here, you have a green light to reopen your booth. When you're ready. I could probably find you some help, if you need it."

She stared at me for several seconds and then sat silently while two women entered the restroom and scooted past us.

She tapped the arm of the chair. "I'm going to assume that Craig would want me to get back to work and check on him later." She nodded, as if another part of her were agreeing with her own assessment. "Yes, that's what he would want."

I pulled open the door and followed her out. As we walked together through the crowded aisles, I spotted the back of Millroy's head. The pair was still lingering around the comic booth. I took Maxine's arm. "Did you notice any odd characters hanging around the booth at all?"

"No, but then again, we've been pretty busy. And some might even say that most comic book lovers tend to be a little odd. Although, thanks to *The Big Bang Theory* and all that, it's the age of the lovable geek. I try not to notice anything off about a customer.

"Unless it's scary."

Chapter 6

Even several yards away from our booth and above the din of the crowd, I could hear Frank doing his best bartering with Jack.

"What if I pay full price and you throw in those purple aliens too?"

Jack had his smartphone out and was punching numbers into his calculator app. He didn't even see me come up.

"Sold," I told Frank, who smiled and handed over a wad of cash.

He held the UFO in one hand, picked up the aliens in the other, and raised them up for my inspection. "You don't think the aliens are too big for the saucer, do you?"

"Maybe it's bigger on the inside," I said, resisting the urge to point out that they were twice the size of the door.

"Is that a thing?" Frank asked. "I mean, a real science fiction-y thing?"

"Oh, yeah. Come to think of it, it is," I said, while in no way stipulating or suggesting that he was purchasing an actual TARDIS. "Or maybe they're just very limber aliens. Or shape shifters. That's also a thing."

When Frank walked away clutching his purchases, Jack's shoulders sank in relief. "This job is harder than it looks."

"Thanks?" I said.

After a brief pause, he caught himself. "I mean, *you* make it look easy." Jack stretched his back. "The accident sure hasn't done much to slow business."

"We can thank the . . . accident . . . for that little bit of business, actually." I went on to explain Frank's plans to fix his layout.

"I like it," Jack said. "Very *X-Files* meets the Island of Sodor."

My face must have blanked.

"You know. Tidmouth Sheds? Knapford Station? Sir Topham Hatt?"

I shrugged.

"Thomas the Train? Come on, now! Even if you never watched the show, you *must* sell the toys!"

I couldn't help the chuckle at his expense. "Yes, any number of them. And Parker used to love it, so I've seen quite a few episodes."

He sent me a playful glare. "So you were just pulling my leg."

"Just a little bit. But if you're worried about it, I can pull the other one so you don't walk funny or anything."

He let out an exaggerated sigh I could hear even over the crowd. "And after I've been slaving away, all during your 'quick' potty break."

"Sorry. I ran into Maxine, and we were talking about the accident. If that's what it truly was."

"You're thinking it might have been something more? Don't tell me you're involved in another investigation."

"Actually, Dad is doing a pretty good job of keeping me out of one. He obviously thinks things aren't as they appear. And I've been his daughter long enough to trust those instincts of his."

"But if it wasn't an accident, what? Do you think he might have jumped?"

I considered the idea for a moment, then shrugged it off. "Honestly, the Craig I know is too full of himself, and he certainly didn't look suicidal. Quite the opposite; he seemed totally absorbed in his future plans."

"Have you learned why he was up there in the first place?"

"Some publicity stunt. Even Maxine didn't know all the details. But Ken went to the hospital to talk to Craig, so maybe he'll get more answers."

Jack's jaw set a little. Was it the mention of Ken? Or concern for me getting caught up in an investigation?

But I didn't have a lot of time to figure that out because Dad strode up to the booth. "I see we still have our shadows," he said.

I had to bite my lip to keep from laughing. Dad had always looked dignified in his police uniform. But the security guard duds they'd dug up for him didn't measure up, literally. The pants, in addition to being a particularly ugly shade of shiny brown polyester with a crooked stripe on the sides, were too short, showing his tube socks. The shirt, still sporting the wrinkles from being folded tightly in a package, gaped over his stomach. He shot me a warning look.

"Shadows?" Jack asked, a little bit too loudly.

Dad grabbed my arm. "You didn't tell him?"

"I didn't have time," I said.

"She was on a potty break," Jack said.

"I found Maxine," I said.

"I can see that." Dad shifted slightly so that he was still facing me, but he could catch Maxine's movements in the background. Then he shifted again, maybe to watch the mobsters with his peripheral vision?

"Oh, come now," I said. "Use those eyes in the back of your head. I know you have them."

"I was just thinking I needed another set. You know, Liz, since you've done a good job of pawning your work off on your boyfriend here, maybe you should see if Maxine needs any help. It'll give you a chance to talk with her. See if she knows more about what happened."

"She doesn't. Apparently Craig never filled her in."

"What about the missing comic books?"

"Missing comic books?" Jack repeated over my shoulder.

I winced and resisted the urge to turn around and face him. Jack was a sharp guy. And it wouldn't take much effort for him to put together the missing comic books with the questions I'd asked earlier about his brother's whereabouts.

His quick intake of breath marked the occasion.

I closed my eyes.

"What?" Dad said. "Did I miss something?"

"Well," Jack said, "I hate to rain on your plans and all, but I really can't stick around. I should probably go hang out with Terry." He pulled his jacket out from under the table, then shook Dad's hand. "Good luck with your investigation."

He faced me briefly but never made eye contact. "Seriously, Liz. Be safe." His voice cracked on the last word as he gave my upper arm a brief squeeze.

Then he walked away. Out of the convention center? Or out of my life for good?

Knowing just how defensive Jack was about his brother, I suspected the latter. After all, when Dad arrested Terry the first time almost a decade ago, it had pretty much put a nail in the coffin of Jack's and my relationship. He'd walked out of my life then, until events last year brought us back together and resurrected the old feelings we had for each other. I seriously doubted they'd survive another trial. And given Jack's proclivity for walking away whenever things got tough, I was beginning to think it might be healthier for me to let him go—and close the door after him—instead of delaying the inevitable.

Dad put his arm around my shoulder. "Don't worry, Lizzie. It'll be okay."

"Will it?" I leaned into him. Maybe the years had softened my dad. He'd never been particularly aware of my love life and never especially sympathetic.

"Yeah. I called Miles earlier," he said. "And Cathy said Parker can swing by after his shift at the wildlife center. As soon as one of them gets here, you can go work with Maxine and see what you can figure out."

# # #

Miles arrived twenty minutes later, and I gave him the thumbnail tutorial instead of the full version. The tech-savvy twenty-year-old had originally come to us to design our website, but he stayed on to set up our social media platforms and eventually wormed his way into handling our online sales and acquisitions.

Dad had never fully explained how they knew each other, but from the few breadcrumbs he'd scattered, I'd gathered that Miles had gotten into trouble in high school when his mother moved him from the reservation to East Aurora, and he fell in with the wrong crowd. He certainly credited Dad with his reformation. Now the two were as thick as, well, thieves, and Miles was a trusted member of our staff, a dear friend, and working his way toward family status.

And since he'd set up our mobile payment system, he certainly didn't need any instructions on that.

I did, however, clue him in on Batman-man and Grandpa. "I don't think there's anything to worry about. They seem more interested in Craig's Comics, but if you notice anything odd, let Dad or me know."

"Got it," he said. "Where will you be?"

"Helping at Craig's Comics." I glanced over to where Maxine was fielding customers, answering questions, and haggling like a pro. "Not that she needs it. But Dad's hoping I can get enough information by osmosis to crack the case."

"Or so *he* could crack the case," Miles said with a bit of a smirk.

"I have caught a killer before," I said.

"Not the way your dad tells it."

I glared at him, but he was probably right that Dad's version of the story differed from mine, just a little. It couldn't have been easy for Dad to admit that I, a woman—or a girl, as I'd probably always be in his mind—with less training than the greenest rookie, had beaten him to a collar. Even harder since he was a seasoned detective who had, as he was prone to remind me, changed my diapers. I decided to take Idina Menzel's advice and let it go.

I first detoured to the concessions area, bought a Coke and a bottle of water, and carried both back to Maxine. I waited until her most recent customer left before offering her a choice of either. "You have no one to relieve you, and I thought you looked thirsty."

"That's so sweet!" She took the water and gulped down half the bottle before pouring a little into the cupped palm of her hand and splashing it down the back of her neck. "Trust me. Don't get old."

"I'll do my best." I took a sip of the cold Coke. "Would you like some help for a little while?"

"You know comics?" she asked.

"A little," I said. "I know most of the major characters, at least the ones who've had action figures made of them. I could handle the easy questions and general sales."

"Then I would *love* the company," she said.

The next half hour offered little time for talking. The customers who approached the booth weren't the gangly teens I'd stereotyped as comic book fans. These were grown men—with one or two women thrown in for variety—who'd probably established that gangly teen stereotype ten, twenty, or even thirty years ago. These were serious collectors, who, if they'd held onto and maintained their original collections, could have some serious dough tied up in the hobby.

One such man in front of me, hunched in an oversized canvas jacket despite the warm temperatures of the room, glanced up from the bin of comic books he'd been perusing, exposing warm brown eyes under a pair of surprisingly long lashes. He pointed to a group of comics in plastic cases. "You have any more CBCS-graded comics?" His eyes crinkled when he smiled.

"I . . . let me get Maxine to help you with that."

Maxine had overheard the question and came to my rescue. "I did have some," she said, "but they got misplaced when we were setting up. I hope to find them, and I can bring in what we have in the shop, if you'd care to check back tomorrow?"

He gave her a nod, let the stack he'd been browsing fall back into place, and wandered off.

"Thanks," I said. "What's all that? Were those the comics in the plastic cases?"

She nodded grimly, a flicker of worry darkening her expression. "CBCS stands for Comic Book Certification Service. We use them for our rarer comic book finds."

"Like appraisers?"

"Sort of. It's more of an evaluation of the condition of a book. We send them the physical books, and they give each an impartial grade out of ten, based on everything from how vibrant the ink is to color of the staples." She rolled her eyes. "All very picky. They seal the books up and put the grade right on the cover. It works great because there's no squabbling over multiple inspections—all of which can damage a comic book. And it's independent, so it protects buyer and seller alike."

"But you don't do it with every comic."

She shook her head. "Too expensive. It doesn't make sense to spend thirty or forty bucks to have a comic book graded unless its value is at least in the hundreds. Otherwise, there's no way of getting that money back. But once we have the grade, we can then look up the value of a particular book with that grade in the pricing guides, so it makes life a lot easier. Of course, the market goes up and down, so you still end up haggling a bit, but overall, the system works."

"And it was the graded comics that went missing this morning?"

"I need to find those." Maxine's posture stiffened. "You don't think someone could've walked off with them, do you?"

I shrugged. "I'd like to think not." I refrained from mentioning the suspected mobsters and ex-con walking around the show.

"I'll search through everything again before I leave, but I don't know where they could have gone. Unless Craig . . ." She screwed up her face. "I'm going to have to ask him."

"That sounds unpleasant."

"I'm hoping"—she crossed her fingers and looked up—"he did something with them, because if they've gone missing, he's not going to be happy. Especially with him in the hospital and all. Even with everything that's going on, I suppose he needs to know. They're worth a chunk of change, and they'd have to be officially reported stolen before insurance would do anything."

"So they *were* insured?"

"Absolutely! We won't take a loss on the missing books. Craig might be upset that I left the booth unattended for a bit. But you can back me up. You know the books went missing before that point!"

"That's right," I said. "You'd asked me if I had seen them."

She nodded. "I just hate to have to tell him. And I hate hospitals. It's bad enough visiting—I always feel like I'm at a pet store or something. Same smells, and all the people are scared and hurting. I never know what to say."

"I'm no pro, but it helps to have someone to go with. Would you like me to come along?"

She jumped at the chance, and we made plans to go after the show closed for the day. But when she started rambling on and on about how kind and unselfish I was, I began to feel guilty. My offer was spurred on more by curiosity than kindness—I wanted to hear straight from Craig the reasons behind his swan dive.

I changed the subject. "Where do you get your vintage comics?"

"Same places you get your vintage toys, I'd imagine," she said. "Mostly folks clearing out garages and attics and wondering if they have anything of value. Also, the occasional Craigslist or garage sale listing." She sniffled. "Sorry, but I was just thinking . . . Craig always likes to joke about buying comics on Craigslist. He calls it 'My List,' like the whole thing was made for him."

"I do a lot of buying for the shop that way too. It's tough, though. I think a lot of people want to be told that the broken toy that's been in their basement is worth tens of thousands of dollars, and that's not usually the case."

"We tell sellers up front we don't do appraisals, but we'll take a look through what they have and offer them a set amount for everything. Usually after that, it's just a matter of checking the price guides and dividing them up into the one-, three-, and five-dollar bins. Every now and then, though, we get lucky and find one that's rare—and in good enough condition—to send off for grading."

"Do you ever get folks who come back in looking to see how you've priced their comic books?" It was one of the harder parts about being a reseller. No matter how lean the operation, no business could survive by paying what an object was truly worth and then selling it for the same price. Still, it can strike some folks the wrong way when the doll we bought from them for forty bucks is on our shelf marked up to eighty.

"Oh, yeah. In fact, it's funny you should ask, because those comic books that went missing this morning? The woman who sold them to Craig has been in the shop a couple times, asking to buy them back. Even before they came back from grading, she was offering double and triple what Craig paid for them."

"Seller's remorse?"

"From what I overheard, they actually belonged to her husband, who wasn't in the picture at the moment."

"Now he wants them back?"

"I don't know," she said. "But we'd already sent them off, you see. And Craig wasn't about to let them go without making a tidy profit. But I'll tell you something else interesting. I saw her here, at the show, this morning."

The hairs on my neck stood up. Our quaint little train show was beginning to resemble Grand Central Station. "Do you have her name and contact information by any chance?"

"Why?"

"My dad's now working security. If it turns out that the comics were stolen, she might be a person of interest."

"I don't want to report them stolen yet—not until I've had a chance to look through the rest of the inventory and talk to Craig. I'd hate to accuse anyone and then discover it was a terrible misunderstanding."

I held my hands up. "Noted. No accusations. Still, I wouldn't mind having that contact information. Might come in handy."

Maxine stretched her neck. "I can look it up for you, if you give me a minute."

"Thanks, Maxine. Might be nothing, but couldn't hurt to look into it."

While she walked over to the laptop, I drained the last bit of Coke and went to place my cup in the trash can I'd noticed peeking underneath the display table. Inside were two foam cups, presumably from this morning's coffee. What drew my attention was a big waxy *H* scrawled on the side of one of the cups. Last I checked my alphabet, there wasn't an H to be had in either Maxine's or Craig's names. I pulled it out of the trash. This cup said "Hank."

This was the coffee I'd bought for my dad this morning. And if I was right . . .

Without saying anything to Maxine, I squeezed between the tables on the way to our booth. Miles was talking to a customer, so I ducked down, found the trash can under our table skirt, and rummaged through it. Sure enough, there was a cup in our trash marked "Craig."

What did it all mean? Had someone switched the cups? Or could they have switched the trash cans?

Then I recalled my father's suggestion that someone run a toxicology test on Craig. Could he have been drugged, and

66

might that have accounted for the erratic behavior that sent him diving from the rafters?

A shiver ran through me. If Craig *was* drugged, was the drug even meant for him?

Or was my father the target?

Chapter 7

The security office was small, somewhere between the size of a typical child's bedroom and a walk-in closet that you see on HGTV. Only this room was painted and furnished in greens and grays that some might find masculine but to me just felt drab. A bulletin board along one wall held charts, graphs, and notices, some in plastic protective sleeves, others yellowed and curled and waving in the air currents created by a nearby vent. Several flat-screen monitors showed the convention floor in grainy real time, and one of the cameras was trained on the comic booth.

"Come on in, Liz," Dad said without budging from his seat in front of the monitors.

"That's no fair," I said. "You could see me coming."

Dad wriggled his fingers toward the screen. "Pay no attention to the man behind the curtain."

I gave him the required chuckle, then turned to Ken, who was leaning against the wall. "How's Craig doing? Did you learn anything about why he was up on the catwalks?"

"As I was telling your dad here, that's going to be hard to sort through. According to the hospital staff, Craig had a number of hallucinations, especially right after he regained consciousness. They said he's quieted down, but I'm not sure they're over yet because he's not making complete sense."

"How so?" I asked.

Ken sent a pained look to my father, and Dad nodded. Parental consent to talk to me about the case? Seriously?

"Look," I said, checking the pique rising in my voice, "I'm out there working on the floor. If there's something going on, I want to know about it. You're not protecting me by allowing me to walk headlong into a dangerous situation."

Ken put his hands up. "That's not what I was trying to do," he said. "Look, this is an official ongoing investigation. I need to be careful what information I share and with whom."

"So you ask my dad?"

Ken scrubbed his face with his hands.

"Lizzie, give the man a break," Dad said, tilting back in his chair. "He's walking some pretty fine lines. You're not in law enforcement. You were a witness to the events. You know Craig . . ."

My heart started beating out a rumba in my ears. "Am *I* a suspect or something?"

"Well," Ken started, "your dad can vouch for your whereabouts . . ."

He stopped when I glared at him. Just a few days ago, I was pressed to decide between Jack and Ken. Now I was *this close* to being shed of both of them in one day. In one very bad day.

Ken rallied. "What I meant to say is that, no, of course you're not a suspect."

69

"Ken needs protection too," Dad said. "If someone comes along down the line and examines his records, it needs to be very clear that he didn't show any partiality or favoritism toward you by not establishing your whereabouts. It's a paper trail, really, for the protection of you both. And to protect any potential criminal case, if one ever goes to trial."

"But now that my alibi has been established," I said, "and permission has been obtained from Hank, the great and powerful, you can tell me what Craig said?"

"Brace yourself," Ken said. "It's a little anticlimactic. He claimed he was trying to reach the balloon."

"Why did he want to reach the balloon?" I asked.

"To get it for the little girl," Ken said. "I asked him twice. He was insistent on that point."

I pulled a strand of hair from my face and digested those words for a moment. "Craig's not the kind to risk his life to retrieve a child's balloon. He's not even the kind to go out of his way. Now, if he'd said he was trying to pop the balloon with a pin and laugh in the child's face, that I might believe, but this?"

"Bitter much, Lizzie?" Dad asked.

I let out a slow breath. Maybe I was. Craig wasn't that same kid who'd tormented me in school. "It's a bit of an exaggeration. Did Craig say anything about the publicity stunt?"

"Oddly enough, no, and then he went off on a random tangent about coffee."

I winced at the word and shifted the bag in my hands. My dad gave me an odd look.

Apparently Ken didn't notice. He went on: "But we did find a stack of leaflets up on the catwalk, promoting some new comic book series. I'm thinking he'd intended to shower them down over the convention floor."

"Mr. Inferno. Captain Inferno. Something like that," Dad said.

I forced my attention back to the subject at hand. "Maxine told me that was the new series he was trying to launch. It's why he wore that ridiculous costume."

"I couldn't get any more out of him. Maybe later when he's more coherent. Or if."

"If?" Dad asked.

"Right now his doctors aren't sure if it's some kind of drug in his system or the pain meds that are making him loopy. They're not ruling out brain injury."

I tried to push away the stray thought that it might just as easily have been Dad lying in that hospital bed. "Maxine was talking about going to see him after we close down for the day. I volunteered to go with her."

Ken was about to protest, but I headed him off.

"Don't worry. With permission of the mighty wizard here"—I genuflected in Dad's direction—"I'll gladly share anything I learn that will help the investigation."

Ken's jaw tightened, but he nodded.

"Meanwhile, there are a couple of other things you both oughta know." I shared with them what I learned about the woman who had sold the missing comics to Craig—and that Maxine had spotted her at the show. Not sure why I led with that. Was it because I really thought everything that happened was all about Craig and not my father? Or maybe I just wanted it that way.

Ken took the paper that Maxine had copied for me. (Unbeknownst to him, I had already taken a picture of it with my phone.) "Jenna Duncan," he read, then addressed my dad. "Mean anything to you?"

Dad hoisted himself out of the rolling chair, the springs painfully squeaking. He craned his neck to read the page in Ken's hand. "Not familiar. Nice part of town, though."

Ken crammed it into his pocket. "Not sure there's a lot I can do, especially since those comics haven't officially been reported stolen."

"Maxine wants to search the booth again, then she'll probably report it," I said. "But from what I gather, those comics were worth a boatload of money. The previous owner wanted them back, which gives her motive to steal them."

"I guess I can run her for priors, if nothing else," Ken said.

"If you do that," Dad said, "see if you can't come up with a picture, and we can look for her on the security footage anywhere near the comic booth, or near Craig. Probably stretching it, but if she was that upset about Craig cheating her, maybe she had motive to drug him."

"About that . . ." And then I froze, unable to get more words out, as if showing them the switched cups and putting the idea out there that my father might have been the target somehow made it more real. Maybe if I said nothing, it would melt away.

"What's wrong, Liz?" Dad said. "You're white as a ghost."

I lifted up the Wegmans bag I'd stuffed the foam cups into, which both brilliant detectives had failed to notice. I pulled out the cup with Craig's name first.

Ken pointed at it. "Nice work. *If* Craig was drugged, there's a chance someone might have put it in his coffee. There could be residue in the cup. Only what did we say about fingerprints?"

I ignored the patronizing tone. "Here's the thing," I said, finally finding my voice. "This isn't Craig's cup. Not the one he drank from, anyway. I pulled this out of our trash. And the cup I pulled out of Craig's trash?" I opened the bag to reveal the one with Dad's name on it.

Dad fell back into his chair. "Well, that puts a new wrinkle on it."

Ken waited a moment, took the bag with both cups from my hand, then pulled out a chair and sat facing my father. He pitched forward, forearms resting on his thighs. "Hank? You got any enemies?"

Dad looked up and met his gaze, just the hint of a sheepish grin on his otherwise stone-serious face. "How much time've you got?"

# # #

We each left that meeting with homework. Ken had the cups to send for forensics. Since results might take a while to come back, they had agreed that it made sense to assume the cup was drugged until it was proven otherwise, so my father was tasked with making a list of potential suspects who might want him dead.

I knew, of course, at least hypothetically speaking, that Dad must have made enemies during a lifetime in law enforcement, but the reality of names being etched onto paper made that much too real. The possibility that someone might now be targeting my father left me literally sick to my stomach, so instead of heading right back to help Maxine finish for the day, I made another trip to the concession stand for a ginger ale—and also to ask around to see if anyone saw anything peculiar when I picked up those coffees this morning.

"Look, if you didn't get what you ordered, you should have come back sooner," the server said. She was the same woman who I'd bought coffee from earlier, but then I had hardly noticed her. Now I took in every detail I could.

She was probably middle-aged, depending on how one defined the term. The older I got, the older middle age became. She carried a few extra pounds but not enough to hide the veins in her hands. Her face was flushed and shiny, and her reddish hair a bit frizzy, probably from the heat of the kitchen equipment. Her nametag was crooked but identified her as Janet.

"No, everything was fine," I said. "I just wanted to know if you saw anyone lingering around. Maybe switching coffee cups." I pointed to the table. "We were standing right there."

Janet shook her head. "We were swamped this morning. I take the orders, take the money, deliver the orders. I really don't have time to watch what goes on out there. Sorry."

"Thanks," I said, then took a gulp of the cold ginger ale, hoping it would clear the lump of worry in my throat. But as I was turning to leave, I noticed the security camera focused on the concession stand. Maybe there *was* a way to figure out how the cups got switched.

My father wasn't in the security office when I passed by, but I made a mental note to mention the camera to him before we left for the day.

Parker showed up just an hour before the show closed at six. At least he could help Miles pack everything away.

That last hour seemed excruciatingly normal. Old collectors trying to beef up their retirement accounts sold off their treasured prizes to younger collectors. Parker, working the toy booth, had an almost boyish gleam to his eyes, reminding me of the hours we'd spent playing together, possibly more than most siblings, since Dad worked late and Mom was often "not feeling well." In other words, sloshed out of her gourd. But Parker had grown to carry more responsibility than he should have, even while maintaining a playful spirit. He was going to make an excellent father, even if he didn't yet know it.

The circle of life. And no, I wasn't about to belt out any verses from *The Lion King*. But life moved full circle, much like all those trains on the tracks, making endless loops along the same paths. There was something both depressing and hopeful about that. Life, in all its mundane continuance.

Unless some idiot fell out of the sky and crushed you.

About fifteen minutes before closing, announcements began. Barely audible over the crowd, they reminded visitors to make their final purchases. We had a brief rush, lasting until about five minutes past six. No vender is going to refuse cash shoved into their face just because it's technically past closing.

Eventually, though, the lights dimmed and the aisles cleared. Without the sounds of conversations bouncing from the rafters, you could even hear the tiny electric motors whining and the trains clicking along on their tracks. That eventually died down too, as the little-engines-that-could were put to rest for the evening.

Maxine stretched, kicked off her shoes, and sighed. "One last search."

"Do you think the missing comics could've been taken out of their cases?"

"Not by accident," she said. "I'm going to lay odds that they're not here, but that's not going to stop me from doing a top-to-bottom search first. I'd feel like an idiot if I reported them stolen and then found them tomorrow when we packed up."

"If you have a list of the graded comics you brought to the show, I can check the bins, just in case."

"I do." She pulled out a three-ringed binder, flipped through a few pages, and ripped one out. She pulled a pen from her apron. "Everything from here"—she made two marks along the left side of the spreadsheet—"to here."

"Gotcha." I studied the list for a few moments to acquaint myself with the titles. There were even thumbnail pictures of the cover images.

Amazing Spider-Man from 1963. *Incredible Hulk: The Terror of the Toad Men*. Now, there's a plot you don't see every day. There was an early *Iron Man* that looked more like a bulked up Tin Man from *Wizard of Oz* than the more developed version we see in the movies. Most of the superheroes were familiar, even in their early incarnations. More unfamiliar was a newer, but apparently rare, book called *The Time of the Preacher*. I squinted at the thumbnail cover. As best I could tell, it was a demonic image hovering over a burning church. To quote the immortal words of Fozzie Bear, "They sure don't look like Presbyterians to me."

With those titles and a few more in my head, I pulled the dollar bin to the floor and sprawled out. Since the building was now almost empty and all the other dealers probably felt as wiped out as I did, there was no sense standing on ceremony. Or standing, period.

Some books were in cheaper flexible plastic sleeves. Others weren't. But I checked all the sleeved comics to make sure there was only one inside and pulled all of them from the box to make sure nothing had fallen underneath them.

Parker came up behind me and started rubbing my shoulders.

I craned my neck to look up at him. "You know, for a brother, you're awfully nice."

"Our booth is all shut up for the night." He sat down next to me. "What are you doing here?"

I held up the page Maxine had handed me. "Looking for these. They haven't been seen since this morning."

His eyes bulged when he read the list. "You *misplaced* an original Spider-Man?"

"That we're not sure about. We only know it's missing."

Parker sucked air through his teeth. "That's a big loss. How about I help you look?" Without waiting for an answer, he pulled down a three-dollar bin and started going through them. He'd gotten three books in when he pulled one out to read.

Our search of the bins turned up none of the missing comics. Maxine also removed the table covers to see if the table-cloths might have been laid over the comics. (They weren't.) And she pulled everything out from underneath the tables, all the coats and extra supplies. (Nothing.) She plopped a gym bag on the table. "Craig's," she said. "I guess I should check it, right?"

Parker said nothing, mostly because he was still reading. I just shrugged. But when she unzipped it, I pushed myself up off the cool concrete floor so I could take a look. There was nothing in there but dirty laundry.

Maxine wrinkled her nose and rezipped the bag. "I'll just take these home and wash them for him."

We even searched the area around the booth. Fabric curtains draped the back wall, covering some ugly utilities, it turned out. But no comic books behind it or under the heavy fabric.

"Well," she said, slinging the gym bag over one arm, "here's hoping that Craig knows where they are."

"Ready to go to the hospital?" I asked. I had a couple of things to retrieve from our booth.

"I should stop home first and feed my cat. And if Craig is doing better, he might want me to pick him up something too. You know hospital food. How about I just meet you there, say, seven thirty-ish?"

I promised her I would, then Parker and I stopped at the security office before we left. Dad was packing VHS tapes into a box.

"Homework?" I asked, shrugging on my sweater. "Make sure you get the one that's focused on the concession stand. I went back to ask if maybe they'd seen anything, but no luck. There should be a nice camera shot of the table though. Oh, and this morning's coffee was courtesy of Janet something or other. Redhead. Ring any bells?"

"No, but I can get her full name from the center and add her to the list Ken's making me come up with."

I must have looked grim.

"Honey, listen. I know you're concerned, and I'm sure I've ticked off a good number of people over the years, but I doubt anyone is out there gunning for me. If they were, they probably would have come for me long before this."

"That's . . . hardly reassuring." I ran my finger across one of the security tapes. "Wait. If this center is so new, why does their security system still use video tapes?"

"Two words."

"Lionel Kelley?"

"Told the center director he knew a guy who could get him a deal," Dad said. "Really not as bad as it sounds. The cameras are decent, and at least the tapes are fairly new. Now if only I can find our old VCR." He placed the last tape in the box and shut off the lights as we walked out.

"Linen closet. Top shelf," I said. "I think."

"Who keeps a VCR in a linen closet?" Parker teased.

"Who keeps a VCR?" Dad said.

"Just be glad I did." I smiled sweetly. "I'll be home to make popcorn after I go to the hospital with Maxine." I turned to Parker. "You guys want to come over and watch?"

"Sounds like fun," Parker said. "But as much as I love surveillance footage, I'm going to have to pass. Cathy put a special dinner into the Crock-Pot this morning. Says we need to talk."

"You in the doghouse, son?" Dad asked. "'Cause we have room on the couch if you need."

"I don't think so, but she's been awful moody lately, so I'll keep it in mind."

"Buy dessert on the way home," I suggested.

"Really?" he said. "I was thinking wine."

I shook my head. "Dessert. Pie's good. Cake. Trust me."

He held his hands up. "Pie it is. On my way."

After Parker walked out, I kissed Dad on the cheek. "I should get going too. I'll run home and change and check on Othello before heading to the hospital."

Dad gave me a look that suggested he was a tiny bit green with envy. Not quite lime green. More like iceberg lettuce. "Maybe I could go with you."

I shook my head. "He's not going to say anything more to you than he will to Maxine—and probably less. I promise I'll share with you, in detail, everything Craig says, including all nonverbal communication, gestures, facial expressions, and awkward pauses. Would you like a diagram of the room and a copy of his medical charts?"

"Well, if you can take a picture of them when nobody is looking . . ."

"It's not like old movies where they hang them at the foot of the bed." I laughed. "I'll get everything I can."

"Thank you, Liz." Then he clammed up tight. Something more he wanted to say but was afraid to say it.

"What is it?"

"We don't know what we're up against yet." He gave me a hug. "Be careful."

# # #

The visitor lot was full when I got there. Well, almost full. I did find a tiny spot in a corner, next to a sports car that was parked at an odd angle. The owner probably figured nobody would park next to him, but never discount the squeezing-in abilities of a Civic owner who's tired and doesn't want to walk ten blocks. Climbing over the cup holder so I could exit through the passenger door was a fair tradeoff.

Maxine wasn't in the lobby when I walked in, so I got Craig's room number from the guard at the desk, then found a spot in the lobby and sank down into the fake leather chair. The cushions of the oversized cube chairs were the only softness in the space. Everything else was angular and made of aluminum, glass, or stone in varying shades of gray and black. It was meant to be sleek but came off a little cold. I thumbed through a couple of magazines and, when no one was looking, tore out a recipe for orange Creamsicle cake.

Maxine came running in at 7:45 carrying a Wegmans bag. "Sorry. I couldn't find a parking spot."

"It was pretty packed when I got here." I pushed myself out of the chair, only to find my legs had stiffened up on me. If this kind of day was hard on me, Maxine, older and a bit more out of shape, had to be exhausted.

"I brought some of those little powdered donuts. Craig's always liked them, but I'll have to ask at the desk if he's allowed to have them." We waited at the bank of elevators for a car to empty and then headed up to the third floor.

Maxine stopped at the desk. Craig was permitted the donuts, and she pulled out the box and stuffed the bag into her pocket.

We followed the signs down the maze of hallways. By the numbers, we had to be getting close to Craig's room when total chaos erupted. Medical personnel in scrubs flew past us, and Maxine and I had to cling to the wall to avoid colliding with a cart someone raced down the corridor.

"Where's the fire?" Maxine asked.

When the foot traffic cleared, we rounded one more corner and discovered that half the doctors and nurses in the hospital seemed to be jammed into Craig's room.

We'd found the fire. And oddly enough, it led us back to Doctor/Mister/Professor Inferno.

"Maybe it's routine?" Maxine suggested. But we both knew it wasn't.

I leaned against the cold tiled wall in the hallway opposite his room and said a little prayer for Craig. I tried to remember him as the boy who'd had so much trouble in his life and had somehow succeeded despite all the obstacles. Occasionally, I'd look at Maxine, and I think she was praying too.

Eventually, the frantic pace of those inside the room seemed to ebb. A few staff members started to leave. Because the emergency had passed?

But when enough medical personnel had left the room so that it was no longer wall-to-wall scrubs, it became clear that not only had the emergency passed, but by the graying pallor of his skin and his lack of response as those around him unhooked him from various machines, Craig had passed as well.

Maxine let out a cry and dropped the box of doughnuts. The container burst open, sending up a cloud of powdered sugar. Mini doughnuts rolled around on the floor by her feet, and one adventurous fellow went tearing down the hallway.

Chapter 8

I pulled into the alley behind the shop, turned off my ignition, and sat there for a moment watching the car windows fog and blur my surroundings. My heart ached, but I wasn't sure why.

I'd never liked Craig. In fact, for much of my life, I'd hated him. But in that moment, I remembered him as I first saw him: the gangly new kid marched into the front of the class in elementary school. He had a homespun haircut with muddy brown locks sticking up here and there, and he wore a snagged, striped knit shirt that hung in places where the original owner had stretched it out. All that was rounded out with a freckled face complete with a chipped-toothed, crooked smile and a voice that was throaty and sometimes hard to understand.

One lone tear ran down my face, and I hesitated to brush it away. I still didn't like the bully he had been or the man he became, but I was glad I had at least one honest tear to shed for him.

When I finally climbed out of my car, Dad was holding the rear door of the shop open. "I just heard," he said. "You all right?"

I nodded.

Headlights lit up the back alley and swung wildly as a police cruiser pulled in next to me. Ken climbed out. "Does she know?"

"I just came from the hospital." I shivered, not sure if it was from the cold or the memory, and my dad hustled us inside.

Up in the apartment, the coffeepot was gurgling its final refrain. Without bothering to remove my coat, I dragged myself into the living room and collapsed on my usual spot on the sofa.

Othello sat on his haunches in the middle of the coffee table, surrounded by VHS tapes. The cat looked up at me for a moment, blinked, then wove his way around the tapes, stopping to stretch before he hopped onto the couch and curled up in my lap.

Dad shoved coffee into my hand. "Drink," he commanded, standing there until I did.

Ken threw his jacket over the arm of the chair facing me and sat down.

I looked up at him, hesitant to ask the question I needed to ask. "Murder, then?" I said quietly, reaching out my hand for Othello to sniff before running it along his head, then along his sleek black and white fur, all the way to tip of his tail. He immediately rewarded me with a purr.

Ken gave a hesitant nod, then locked his gaze with mine. "Still not sure. Going to treat it as such, though, until we know otherwise."

Dad returned with two more cups and set them on the coffee table.

I pointed to the stack of VHS tapes balancing precariously on the glass. "Did you come over to watch?"

"Considering what happened, I thought I'd better." Ken reached into the pocket of his jacket, pulling out papers held together by a rubber band. "By the way, there's no record on Janet, our barista, except that she likes to drive a little fast. I've got a couple of guys tracking down the whereabouts of the other names on Hank's list. So far, most of them are either still in jail or have moved out of the area."

I looked up at my dad, whose face was grim. I wondered if he'd included Terry on that list. He'd have motive, I suppose. And the opportunity. Though if he had drugged the coffee—assuming the coffee had been drugged in the first place—his motive might have been less than murder. A practical joke, perhaps? Something that would maybe make Dad sick or loopy, perhaps embarrass him? All things that might have happened if the person who'd ingested this still hypothetical drug hadn't donned a spandex suit and climbed a ladder.

"How do you do this?" I asked. "Manage all these what-ifs? It's a tangled mess."

Dad put a hand on my shoulder. "You follow every possible lead until they dead-end."

"And on that note," Ken continued, "I was able to get a few things on our mystery woman, the one who sold Craig the comic books. Including a picture." He pulled that sheet out of the packet and handed it to Dad.

Dad reached for his reading glasses, offering me a glimpse of the picture as he did. Jenna Duncan was a hard woman to characterize. Brunette, yes. Pretty, yes. But that was the easy part. Classic and elegant would be her style. A little Jackie O, but with a lot more swagger. I suspected that if any of her features had dared stray outside of the limits of perfection, she'd've had them surgically altered years ago.

"Anything pop up when you ran her background?" Dad asked.

"No priors. She's clean, but it's who she's married to that makes this all a little interesting. Y'ever hear of a lawyer by the name of Joshua Duncan?"

Dad sat up a little straighter. "This is Josh Duncan's wife?"

Ken nodded.

"Who's Josh Duncan?" I asked.

"Ah, he's . . ." Dad let that word end in a hiss. "Uh, rather, he *was* a local lawyer. Still alive, but disbarred and kind of in prison."

"*Kind of* in prison?" I repeated.

"He's definitely in prison," Ken said.

"I put him there," Dad said, scratching his cheek. "At least, I started the investigation based on some initial complaints. I was out of my league so I handed it over to the FBI, who put their white-collar investigators and forensic accountants on it and found even more. Duncan claimed he just took on too many clients and got in over his head. But he'd falsified documents to make it look like he was doing a stellar job, even though his mistakes hurt his clients. One poor sap even found out his divorce was phony. His new wife was *not* happy to discover she'd married a bigamist, despite the reality TV potential."

"How did I miss all this?" East Aurora always seemed like such a quiet hamlet when I was growing up. And it still looked the same. Maybe it was time to get those rose-colored glasses checked.

"It brewed over when you were living in Jersey," Dad said. "When it came to trial, sentencing guidelines said he could've been given anything from a slap on the wrist to serious jail time. Only Duncan apparently had a habit of acting pretty cocky in court, so not only did the judge throw the book at him, but I think she adjourned before passing sentence so she could go home and search for a bigger book."

"So while he's locked up, his wife cleans out the attic and sells Craig her husband's prized comic book collection," I said. "And from what I gather, at a steep discount. And now she's mad."

"But who's she mad at?" Ken said. "The comic book dealer who cheated her? Or the cop who sent her husband away?"

"Given all that activity around the comic booth, I'd lay serious money on the former, but that's not the only question," Dad said. "As I recall, Duncan also had a chunk of change to pay back in restitution. How is it that Jenna Duncan managed to stay in this house?"

"Maybe she has money of her own?" I asked.

"I guess I should check with the FBI to see if she's on their radar," Ken said.

"Talk to Mark Baker," Dad suggested. "He's the forensic accountant who worked the case. Tell him I sent you."

"Thanks," Ken said.

"Meanwhile, I'd like a replay of what happened at that comic booth." Dad stood up and put a tape into the VCR. Soon a grainy picture popped up on the screen.

"So we're looking for this Jenna woman?" I asked. "And Batman-man and Grandpa?"

"Edward Millroy," Ken said. "And the other guy's name is Don Eicher. We should also try to follow Craig's movements."

"He disappeared for a while this morning," I said.

"We'll want to watch everyone who approaches and see what they do."

"Including Terry Wallace," Ken said softly. He looked at me as if he wanted to say more.

"Terry had no reason to hurt Craig," I said.

Ken tapped out an unrecognizable rhythm on his legs before answering. "With all the action taking place near that comic booth, it suggests that if anyone was drugged, Craig was probably the target. But I'm not ready to discount other possibilities." He stared at my father. "And for your own safety, I don't think you should write them off either. If we go with the working theory that someone tampered with the coffee cup, then we still have to allow that Craig might not have been the intended victim."

Dad didn't answer. He picked up the remote and pressed *play*.

# # #

When I woke up, I had a kink in my neck and a little string of drool connecting me to the throw pillow. I quickly wiped it away as I realized I wasn't alone in the living room.

Dad was sound asleep in his favorite chair, while Ken smiled up at me from where he'd stretched out on the floor with his back against the sofa, the remote still in his hand. I picked up my phone and glanced at the time: 2 AM.

"You shouldn't have let me sleep."

"You probably needed it," he whispered.

I sat up, squinted into my empty coffee cup, and set it down on the table amid the collection of cups, glasses, and the oversized popcorn bowl that now held just a few kernels. "Did you find anything?" The last tape I remembered had shown nothing suspicious, unless you counted Craig flapping his cape, swooping in on people, and annoying everyone in sight.

Ken pushed himself up off the floor and sat next to me on the sofa. "I'd like you to see this." He rewound the tape and let it play.

This camera angle caught the comic book stand perfectly—and Maxine who was working behind the counter. To the left, Jack stood next to Terry who was paging through comic books from the five-dollar bin, and you could make out Maxine's face turning in that direction, as if she was talking with them. I was so focused on them that I didn't catch the movement to the right of the table until the person walked away, but then I realized it was Batman-man.

"Wait, replay that."

Ken did, and this time I watched the right end of the table. When Maxine was talking with Terry, Batman-man approached the table. Even from a distance, something was odd in the picture, as if he was fumbling with something from the pocket of the coat that was slung over his arm.

"Back again?" I craned my neck forward to watch.

This time it was pretty clear that Millroy was doing something with his coat. Hiding something inside? Or pulling something out?

"Sorry, rewind again?"

Ken rewound, and even while the tape was progressing backward, I looked for the coffee cups. There was one on a table in the back of their booth, but midway through the tape, Maxine took a sip from it.

"There. Could you freeze it?"

Ken froze the tape in the spot just before Millroy approached the booth.

I got up and walked to the television. "Right there." I pointed to an object barely visible behind one of the comic bins to the right of the screen. "Is that a coffee cup?"

Ken came up behind me. Close enough behind me that I could feel his breath on my neck. "I think so."

I took the remote from his hand and stepped the tape slowly through the whole sequence. Ken remained close, watching it with me. I could feel his warmth against my back and smell his musky scent. I resisted the urge to pull away to protect my personal space. After everything that happened today—or rather, yesterday—the human connection felt like a tonic. I breathed it in.

I paused during Millroy's fumbling with his jacket. "Is he hiding something underneath it, like comic books? Or is he getting something out of it?" A few more frames after this, he'd hunched over the comic book bin. It would've been easy, if he had good aim, to drop something right into the cup behind it.

"Inconclusive," Ken rumbled, very close to my ear. "Could be either. I don't see Jack's brother making any kind of moves like that, unless he's deliberately distracting Maxine."

"Why would he help those guys? He has no connections to the mob."

"Unless he made some in prison. A lot of men who go in don't come out for the better. Unless you count the new criminal skills they learn and contacts they've made."

I nodded. So Terry still wasn't completely in the clear.

Ken reached his arm around my waist. "I hope you're not mad at me. About earlier."

I hugged him tighter and let my head rest against his shoulder. "It's just an ugly situation. I never liked Craig, so I can see why you had to rule me out, and I'm glad you did."

"It was easy when I saw you never went anywhere near the coffee."

I had closed my eyes, still relishing the closeness and safety. When his words sank in, my eyes popped open and I pushed him away to arm's length. "But I did. I did have access to the coffee."

"I don't see you anywhere near it at the booth."

I shook my head. "Not at the booth. Maxine was behind me in line. We both set all our cups down at a table. Jack and Terry were there. You. *You* were there."

Ken's face blanched, clearly visible even under a deep five-o'clock—or rather two-AM—shadow. "There was coffee on the table."

"There were cameras," I said.

Ken froze in place, and I fumbled through the stack of videotapes, holding the labels up to the light coming in from the streetlight outside. I ejected the paused one and put the concessions area tape in the player, then fast-forwarded it, keeping my eye on the time stamp. I pressed *play*, and the concession stand came into near focus. I stood in line with Jack and Terry with Maxine right behind. I watched as she got her coffees, I grabbed mine, and Jack and Terry got theirs, and we all set them on that wobbly round cocktail table. All the cups were clearly visible, no tampering possible, until Ken walked up. His position obscured the camera view, and shortly after that he accidentally jostled the table and we all made a grab for the cups.

Ken backed up the tape, played it again, then let out a chain of epithets that could raise the dead.

My father awoke with a snort. "What?"

Ken replayed it and Dad raised a fist to his mouth.

"What?" I said.

"*I* could have done it," Ken said, shaking his head.

"But you didn't," I said, shifting my gaze between Ken and my father. They seemed to be in the middle of an intense telepathic communication.

"That's not the point, sweetheart," Dad said. He turned to Ken. "Who's your best man? Howard Reynolds?"

Ken nodded. His lips were drawn so tight, I was worried someone would have to take a crowbar to pry them apart.

"It'll be okay," Dad said. "He's a good cop."

"Don't mind me," I said. "Apparently I don't need to know what's going on. Does this mean you have to excuse yourself from the investigation?"

"Recuse," Dad said, "and there's actually no rule that he has to. But should a case come to trial and some savvy defense lawyer picks up on any hint of impropriety or evidence tampering—"

"But he wouldn't do that," I said. "And they certainly couldn't prove it. Besides, aren't you like ninety-nine percent sure that Craig is at the center of all this?"

"I still think he is," Dad said.

"Then what does it matter who drank out of whose cup?" I asked.

"Because just putting that idea out there," Ken said, "can weaken a case in the eyes of a jury. All any savvy defense attorney needs is reasonable doubt. For instance, you didn't like Craig."

"Yes, but I wouldn't kill him!"

"And I wouldn't tamper with evidence. Would a jury who doesn't know either of us have the same confidence?"

Ken waited for a response, but I didn't have one. "I'll let Howard know this is his case in the morning—somebody might as well get some sleep." He picked up his coat. "You both should too."

While Dad walked him to the door, I gathered a few dirty glasses and the popcorn bowl and put them in the kitchen sink.

"Don't look so worried, Lizzie," he said when he returned.

"I don't know Howard Reynolds. Any good?"

"Best as they come. Iraq War vet. Level-headed. Thorough. Doesn't back down from a fight but doesn't go looking for one, either."

"I suppose that'll make me a suspect, then."

"He'll want to talk to you. He'll want to talk to me. Will he consider either of us as suspects? That'll depend on how the evidence comes in."

"I don't like this one," I said. "It's coming too close. To all of us. I could be a suspect. You might have been targeted and could have been killed. Ken is off the case. Jack and Terry are under suspicion as well. What in the world is going on?"

Dad gave me a hug. "I don't think we're going to find any answers to that one tonight. Get some sleep, sunshine. Maybe in the morning something will dawn on you."

I was halfway to my bedroom before I recognized the puns, but I was too tired to groan.

Chapter 9

I awoke to pressure on my chest and a black tail swishing my face, but before I had time to swat it away, Othello dug in his rear claws and launched off, running to the sound of a can of cat food being opened in the kitchen, no doubt by Dad.

I fumbled to find my glasses on the nightstand and glanced at the clock: 6 AM, on the dot. Later than I'd wanted to sleep, but I still had plenty of time to get ready and start the second—and last—day of the train and toy show by eight.

I reluctantly threw off the covers and crossed to the window to pull back the curtains.

Main Street still looked the same. Same faux brick street. Same delightfully quaint shops, most still closed, of course. A few cars ventured down the street, windshield wipers slapping off a little condensation. A stray reflected headlight pierced the morning twilight and drew my eyes to Craig's shop. It brought a lump to my throat. He'd accomplished so much, converting that once-vacant storefront into a thriving business, and he had died leaving so many plans unfulfilled.

What would happen to the business and to those comics he'd been working on?

When I padded out to the kitchen, Dad, wearing an apron over his security uniform, had already started the coffee. Bacon popped and sizzled in a small pan on the stove, and he rushed to turn down the heat.

"You seem chipper this morning," I said, reaching into the cupboard and pulling out the largest mug I could find.

"It's all those years operating on little or no sleep. I'm rather used to the long hours. How are you doing?"

"Funny thing," I said. "My alarm clock didn't go off this morning."

"I may have sneaked in to turn it off," he said. "I texted Parker and Miles, and they're both willing to pitch in today. I figured Parker could work the store, maybe Miles and Cathy run the booth."

"And I could, what? Sleep in and have my nails done, maybe catch a movie? Dad, yes, I was upset about Craig, but I think I can handle working today."

"Actually, I thought you might like the chance to just walk around the train and toy show."

"Take in the scenery? Check out the competition?"

Instead of answering, Dad pulled a plate from the cupboard, lined it with paper towels, and started draining the cooked bacon. "I was hoping you could be my eyes and ears. You did good yesterday, kiddo. The coffee cups. The missing comics. Jenna Duncan. They're all details that might've gone unnoticed because it all looked like an accidental fall. You gave the police several leads and may have preserved key evidence."

As he heaped on the compliments, I could feel my head swell, but at the same time, my internal early warning system was activated. Dad's praise was seldom unconditional. The safe, *rational* thing to do would be to put my foot down and drag both of us out of the investigation. But Dad had spun his words as adeptly as some cult leader, playing on my pride, my craving for his approval, my sense of justice, and that infernal inherited curiosity.

I said nothing, but my next sip of coffee tasted an awful lot like Kool-Aid.

"This is the last day of the show," he said. "I'm assuming all the major players from yesterday will show up again. They seem to have some unfinished business."

"And you trust me to do this on my own?" I pulled out a chair and plopped at the table with my coffee.

"Why wouldn't I?"

"You're going to send your little girl, out all alone, wandering the mean aisles of the East Aurora Train and Toy Show?" I forced a casual smile. "Why, I could trip over a teddy bear, step on a Lego, or even get my eye poked out by a lightsaber."

"Just as long as you don't run off with that Howdy Doody doll a few booths over."

I batted my eyelashes at him. "But Howdy is so sweet. You don't know him like I do. And I can earn enough to support both of us until he finishes school."

Dad set the plate of bacon on the table and sat down. "A pretty girl like you, I doubt you'd be alone for long," he said airily and picked up his newspaper.

I crumpled the top of his paper so I could see his face. "What have you done?"

He shook the crinkles out of the paper and set it down. "I just mentioned to Ken that you'd be there. Since he handed over the investigation to Howard Reynolds, it seems he's decided to take some time off."

I narrowed my eyes. "What's your game?"

"Lizzie," he said, his expression grim, "this isn't a game. The more I think about it, the bleaker it looks. We've got one dead man, and we can't even call it murder, not for sure. And all these characters are walking around, and we've no idea what they're up to or who they're after. And the clock is ticking. I know I can't keep you from the toy show, but if you're going to be there, you might as well see what you can find out. And I figured you'd be safer with Ken along."

"For my protection."

"Yes."

"And that's the *only* reason?"

He half-hid his face behind his coffee cup. "I thought you might enjoy the company. You do seem to get along."

"So a little investigation, a little matchmaking. And you've already talked to Parker, Miles, and Ken. What time did you get up, anyhow?"

"A little after five. But I've been multitasking like the wind. I also looked up the value of those missing comic books." He pushed a neatly written column of numbers in my direction.

I glanced at the total at the bottom and nearly spurted coffee out of my nose. "*Ninety thousand dollars?*"

"Closer to ninety-five, but in that ballpark."

"That's some ritzy ballpark. Ninety grand would pay for a lot of peanuts and nachos." I set my mug down, pulled off my glasses, and started to run down the list of comics. "These have to play some part in what happened. I had no idea they were worth this much. I wonder if Maxine does."

"Beats me," Dad said. "But Jenna Duncan just got a lot more interesting."

I leaned back in my chair. "So did Craig. Who would even bring ninety thousand dollars' worth of merchandise to a local collector's show?"

Dad rested his elbows on the table. "That's a very astute question. You have to figure Craig brought them because he was reasonably convinced he had a buyer for them."

I looked up at him. "The mob guys?"

"Maybe, but why?"

I shrugged. "Jenna Duncan might want them back, but if Craig knew what they were worth and he got them fair and square, he's not going to give her a bargain."

"True," Dad said. "And then there's the age-old question—who gains the most from Craig's death?"

"Maxine did say that they were insured. I'm going to lay odds that he carried life insurance as well."

"So who benefits?" Dad asked. "And when we find that out, we also need to know if those beneficiaries were at the train show."

"They wouldn't have had to be," I said. "They could've hired someone. What if the mob guys were there as hired guns to kill Craig? Or you? Or maybe nobody tried to kill anybody, because we still don't know for sure that Craig was drugged. And even if he was, we don't know the goal was murder."

He winked at me. "You're very good at this."

"How can you say that? I have a million pieces and none of them fit."

"Exactly. Most mistakes at this stage of the game are made because of assumptions. You're gathering pieces, figuring out different ways they might go together, but you're not trying to jam them to make them fit. Seriously. You're a natural. Must be good genes."

"I'm afraid my good jeans are in the wash."

"And it always comes back to clothes." Dad rolled his eyes. "And I had so much hope you'd keep your mind on the case."

"I'm just figuring out what I should wear today. Seems I have a date with a policeman."

# # #

I never got a chance to "accidentally" run into Ken at the toy show, since he was waiting for me at the kitchen table when I emerged from the bathroom, showered and dressed and looking for my earring.

"You look nice," he said, coming over to kiss my cheek.

"Thanks. Where's . . ."

"Your father let me in as he was leaving. He went over early to check things out at the show."

"And you're my protector for the day?"

Ken shrugged, and I thought I detected a hint of a blush. Was he onto Dad's other motive for setting this up?

"Are you sure it isn't my father who needs protecting?"

"My guys are still running down that list, but I was thinking. If someone drugged that cup intending it for your father, it would have had to happen early on, probably in the concessions area. That's all on tape, and not too many people had opportunity, and even fewer had any reason to hold a grudge against your father."

He didn't mention the glaring exception. *Terry.* I'd definitely keep my eyes open for him at the show today.

I finally spotted my earring in the corner under the kitchen table. Funny thing about earrings, you can't always find them where you left them, especially if you have a cat.

"Just let me go clean this off," I said, heading to the bathroom.

I stared at myself in the mirror. "Is this what you want?" I whispered. Assuming my relationship with Jack was DOA, as our last conversation suggested was inevitable, was I ready for some kind of committed relationship with Ken? My feelings for him personally aside—and he was a great guy and certainly Dad's fan-favorite—did I want to get more seriously involved with a cop?

I knew the long hours and the stress all too well. I hadn't worried too much about Dad when I was little. I recalled being more resentful than anything else, especially when fun plans were cancelled and promises broken. But that changed when I began to understand the dangers of his work—and any vestiges of resentment remaining were surgically extracted at the instant I'd learned that he'd been shot in the line of duty.

Someone needs to run in the direction from which bullets are coming, and I had a lot of respect for the men and women who did. But I wasn't quite sure *I* wanted to be the one at home with her stomach tied into a macramé plant hanger, waiting to see when—or if—someone I loved would ever walk through the door.

I shook my head at my reflection. It was nice to have someone to go to the movies with, or to philharmonic concerts at Knox Farm. And maybe that's all that Ken wanted too. He'd never seemed in any particular hurry to advance a relationship. But perhaps my friendship with Jack had something to do with that too.

But today Ken was to be my partner-in-crime, and not my partner-for-life, so I did my best to shake the thought from my mind.

Seriously, how close can someone be to having a complicated love life without having one at all?

# # #

"Where are we headed?" I asked Ken, still thinking about the relationship conversation with my reflection.

"I thought we could go to the station first," Ken said, taking my words at face value. "Howard Reynolds is going to want to talk with you, so I thought maybe we could get that out of the way." He hazarded a glance at me as he waited for a break in traffic to make a turn. "Maybe pick up a little information while we're there, if we're lucky."

"So in other words, you're still working the case, just not officially."

He nodded. "It's not that I don't trust Howard or the rest of the guys. They're great. But there's too much riding on this whole situation for me to cool my heels at home or pack up and go hunting."

I merely nodded while he pulled into the parking lot and slid into his reserved spot.

Lori Briggs, the mayor's wife, whose apparent interest in the police chief had sparked more than a few rumors around town, gave me a frozen grin as she met us midway to the door. "Why, Liz! Ken. Funny to run into you here." Her attention was all on Ken, which was pretty typical. "They just told me you'd taken today off."

He dipped his chin and took my arm. A signal to her? "Yes, ma'am. Just needed to stop by for a few minutes."

"I thought you'd be working the case," she said.

He shrugged. "Not sure yet whether there is a case, but it's in good hands."

She narrowed her eyes. "Be careful. I'm not saying Craig McFadden was all that well liked around here, but the folks on Main Street are a little worried this is becoming a trend. First that ugly business in the toyshop last year, and now . . ."

"What are people saying?" I asked. "Because from where I was standing, it looked like Craig fell."

"They're saying drugs. Something trippy, like LSD or PCP. And it might not be any of my business, but now's not the time to slack off. It's time to find his dealer or whatever and send a clear message that we have a zero-tolerance policy on illegal drugs."

"I assure you," Ken said, "nobody is slacking off, and if it turns out Craig's death was due to some kind of drug over-dose, every asset of my department will be used to root out the source." Ken's words had grown in vehemence.

Lori was a little taken aback, quite literally, and stumbled into the mulch lining the walkway, her high heel sinking into the loose ground. Ken reached out to keep her from falling.

She held onto his arm a little longer than was necessary. "Alrighty then," she said, her face flushed. "I guess I'd better leave you to it." She sauntered to her Volvo, once again parked in the tow-away zone out front.

Ken watched her go. "One of these days, I'm going to have that car towed." He pulled open the door. "Shall we?"

"I notice you didn't correct her. Do you think Craig might have taken some kind of street drug?" I'd been so fixated on the coffee cups and the idea that my father could have been targeted that I'd never even considered that if anyone drugged Craig, that person might be Craig.

He shrugged. "She's just guessing. But it's certainly possible. That, and perhaps some kind of overdose or side effect from a legitimate medication. I hope the toxicology results come in quick so we know what we're dealing with. If it is some kind of new designer drug moving in, I want to move it out just as quick."

The air seemed stagnant as we made our way inside. Ken was immediately buzzed in, and I followed him to a desk at the back of the bullpen. At it sat a thirtysomething African American man. He was bulky without suggesting a lack of fitness, and he already looked tired. I suspected he'd been working for hours.

"Detective Reynolds, this is Liz McCall. I thought you might want to talk with her. She was a witness to the incident yesterday."

Reynolds rose from his desk and offered a hand. I shook it, trying hard not to be surprised as I noticed several fingertips were missing. The war? I'd been told he was a veteran.

"Thanks, saves me a trip." He sent a friendly, reassuring smile in my direction while gesturing to a chair next to his desk. "How are you doing this morning, Miss McCall?"

"Liz is fine," I said, smiling while I sat down. In the corner of my mind was Dad's voice saying how a good interrogator always acted like your best friend. And suddenly I was less reassured.

"So you knew this Craig McFadden?" His tone was even and conversational. Fine. I had nothing to hide.

"Yes, sir. I went to school with him, for a little while anyway. Later he moved away."

"What did you think of him?"

Ken, who hadn't made any move to leave, cleared his throat.

I sat up a little straighter. "Honestly, in school he was quite a jerk. But I was trying to give him the benefit of the doubt that he'd turned his life around."

"And you got along with him now?"

"I didn't see that much of him," I said, not mentioning that I tended to go out of the way to make that happen.

"So you probably couldn't tell me if he was acting out of the ordinary at all."

I shook my head.

Ken leaned forward. "You might want to check with his doctor to see if he was on any medications . . ."

"Got it covered." Detective Reynolds rubbed an eyebrow and turned back to me. "Your businesses are in competition, I gather."

"Not really," I said. "He sold mostly comic books, and we mainly sell toys. There is only a small overlap."

"Yet you still offered his employee a job at your place based on her experience."

Rats. "You've been talking with Maxine."

He nodded. "She's a bit torn up about the whole thing."

"She knew Craig a lot better than I did, and now she's got to be wondering if she has a job."

"So Craig's death opens the door for you to acquire a valuable employee," Reynolds said.

I laughed. I couldn't help it. A few heads around the bullpen pivoted to look in my direction. "Are you entertaining the idea that I killed Craig so I could steal Maxine? For the record, I wasn't trying to steal Maxine as much as I wanted to borrow her for the holiday rush. She's an amazing worker, and yes, I did want to capitalize on that knowledge base a little bit. Not many temporary employees could pick the Bionic Six out of a lineup of action figures. When you find one who can, they're good as gold." I made a mental note to ask her if she was still available.

He scooted back in his chair, and Ken's head drooped. Time to start holding my tongue a bit.

"You might be right there," Reynolds said. "As a motive, it's a little sketchy. But tell me what you know about Maxine."

"Not a whole lot. Just what I saw at the show yesterday. She's very efficient and personable. She dealt well with customers and seemed to get along with Craig okay, which couldn't have been easy."

"You didn't notice anything off in their relationship?"

I shrugged. "They didn't have a relationship, in that sense. At least I hope not. Not unless she's some kind of cougar." *With very low standards*, I added mentally. "Still, she put up with more of his nonsense than I would have."

"How so?"

"He was abrasive and rude. And she went above and beyond the call of duty, especially for that kind of job."

"Did she say what she thought of her employer?"

"She seemed to make excuses for him a little," I said, noticing this for the first time myself. "I figured she was just very loyal. Old school."

Reynolds nodded, but his brow creased ever so slightly.

"Is Maxine a suspect?" I asked.

"We don't have suspects," Reynolds said. "Not until we can be sure a crime has actually been committed. Right now I'm just trying to learn who the players are."

I nodded, thinking my dad would've liked that assessment. "Does that mean you're not going to tell me to not leave town like they do in all the old TV shows?"

"As if I had the power." Reynolds tossed his pen on his desk. "But if you are planning any trips, I'd appreciate a heads-up."

Chapter 10

"What did he mean by that?" I asked Ken after he started his car.

He waited until we were on the street heading toward the conference center before answering. "He's just yanking your chain, I think. I hope. And, Liz, you're not at the point of needing to lawyer up or anything, but must you be *so* forthcoming?"

"Sorry. I've been told I'm a very open and genuine person. Some think it's my most redeeming quality."

He tapped the steering wheel a few times. "That's new. Stuck on a girl who's too transparent for her own good."

"What does that mean?"

"Nothing. I just usually go too far the other way and fall for the ones with too many secrets." He sent me a smile. "You're refreshingly different."

His mood sobered, leaving me wondering if I'd evoked a memory of someone in his past with "too many secrets," or if he'd just caught sight of the convention center parking lot, which was now jammed with cars and more than one news van. Multiple lines snaked in front of the building as people waited for the doors to open.

"Are the reporters covering the train show or the . . . incident?" I asked.

"I think we're about to find out." Ken reached for the car door handle. "Good thing I'm off duty and don't have to give any interviews." He glanced at the lines again. "This place have a back door?"

I texted my dad, and Ken kept his head down as we speed-walked around the side of the building until Dad emerged at a door marked "caterer's entrance." Still, a voice called out, "Chief!" But Dad pulled the door closed behind us and locked it as we hustled into a dim and empty kitchen area.

"Thanks," Ken said. "It got busy out there."

"I guess they covered the incident on the eleven o'clock news," Dad said. "Only the story was Craig McFarrel was somehow hit by a train. I'd like to think that the increase in attendance was caused by a whole bunch of people who'd never heard of the show deciding all of a sudden that they like trains and toys. But I'm just not that naïve."

"You got enough security?" Ken asked.

"I called up a couple of retirees from the force to cover the entrance," Dad said. "They sounded excited to come. I'm hoping it's the paycheck they're after. One guy's here already. The other should be here any moment. We're letting the camera crews in one at a time to get crowd shots. Other than that, we've asked the media to stay in the parking lot."

"I'll bet they love that," Ken said.

"They weren't happy, but they're cooperating."

"So business as usual?" I said. It hardly seemed a worthy tribute, even to someone like Craig.

Dad shrugged, and then we followed him through a series of doors, the last of which opened into the main area, already abuzz with conversation as the vendors readied their booths and the model engineers warmed up their engines.

Conductor Frank waved us over as Ken and I headed toward the toy booths. I wasn't sure if he wanted to talk to me as his UFO vendor or to Ken as the chief of police—or maybe a little of both.

"What do you think of her?" Frank asked, pointing to his layout.

I stepped closer to take a look. He'd added some scorch marks to the outside of the flying saucer—which I hoped Dad hadn't seen because he painstakingly cleaned it when it first came in the shop. But most of it was embedded in the hillside and a thin ribbon of smoke rose upward from the crash site.

"The smoke's a nice touch," I said.

"Did you see the aliens?" He pointed to an area a few feet away. The purple aliens were arranged in a field, more in the foreground, so that the size difference wasn't easily recognizable. They were gathered around a large cauldron over a glowing flame. At regular intervals, the pot lid hinged open just enough to reveal the wide, frightened eyes of a human figure.

"That's wonderful!"

"I got it from an old *Twilight Zone* episode."

"'To Serve Man'?" I asked. "I thought you weren't into science fiction."

"Just the *Twilight Zone*, on account of my nephew used to do some odd jobs for Rod Serling."

"I'd forgotten Rod Serling lived around here," I said, making a mental note to look for action figures from the show. Toys with ties to local interest tended to move off the shelves a lot quicker, which is why Fisher-Price and Howdy Doody were such hot sellers.

"More toward the Finger Lakes, I think," he said. "But local enough."

Frank wagged a finger at Ken. "You're the new police chief, right?"

"Yes," he said hesitantly. "But I'm off duty right now."

Frank rubbed his chin. "Is it true what they're saying about the guy who fell?"

"What have you heard?" Ken asked.

"I heard he was dead, for one thing," Frank said. "Those reporters were camped out when I got here at six."

"Unfortunately, that's true," I said. "He died last night."

Frank looked down. "Now I feel bad. Yesterday I was mouthing off about how he was such an idiot."

"Did you know Craig?" Ken asked.

"Just around the shows," Frank said. "The costume was new though. Never saw that before."

"So you saw Craig before he fell?" Ken asked. "We're trying to put together a timeline."

"Yeah, I saw him," Frank said. "If I'd a known he wasn't long for this world, I might have paid him more attention. But he was running around here, flapping that cape of his, and I hadn't finished putting my layout together."

"What did he say?" I asked.

"I don't recall. But he did hand me one of his pamphlet thingies. You want it?"

"Yes, that'd be great." I remembered someone saying they found a stack of leaflets on the catwalks, but I hadn't seen one for myself.

Frank fished it out from underneath the table skirt and handed it to me.

Ken looked over my shoulder. "Those are like the ones he had on the catwalk. I'm glad he never had a chance to drop them."

"They could have hurt someone," I said. They were glossy trifold brochures of a decent weight that never would've fluttered like tickertape. They'd have gone straight down, and heaven help the man standing directly under Craig.

"He was going to throw a bunch of those?" Frank said, looking up at the catwalk directly above his layout. "Man, that guy really was an idiot." He glanced toward the door. "Do you think I ought to go out there and set those reporters straight? I'd hate for folks to stay away because they think it's not safe."

"You obviously haven't seen the line outside," I said. "I don't think you need to worry about a drop in attendance."

"If I were you," Ken said, "I'd just tell them that a man fell from a restricted area. The police are investigating, but the facilities are safe for the public. If they ask anything more, send them to the police."

As Frank walked to the door, straightening his uniform, Ken and I headed toward the comic booth, but Cathy intercepted us. At least I think that's what she was trying to do. She was leaning over the table and waving like a windmill. "Liz!"

"Thanks for coming in," I said. "Are you up for this today?"

"No worries. I got this, at least once I figured out that last sale. Parker must have been swamped last night just to leave cash on the table like that."

I winced. "I didn't even get to check the booth last night. How did it go with Parker? Did you tell him?"

"I chickened out."

"Cathy!"

"I tried! We had such a lovely dinner. And he even brought home a pie. And then over coffee—don't worry, I had decaf—he got to talking about how he loved spending alone time together, just the two of us. And I started thinking about how a baby is going to change all that. I couldn't tell him."

"Cathy, he's going to be thrilled."

"But what if he's not? What if he's disappointed? This is going to change both of our lives forever."

"Cathy"—I took her face in my hands to get her to focus—"he's going to be thrilled. Trust me. Now breathe."

Cathy breathed in deeply, and I let go of her. "What if we're lousy parents?"

I shook my head. "You two are going to be amazing parents."

"Liz?" Ken touched my arm.

"Just a minute," I said.

"No, I think you'd better see this."

I spun around to face him and caught a glimpse of Maxine whipping the last of the covers from her tables. She stood back, put her hands on her cheeks, and just stared. The comic book tables that we'd painstakingly searched through the night before—and then left in apple-pie order—were now in complete disarray. Some comics lay in heaps on the table. Others were ripped apart.

Maxine continued to stare, then her hands started shaking.

"Get me a bottle of water," I told Ken. "And get Dad!" I rushed over and helped Maxine to a chair, pushing their cart, loaded with a laptop and a fresh supply of graded comics, to the back of the booth.

"Who would do this? Who would destroy these things? I don't understand."

I knelt next to her chair and patted her hand. I had no answers. Instead, all I seemed to have were more questions.

# # #

Dad and the water seemed to arrive at the same time. I handed the bottle to Maxine, who took it with still-trembling hands.

Meanwhile, Cathy had come over and put the tablecloths over the vandalized comic books. "We don't want customers right now," she said as she stashed the loaded cart behind the drapes at the rear of the booth.

I thanked her and was glad for her timing. The doors opened, and those who didn't have to stop to buy tickets were already streaming in. I was wondering if we should try to take the distraught Maxine away from the booth, which was probably going to be considered a crime scene, when Dad voiced the same idea.

Maxine vaguely nodded, and we followed him to the door that led to the corridors that held that empty kitchen, only this time we jogged a little to the left and ended up in some kind of small lounge area, with lockers, vending machines, a couple of small lunch tables, and a bank of semicomfortable seats along one wall.

"Employee lounge," Dad said.

"You're getting to know your way around this place," I said.

Dad patted his security ID. "All part of the job, ma'am."

We got Maxine settled on the couch, and I bought her a pack of chocolate chip cookies from the vending machine. Dad also found a blanket somewhere, and Maxine pulled it tightly around herself. Considering all that had happened in the last twenty-four hour period, she was certainly entitled to a little bit of shock.

"If those security cameras were on last night, they should've gotten a good shot of whoever did this," I said. "They will catch them."

"You probably think I'm acting foolishly over a bunch of comic books," she finally said. "It's just when I saw those books torn up like that, it made everything else more real. Torn and discarded. That's what happened to Craig."

"You really liked him, didn't you?" I asked.

Dad's radio erupted with a chain of static, and he excused himself to go answer it.

Ken sat down in a nearby chair.

Maxine put a hand over her mouth, deep in thought. "It's not about liking Craig. It's a lot more complicated than that."

"Yeah, I know. Craig could be a jerk sometimes."

"That wasn't where I was going . . ."

"No, those things are hard to say. Sometimes the people in our lives are difficult, but we learn to get along. To make do. We remember the good times. We hope they'll change.

And when they're gone . . . yeah, we feel loss, but then there's almost a sense of relief. But then you feel guilty for feeling that, especially when everyone else is sad."

Maxine took my hand. "Who did you lose, child?"

Man, Ken was right. I was transparent.

"My mother. She had an alcohol problem. Those last few years were . . ."

Maxine stared off into space. "You're right, you know. Craig wasn't the nicest man. I tried to take into account what he'd been through. You're familiar with all those years in the foster system, right?"

"That must've been hard on him."

"Some make it out okay. Others never find their way. Craig was just learning to find his way, I thought. Learning those things that maybe he should have figured out years ago. Getting along with people. Having a little empathy for others." She shook her head. "I've known people who came out of the system far worse. I thought he had a chance. I actually thought . . ."

She trailed off into her own thoughts while I entertained a few of my own. Yes, I still had emotional baggage. I loved my mother, but those feelings were challenged by the frustrations of living with an alcoholic parent. Even then, I still had Dad, my ever-present rock.

What must it have been like for Craig, shuffled from foster home to foster home, like a holiday fruitcake? No mooring. No safe harbor. Although that mixed metaphor created the odd mental picture of a fruitcake tossed by the waves in a stormy Lake Erie.

Yeah, there were times when my childhood was no picnic, but Craig had it a lot worse. I only wish I'd found "a little empathy for others," as Maxine had put it, when I knew him in school.

"Liz."

I jumped at my dad's voice. I was so lost in my thoughts that I didn't hear him come into the room. He slid into a chair facing Maxine and me.

"I just got a call from the police."

Ken's posture stiffened a bit.

Dad went on. "I'm afraid there's more bad news. They're sending an officer to escort Maxine to the comic book shop. There's been a break-in, and they want her to look around to see if she can figure out what's missing."

Maxine closed her eyes. "When it rains . . ." She squeezed my hand. "Will you come with me?"

"As long as the police don't mind," I said.

"They shouldn't," both my dad and Ken said at the same time.

"Then of course." I reached in and gave her a hug.

# # #

I wish I could say I'd never ridden in the back of a police car before, but the truth was I had. If you want to avoid the feeling of claustrophobia, you try not to focus on the fact that there are no handles on the inside. And taking my dad's advice, you try really hard not to touch anything.

This was a short trip, though, just back to Main Street. The police car double-parked another out front, but the young officer didn't stay. He just escorted us to the doorway where Howard Reynolds was standing, then took off.

"Maxine asked me to come with her," I volunteered, then realized I probably shouldn't say too much more. I didn't have Ken to keep me from putting my foot in my mouth. He'd gone to the station to see what he could find out. Meanwhile, Dad was going over last night's security camera footage, looking for any good shots of the vandals.

Maxine hung onto me for support, and that might've been all the convincing Reynolds needed, because he nodded and held open the door.

I followed Maxine in. Whoever broke into this place had done a thorough job. Display cases were smashed, and the floor glittered with broken glass. Bins were upended, and comics were strewn knee-deep in spots.

"You want me to try to figure out what's missing?" Maxine asked. "I mean, even with an inventory list, that's going to take a while."

Reynolds put his hands up. "For now, concentrate on the things of greatest value. Anything that jumps out at you."

She exhaled a forced breath and began a survey of the room. "Craig's computer," she said, pointing at the desk.

"Do you know what kind?" Reynolds asked.

"I think it was a Dell," she said. "He had all these stickers—Garbage Pail Kids—stuck on the case. He thought they were hysterical." She continued to scan the room. "None of the action figures seem to have been touched, and we have a Boba Fett worth a couple grand." She gestured to a shelf behind the register. "They didn't touch any of these, so I don't think whoever did this knows the business."

Reynolds wrote that down.

"But they went through the comics," I said. "Just like at the show."

"The show?" Reynolds asked.

"We found out about it moments before your guy came," I said. "The booth was ransacked as well." I turned to Maxine. "Did they take any graded comics from the store?"

She shook her head. "I came by last night and took the rest of what we had with me. I promised a couple of collectors that I'd have some today at the show."

"What time was that?" Reynolds asked.

"Ten?" she said. "I was kind of shook up after the hospital. I had just turned on the news when I remembered that I'd made a promise to bring those graded comics." She looked up with a start. "I left them sitting on the cart at the show. The laptop is there too. If Craig's computer is gone, the laptop has the only other copy of the store's inventory. Well, except for the printout, but that's not as up to date."

"Don't worry," I said. "Cathy pushed the cart out of sight. It's behind the drapes at the show."

Maxine leaned against a stool adjusted perfectly to her height, probably the one she used every day at work. "I don't even know what I should be doing," she said. "Should I be cleaning up?"

"No, not yet," Reynolds said. "We'll process the place for fingerprints, and we'll do the same for the booth."

"What about the stuff on the cart?" I asked.

"Some of those comics were worth a few hundred," she said.

"How about I take them in, for now, as evidence." Reynolds rubbed his cheek as if he were massaging a sore molar. "Did that laptop have a copy of everything that was on the missing computer?"

Maxine twisted her hands together. "It's supposed to. If Craig updated all the files."

"You think the thieves were after some information from the computer?" I asked Reynolds. "And maybe the comic books are a diversion?"

Reynolds shrugged. "No idea. But probably worth getting a forensics guy on the computer." He tapped his pen on his paperwork. "Was there anything on the computer that you think someone would want?"

"I can't . . ." Maxine said.

Reynolds rubbed his fingers together, as if the friction could spark an answer. "What was on there?"

Maxine jerked to attention and started ticking items off on her fingers. "All our business records. Sales tax. Inventory. That kind of stuff. Purchase records. All the receipts for our graded comics."

"What about Craig's new comic series?" I asked.

Maxine quirked an eyebrow. "That was on there too. He got a humongous hard drive to store all the images." A shadow crossed her face.

"Something else?" I asked.

"Customer contact information. Maybe some personal pictures. I think he backed up his e-mail there." Her brow pinched a little, but Reynolds didn't seem to notice.

For the next few moments, Maxine wrote down all the passwords she could remember. While she did, I took a more thorough look around the shop. Without moving, of course, since touching anything might contaminate any evidence they'd not processed.

The shop wasn't that large. Some of the connecting shops on Main had long been subdivided; when a business ran out of space and if their neighbor had extra, cash exchanged hands, and walls were repositioned. That was probably the case here, with one of the neighboring shops enjoying the L-shaped square footage.

On the back wall was a montage of photographs. There was Craig, closely surrounded by a youth soccer team, all bearing the "Craig's Comics" name on their uniforms. The next picture was a baseball team. The young boys in this picture wore a different uniform, but one still sporting Craig's name as they crowded around and hoisted a trophy. Similar pictures showed other youth teams—lacrosse, football, swimming. Mixed in with the team shots were candids of players in action. Huh. I'd never known Craig was so community-minded. It might explain his high Yelp rating.

"So what should I be doing?" Maxine asked Reynolds. "Do I even still have a job?"

"A lot of that will depend on the next of kin," Reynolds said.

"They've found a next of kin?" I asked. I'd pegged Craig for a loner.

Maxine looked just as amazed at the prospect as I was.

"He's coming in later today with his mother," Reynolds said. "I'll expect she'll be the one deciding what happens with the business since he's a minor."

The realization hit. "Craig has a son?" I asked.

Reynolds nodded. "He's listed as the beneficiary of Craig's life insurance. Craig never married the boy's mother, but the son is his closest blood relative. The only blood relative on record, actually."

Maxine plopped down on the stool again and stared up at the ceiling. "A son." She looked at me. "Craig had a son."

Chapter 11

By the time the officer dropped us off at the convention center, Maxine looked in no condition to operate a motor vehicle, so I offered to drive her home in her car, a beat-up Subaru that looked quite at home in the pot-holed parking lot next to the dumpster. I figured she might enjoy the company. And if I happened to glean any helpful information about Craig, all the better. I phoned Ken, and he promised to meet me at her place later.

It was only a ten-minute drive to Maxine's place. Or it *should've been*. I made the mistake of looking into my rear-view mirror and spotted a red pickup that seemed be following a little too closely. The sun was hitting the window in just the wrong place, so I couldn't identify the driver.

I also noticed when I turned off Main Street, the pickup did as well.

I had finally succeeded in prying a few words out of Maxine, but after that pump was primed, the words kept coming in a flood of nervous energy, and she was still bantering about how much she loved East Aurora. I kind of tuned her out. I made a quick unplanned right with no signal and watched as the truck followed.

"Where are we going?" Maxine asked.

"Do you know anybody with a red pickup?" I asked. "Don't turn around."

Despite my warning, she turned around. "Someone's following us? Doesn't look familiar. But I don't know a whole lot of people here."

I took a few more random turns, and the red pickup stayed with us. My brain conjured up any number of images of desperate rogues who might be driving—the two mobsters from the toy show ranked high on that list.

"What are you planning to do?" Maxine clenched the door handle with one hand and braced herself against the dashboard with the other. That poor woman. She'd had a rough few days.

"I could head to the police station," I said. I wasn't sure that was the best option, though. I'd been heading farther and farther away from Main, and I'd changed direction so many times, I'd gotten a little lost myself. I hit the throttle and picked up speed.

The pickup seemed to fall back. "Oh, don't get all law-abiding on me now," I said.

As I sped past the flea market, I spotted a patrol car parked in the lot. "Hang on!"

"I'm hanging," Maxine squealed as I did a superfast three-point turn and doubled back, meeting the pickup right in front of the entrance for the flea market.

I jerked the wheel with no warning, the rear tires skidding on the stones and sending up a cloud of dust. I pulled up right next to the police car, slammed on the brakes, pulled off my seat belt, and climbed out, looking for the driver of that police car.

No, I did not say I took the car out of gear. And no, I did not say I turned off the car.

I realized my mistake as soon as the car started rolling forward and Maxine screamed from inside.

I made a grab for the door and was able to hold on, but the car was moving too quickly for me to reach the brakes.

The last I saw, Maxine was bracing herself for impact with both eyes firmly shut as her rusty Subaru rolled straight toward the homemade pie stand.

"Move! Move!" someone shouted. It might have even been me.

The pie vendor looked up, his eyes widened, and he jumped out of the way just in time.

I watched as Maxine's car crashed into a wooden display shelf fully loaded with pies. They hit the car, making colorful splashes of cherry, pumpkin, blueberry, lemon, and chocolate, all along the windshield and hood in a display that might've found a spot at a modern art museum—if the curator had a sense of humor.

Fortunately, after taking out the entire pie booth, the car struck a curb and came to a stop, leaving Maxine unharmed but still screeching inside.

And she wasn't the only one. There was quite a bit of screaming going on. The driver of the police car came running over.

"Officer!" I said. "I need your help. Someone is following me. The red pickup!"

By this time, the red pickup had parked. The driver climbed out and whipped off a pair of mirrored sunglasses.

I drew closer to the uniformed officer for protection, keeping free of his holster and gun, in case it should come to that.

But the officer just raised his hand and waved. "Tony, what's up?"

Tony? I blinked at pickup driver. Tony Calabrese? He was new on the force.

"Wait," I said, spinning to face the cop. "He was following me." I turned back to Tony. "Why were you following me?"

Tony shuffled a little, kicking the small stones of the parking lot around with his feet. "I was just supposed to keep an eye on you. Sorry to spook you."

Meanwhile, the owner of the pie booth, sporting a few small scrapes on his knees, visible through now-torn jeans, came over. More yelling ensued.

Finally the cop whistled for silence. He beckoned to the pie vendor. "Are you okay?"

"Yeah, but my pies!" he said.

"We'll get to that in a minute." The officer reached into the vehicle, shifted it out of gear, and turned it off. "Are you all right?" he asked Maxine.

"Fine, I think." She unbuckled her seat belt and climbed out of the car, breathing heavily and with her hand on her chest. "Yeah, I'm fine." She took a slack-jawed look at her car, covered in pie.

The officer's shoulders rose in a deep breath before he returned his attention to me.

I gulped. "I thought I was being followed."

The officer glanced up at Tony.

"It's true, I'm afraid," he said.

"You were following her? In your private vehicle? Why?"

Tony shrank back and bit his lower lip before responding. "The chief asked me to."

"Chief Young asked you to trail this woman? Is she wanted?"

Tony blushed fiercely. "Not in that sense."

"In what sense, then?"

"He just asked me to keep an eye on her. This"—he gestured in my direction—"is *his* woman."

# # #

A couple of hours and a whole lot of paperwork later, I sat in Ken's back seat as he drove Maxine home.

His woman? Wasn't sure how I felt about that. Guilty about leading him on? Flattered that he thought that of me? No, mostly irritated that he'd called in some favors and actually enlisted someone on his force to follow me, albeit unofficially. And those thoughts paled in comparison to the embarrassment I felt—and would feel again as soon as the next edition of the *Advertiser* came out, since one of their photographers just happened to be shopping at the flea market when we made our grand entrance.

When Ken pulled into the lot of Maxine's apartment complex, he put his car in park and turned off the motor. Show-off.

"Um, if it's okay, I'd like to walk you in to make sure things are as you left them," he said. "I didn't get a chance to tell either of you, but when Craig's next of kin arrived in town, they reported there had been a break-in at his house."

Maxine shook her head. "What is happening?"

"I wish I knew." Ken scratched his head. "If you want, I can go first."

Maxine dug in her purse and pulled out her keys.

Ken took them. "I'll wave you in when it's safe. If you don't hear from me in five minutes . . ."

My irritation melted into worry as I watched him pat the hip where he kept his off-duty weapon and walk toward the apartment building.

It felt like an eternity, but in actuality it was only four minutes later when Ken came into view, a black cat in his arms, and waved us in.

Maxine's apartment was on the ground floor of one of many in a series of identical brick boxes grouped tightly together and labeled with a quaint name, followed by the ubiquitous "Estates," as if the developers were fooling anyone into thinking the rich and famous frolicked in the dilapidated swimming pool, now empty and surrounded by a rusted chain-linked fence.

Her door—just past a run of dented mailboxes and thread-bare steps leading to the upper apartments—opened directly into a surprisingly bright living room.

"Careful of the cat," she said.

As soon as Ken put her down in the apartment, she took off at a dead run for freedom.

I managed to close the door behind me just before she made her escape.

"She can't get outside because of the main building door," Maxine said, picking up the small, sleek cat. "But that's not for lack of trying. Meanwhile, I hate chasing her up and down the stairs." She held the cat up and looked into her eyes. "Isn't that right, naughty girl?"

"The lock didn't look tampered with, and nothing looks out of place," Ken said, but when he caught my eye, he tipped his head to a nearby hallway.

While Maxine took some comfort in her cat, I shrugged off my sweater and looked around. She had a sofa, chair, and small television in the living room, and a vast array of plant life in front of a sliding glass door that offered a bit more privacy than originally intended, since the seal between the double panes was broken and the condensation blurred the parking lot on the other side.

Off the living room was a miniscule kitchen—neat as the proverbial pin, if said pin had been scrubbed, shined, and roped off with museum barriers—and an even smaller eating nook. There weren't even any stray cat hairs wafting in the air or the smell of a litter box. If I didn't know better, I'd say the cat was a holographic image or robot. I'd definitely need to get her secret.

"What lovely plants," I said, but instead of getting closer to them, I walked over to where Ken was standing, with a view down the hallway. "You certainly have a green thumb."

That got her distracted. As she hovered over her plants, pointing out various ones, I hazarded a longer glance down that hallway. Through the opening of the bedroom door, I could just make out a picture frame sitting on her nightstand. And if I wasn't mistaken, it was a picture of Craig.

I raised my eyebrows and looked at Ken, who shrugged. Why would Maxine have a picture of her employer on her nightstand? Unless he was more than her employer. But what?

A secret crush? Her lover? A good friend? Maybe she was just grateful for the job.

I supposed her affection for Craig could be innocent enough, especially if she were lonely and most of her other social interaction was spent talking to plants and one very hygienic cat.

If Maxine held a grudge for what I did to her car—the garage said she could have it back by Tuesday—she didn't show it. And in the end, I left with more questions about her relationship with Craig and a spider plantlet that, knowing me, would be lucky to make it through the night.

# # #

"Do you think that the picture of Craig on Maxine's nightstand is suspicious?" I asked Ken, then downed half my Coke as we waited for the rest of our order.

Ken looked at the people around the counter and proposed we delay that conversation until after we sat down. He'd first suggested we eat at Wallace's, and normally I would've jumped at the chance. But given the last bit of conversation Jack and I had experienced, I wanted an opportunity to clear the air before we ran into each other in an awkward social situation. And arriving for a nice late lunch/early dinner with Ken would probably be pretty awkward for all of us.

We'd settled on a local hot dog joint just off Main. And since I hadn't eaten since this morning, except for a dollop of pumpkin pie filling that had landed on my hand, I'd pigged out a little and ordered two hot dogs, a side of onion rings, and a dark chocolate and peanut butter shake, and then added the

Coke because I was thirsty. I considered making it a diet, but I didn't want the nice lady in the orange apron to laugh at me.

While Ken got the rest of our food, I gathered napkins and ketchup packets and picked a table away from prying ears.

When he set the tray down, I practically dove in. There's nothing like that first bite of an onion ring right out of the fryer.

"Does this mean I'm forgiven for having you followed?"

I wiped my mouth with a napkin. "I'm working on it. I'd like to know why."

"The case was getting too dangerous. Craig, dead. The comic booth and the store, ransacked. I hadn't even heard about his house being broken into. And you were driving around with Maxine. I worried that her closeness to Craig would make the two of you some kind of target."

"I worried the same thing. I thought the pickup driver might have been one of those mob guys. I half expected them to shoot my tires out with an Uzi."

Ken looked down. "Sorry. You should have called, though."

"You should have told me."

He crumpled up his empty hot dog tray. "Other than that—and not putting the car in park—you probably did the right thing."

"I'm not sure I could have called while driving." I tilted my head and sent him a flirty smile. "Besides, isn't that illegal in this state?"

"But preferable to taking out half of the flea market."

"One stand. I hit *one stand*. Nobody was hurt. And technically, I wasn't even in the car."

Ken hid his face behind his hands with a sigh but ended up laughing. "Only you, Liz. Only you."

"What does that mean?"

Instead of answering, he bit into his second hot dog, and the next few minutes were filled with appreciative food grunts that can only be understood by those who've experienced a Sahlen's hot dog. To everyone else, they might have resembled the soundtrack to a cheap porn flick.

It was only when he wiped the mustard from his hands that he answered. "About Maxine. I don't know what to make of the picture. You're a woman. You've spent more time with her than I have. What do you think it could mean? I mean, do you have any pictures of men on your nightstand?"

The question gave me butterflies. "Just my father's," I said. "And Parker's. It's a family picture."

"So not necessarily romantic love," he said, "but some kind of affection."

"Hers could be romantic, I suppose," I said. "Maxine seemed awfully devoted to him and terribly stunned by his death."

"More than just the possibility of unemployment?"

"She won't be unemployed for long. If Craig's heir decides to let her go, I'm calling dibs."

"So you're going to see her again, then," Ken said.

"Yes, and maybe I can figure out what exactly her relationship was with Craig." I tossed my napkin onto my plate, hiding a small piece of the second hot dog that I just didn't quite have room to finish. "Speaking of relationships, I—"

But a buzz from Ken's cell commandeered his attention. "Sorry." He glanced at his phone, then read whatever text he'd received again.

"Just got some toxicology results on Craig."

"Isn't that awfully fast?" I asked.

"Usually takes weeks. This is from the blood work the hospital did when they were trying to figure out how to treat him. Apparently nobody informed the lab that he was dead, which this time worked in our favor." He continued to stare at the phone.

"So what did they find?" I asked.

"Something called scopolamine," he said.

"I've never heard of it."

"Neither have I. Reading the rest of the report now."

While he was doing that, I pulled out my phone to see what the good folks at Google had to say. The first site I found talked about scopolamine's use in preventing motion sickness. But just a few lines down, they talked about the drug in connection with crime in Colombia.

"Organized crime," I said.

"On another continent," he said. And we both kept reading. Just two typical thirtysomethings, out on an apparent date, each buried in our own phones.

It seemed scopolamine wasn't a recreational drug at all, but one administered to hapless victims, rendering them susceptible to suggestion. According to one article, these victims were often then raped, kidnapped, or ordered to empty their ATM accounts. And they complied without putting up a struggle.

"This can't be real," I said, immediately searching for scopolamine on Snopes. At first I was rewarded. An e-mail talking about victims becoming human zombies by simply touching a scopolamine-laced business card was proved false.

But underneath that was more information. News stories from Colombia. State Department warnings. If these reports could be believed, scopolamine, also known as *burundanga* from the tree on which it grows, was a very real problem, at least in Colombia.

"What's it doing up here?" I asked.

Ken shook his head, his eyes still glued to his cell.

"So this isn't recreational drug use," I said. "And I doubt someone was trying to date-rape Craig. So what then? Rob him? Get him to do something he wouldn't do?"

"Like jump from the catwalks?" Ken said.

"If he was under the influence of this scopolamine, someone could've made him hand over those pricy comic books and then told him to take a flying leap."

Ken stroked his chin. "So the death that hundreds of witnesses in a crowded convention center see as an accidental fall could be murder after all."

"I *knew* he wasn't the type to kill himself."

"But who would have drugged him?" Ken said. "And remember, it's only supposition that it has anything to do with those missing comics."

I folded my hands over my mouth. He was right, of course. Dad had warned me not to try to force any pieces to fit. "It has to be someone who'd have access to scopolamine and access to Craig's drink. Assuming it was in his coffee. Do we know that yet?"

"Tests on the cup will take a while."

"So we know someone drugged Craig. We know someone walked off with a bunch of pricy comics. Comics that Craig had cheated a local resident out of. We also know that someone is still looking for something, either comic books or information. And they want it desperately enough to break into a convention center, a Main Street storefront, and Craig's house. So we can assume they haven't found what they wanted yet."

"What a mess," Ken said. "And I'm not even technically on the case anymore."

This time my phone beeped. "A text from Dad." I looked up with a smile. "He wants us to come back to the show. He said it took a while, but he knows who ransacked the comic booth."

Chapter 12

The security office had become the strategy room. Dad still sat in his squeaky chair. And since Ken had decided he'd better opt out if he was going to maintain any illusion of being off the case, Detective Reynolds was leaning against the wall next to a couple of uniformed officers. Not sure how I rated an invite, but I wasn't about to leave.

Dad queued up the video to point out the two men. They'd managed to avoid being caught by the camera that had been focused on the comic booth. Apparently they'd spotted it and managed to change the aim so that it only caught images of the ceiling. So while we couldn't actually see them vandalizing the booth, other cameras had caught them as they pulled open a back door to the center. They were no longer dressed in a Batman tee or bolo tie, opting instead for plain dark clothes. But they were definitely the same two Dad had pointed out to me at the show, suspected of mafia ties.

"So, what? We got them on breaking and entering?" Reynolds asked, rubbing the stubble on his chin. "Or do we even have that? Why isn't that door locked?"

"I wondered the same thing," Dad said. "I know it was locked when I left. I locked and double-checked everything personally. So I ran the tape back." Dad rewound the tape and told us to pay attention. Most of the time it just showed a closed door, but eventually it caught what looked like a man bursting through the door and sprinting backward toward the parking lot. Dad stopped the tape and ran it forward at normal speed. A very familiar figure of a man entered the frame, using a key to unlock the door.

"Who's that?" Reynolds squinted at the screen as Dad paused the picture.

"Lionel Kelley?" I said, guessing based on the man's slim build and posture, which was impeccable.

"Kelley?" Reynolds said. "That twerp? What's he doing with a key? And why's he letting them in?"

"Now," Dad said, "don't jump to conclusions. Until very recently, Kelley was head of security here."

"And he should've relinquished his keys. And he definitely should *not* be opening doors for known felons," Reynolds said.

"All true," Dad said. "But I don't think he opened the door for those guys. I have a feeling they were hanging around for a while, saw him go in, and took advantage of the open door. Yes, Kelley should've turned in his keys, but I suspect his plans were a little less nefarious. In fact, I can prove it."

"You have him on other cameras?" I asked.

"Yes, and never near the comic books."

"Well, let's see it," Reynolds said.

Dad looked uncomfortable. "I don't suppose you'd take my word for it?"

"Roll film," Reynolds said, folding his arms in front of his chest.

Dad faced the monitor with a resigned sigh and called up footage that showed Kelley walking around the conference floor.

"Didn't he know he'd be caught on camera?" I asked.

"I think he was counting on nobody watching the footage," Dad said. "Which is what happens 99.9 percent of the time when there's not a problem. It's also why I don't think he let in those two men. He wouldn't want anybody to watch this."

Kelley made his way over to our toy booth and lifted the table cover. I squinted at the grainy screen. "What's he . . . ?" And then I remembered what Cathy had said about Parker leaving money on the table. The serious, stalwart ex-security guard and former officer pulled out his wallet, carefully counted out cash, and put the amount on the table. He then picked up a My Little Pony headband and stroked his fingers through its rainbow mane as if he were petting a prized stallion. He placed the headband on his head, adjusted the plush ears, and shook his head to toss the mane around, like a sultry, long-haired model in a shampoo commercial. And then he picked up the matching rainbow tail.

"Oh, for the love of . . ." Reynolds started.

"He's a closet brony!" I said, laughing in spite of myself. I wasn't the only one laughing. The uniformed cops gave up trying to hide it.

"What's a brony?" Reynolds asked.

"It's a combination of bro and pony," I said. "Adult men who like My Little Ponies." I shook my head. "And I shouldn't laugh. Nothing wrong with being a brony. There are far worse hobbies. It just took me by surprise, is all. Most bronies are good people."

"That's for real?"

"They have an annual convention," Dad said. "Brings in over ten thousand, last I heard, from all over the world."

"Ten thousand men . . . dressed like that?" Reynolds pointed at the frozen screen.

"Some don't cosplay at all," I said, "and some dress up as other pop-culture characters. And before you ask, no, it has nothing to do with sexual preference. There are both gay and straight bronies. They just like the show. There are women too. Some call themselves bronies. Others call themselves Pegasisters. And there are more bronies in the area than care to admit to it. We do a fair trade in ponies."

Eventually the smiles and smirks stopped, and the mood grew somber again. We watched as Dad jumped from camera to camera as Kelley hit the toy vendors, picking up an armful of My Little Pony paraphernalia, always leaving cash behind and the tablecloths replaced neatly over the merchandise.

"Do we see him leave?" Reynolds asked.

"Yes," Dad said. "He takes his bounty into the employee lounge, opens a locker, and stuffs all his . . . purchases into a duffel bag, plus more he'd apparently kept there. He then opens another locker and urinates in my uniform shoes."

I looked down to see Dad wearing his sneakers. "Ew."

Dad shrugged it off. "If that was the worst thing anyone's tried to do to me, I'd say I've lived a charmed life. But then he takes his stuff and leaves, locking the door behind him."

"He didn't want to be seen with the My Little Pony stuff," I said, "so he came back at night when he didn't think anyone would be here."

"And the other two just took advantage of that fact, yes," Dad said. "They were very clever to avoid most of the cameras. It's only after Kelley leaves that this happens." Dad called up a bit of footage. At first, there was a clear shot of the comic booth, and then the camera tipped up so that it was focused elsewhere.

"So they were on the catwalks?" I asked.

"Must have climbed up there somehow," Dad said. "We could check for prints."

"We got them coming in where they're not supposed to be," Reynolds said. "Trespassing, at least."

"But we also have this," Dad said. "They got cocky and missed a camera. Here's an angle they weren't counting on." Dad rolled more tape.

The two men were skulking toward the door. One had something in his hand. Dad paused the video, and we all squinted at the screen.

"It's a comic book," I said.

"That's *criminal* trespassing." Reynolds smiled.

"It's still a far cry from murder," Dad said.

"Yeah, but while we got them, we might be able to get a search warrant to look for the missing comic books," Reynolds said. "Maybe we'll luck out and find something else. But we wouldn't be able to hold them long on those charges."

"But if you don't take them in now," Dad countered, "how do you know they don't ride off into the sunset right after the show ends?"

"They're still here?" Reynolds asked.

Dad nodded, called up the security cameras in real time, and a few moments later pointed out the two suspects.

Reynolds gestured to his men. "Go get 'em." He saluted my dad. "Let me know if you catch anything else. On the video, I mean. I'll be back for those tapes later."

"Will do."

As they filed out to make their arrest, I stood behind Dad's chair to watch. Before the cops approached the men, Ken opened the door and joined us. "What happened?" he asked.

Dad pointed to where the arrest was taking place. But another face on a different monitor drew my attention. Jack Wallace was back at the show. He wore a heavy sweater yet carried a bulky coat draped oddly over one arm. And he looked nervous, not that I could see his facial expression in the camera, but his movements were stiff and jerky.

"Got them!" Ken said, obvious pride in his voice.

"I only hope you can hold them," Dad said. "They're going to lawyer up pretty quick."

"Liz?" Ken asked.

I waved him off. I was still following Jack as he navigated the crowded maze of aisles.

"What are you looking at?" Dad asked.

Ken spotted him first. "What's *he* doing here? Looking for you?"

I shook my head. He was headed straight toward the comic booth. He stopped short. Where the comic booth had been, large fabric dividers had been set up.

"I did that," Dad said, anticipating my question. "So the police could process the area without being disturbed by the show, and vice versa."

"Is anyone there now?" I asked.

"I think they finished up a while ago," Dad said. "It didn't make sense to remove the barriers if the booth wasn't going to reopen."

Jack stood in front of the curtains for a while, looking—or pretending to look—at the nearest train layout. He nodded to a passing shopper, then ducked behind the drapes.

"Let's go," Dad said. Ken and I followed him, taking a shortcut through a side hallway not open to the public. When we emerged, Jack was just coming out of the draped off area, his jacket now hanging limply at his side.

"Jack!"

He looked up. If guilt had been written on his face, it would've been in all caps and in indelible ink, followed by a blushing emoji.

"What are you doing?" I asked.

But Dad and Ken forged ahead and pushed aside the draping.

"Liz," Ken said.

I looked away from where Jack was now hanging his head. There in the booth, sitting on top of the previously ransacked table, was a stack of graded comics, still in their plastic cases.

"I can explain," Jack said. "It's not what it looks like."

"I don't know what it looks like," I said. "But a lot of people went through a whole lot of trouble to find those comics, including possibly killing a man." I put my hands over my mouth. "What have you done?"

Jack sent me a pained look. "I *just* found them."

"Let me call Reynolds," Ken said.

"Maybe we should go to the office and talk about it," Dad said.

"How much trouble am I in?" Jack asked, keeping his focus on Dad.

"It depends," Dad said, trying to hold off Ken who had already pulled out his phone. "Where did you find them?"

Jack's gaze swept the room, looking first at Ken, then Dad, and finally at me. Then he pinched his eyes shut. "In Terry's room."

Chapter 13

Ken put away his phone at Dad's suggestion, but he didn't look entirely convinced.

Instead of heading to the security office, Dad led us to the empty employee lounge. He fed coins into the vending machine to buy a bag of Doritos and tossed it on the table. He had apparently remembered Jack's fondness for the chips. But if he was trying to soften Jack up, his effort was probably wasted. Any softer and Jack would be blubbering all over the place.

Jack didn't touch the chips, though. He was too busy clenching the arms of the chair and not looking any of us in the eye.

Dad pulled up a seat. "Might as well tell us all about it."

Jack pitched forward, his forehead now resting on his fists. "I wanted to believe him." He looked up. "I still want to believe him."

While Ken paced the other side of the room, I pushed my chair closer to Jack's. "What did Terry have to say about the comics? Did he confess?"

"To taking them, yes. But not to stealing them." Jack turned to Ken. "How much trouble could he be in?"

"Well," Ken said, still pacing, "considering the police just arrested two suspected mobsters for the same offense, and of course they'll hire the best lawyers in the country in what will no doubt be a successful attempt to make our entire force look as adept as Sheriff Amos Tupper . . . Even if I'm not there to throw the book at your brother, someone on the force will be more than happy to."

"Amos Tupper?" Jack asked.

"Sheriff in Cabot Cove," I said. "*Murder, She Wrote.* Half the town dead. Sheriff couldn't solve a thing without the help of a retired school teacher turned mystery novelist. No action figures, but we do have the board game in stock."

"There's a board game?" Ken asked. "Seriously?"

"You a fan?"

"Let's just say I have an unusual attraction for amateur sleuths," he replied with a sheepish grin.

Jack rolled his eyes.

"Let's get back to the subject at hand," Dad said to Jack. "I know you love your brother, but he could be in a lot of trouble. *You* could be in trouble for helping him. We're talking a felony."

"But they're just comic books," Jack said.

"That are worth over ninety grand," Dad said softly.

Jack blanched. "I . . ." He started choking. I bought a bottle of water from the vending machine and handed it to him.

"You didn't know they were worth that much," I said. "Did Terry?"

Jack shook his head. "I don't think so. He didn't act like it was such a big deal when I confronted him. He said he found them somewhere."

"Where?" I asked.

"He told me he stepped out for a smoke—another bad habit he picked up in prison—and they were lying by the door."

I looked at Dad. "You know, that actually makes sense. I didn't see any point on the camera footage where Terry might've taken them from the booth."

"I should really call it in," Ken said.

"Wait!" Dad and Jack said at the same time.

I knew why Jack didn't want that to happen, but Ken sent my father a curious look.

"Think about this for a moment," Dad urged, his face grim. "What is going to happen immediately after you call?"

"They'll have to let those two guys go," Ken said.

"And no judge is going to issue a search warrant for their hotel room once that happens," Dad said.

Ken froze in place. "You're asking me not to report this? To risk the reputation of the police department on a gamble? To hide the fact that we've recovered stolen merchandise?"

"Are you even sure these are the comic books you're looking for?" I asked.

"Don't pull an Obi-Wan on me," Ken said.

"What Liz is saying makes a lot of sense," Dad said. "That's your protection, right there—you haven't had a good look at them. Should it come into question later, that's your out."

"Besides," I said, "you look pretty off-duty to me."

"I can't turn a blind eye to this," Ken said, resuming his pacing.

"Not asking you to," I said. "Just . . . delay it a little. Give it until morning. Let Jack and Terry take the comic books to the police station. If they surrender them voluntarily, it looks better for Terry."

Jack sent me an appreciative glance.

Dad nodded and added, "By then, the police would've executed their search warrant. And hopefully a second if they uncover anything related to the murder."

"Murder?" Jack said, his eyes getting wide again. "Craig? I thought that was an accident."

I laid my hand on his. "Did you or Terry have any recent dealings with Craig?"

Jack shrugged. "Saw him at some of the games."

"Youth sports?"

Jack nodded. "You know I sponsor a team. Or rather, the restaurant does. So does Craig. Usually in the championships, our teams went head to head."

"Friendly rivalry?" Dad asked.

"Not always," Jack said. "Craig could be a bit of a . . ."

"Jerk?" I offered.

Jack nodded. "Not to speak ill of the dead, but yeah. Taunting. Bad sportsmanship. And it's not like he was a coach or anything. All he did was buy uniforms."

Ken sat down at the table opposite Jack. "Hank is right. You and Terry go to the police station and surrender those comics tomorrow. Admit you found them but didn't know they were stolen. You just heard they were valuable."

"Do I take them home?"

"No," Dad said. "I can lock them up here. There's a safe. Liz can go to the station with you in the morning."

Jack looked up at Ken.

Ken held his hands up. "What can I do? I'm on vacation, can't you tell? Let's just hope the police find something . . . anything in that hotel room."

"I'll talk to Terry tonight," Jack said, finally reaching for a Dorito. "I think it'll be okay."

"Jack, do you or Terry know anyone who was recently in South America? Colombia, in particular?" I asked.

Jack immediately shook his head. "Do I want to know why?"

"No," Ken said, shooting me a warning glance.

Jack gathered his coat. "See you tomorrow?" he said to me. "Nine, maybe?"

"Nine is good," I said.

He spared one last curious glance at Ken, then at me, then left the room.

Chapter 14

Ken grabbed my hand as we started to walk aimlessly around the toy show, and I let him. He'd gone up at least two notches in my estimation by the compassion he'd shown Jack and Terry.

Less than two hours, however, remained before the show would end. Vendors would start loading up their wares, and the hobbyists would carefully pack their elaborate train layouts and return them to the basements, attics, and garages from which they came. With two lead suspects for Craig's murder in jail and the missing comic books found, there was nothing much for us to look for. And with the events of the last day and a half, the toys and trains had lost some of their sparkle.

I stopped at a competitor's booth and admired the *Charlie's Angels* figures, still in their boxes. I poked Ken playfully in the arm. "Quick. Which Charlie's Angel do I remind you of?" I offered up a goofy action pose.

He chuckled, then stepped back to look. "Sabrina."

I gave him a pouty look. "Not hot enough to be Farrah, huh?"

He put an arm around me. "Plenty hot enough."

"But more of a curly brunette, like Jaclyn."

"True," he said, "but Sabrina was always the smart one. She was my favorite."

"So you honestly and truly love me for my mind?" Blame the fatigue. I'd used that fearsome L-word. No taking it back now. Maybe he'd just consider it a figure of speech. That's what it was . . . right?

He pulled me closer. "Yup."

That started my head spinning. It came closer to a declaration of love than I was ready for.

While I was still pondering what my verbal slip and Ken's monosyllabic response meant, if anything, to the future of our relationship—and trying to decide what I thought about that—we resumed our slow meander through the various aisles. Santa was doing a fair business with the kids, ho-ho-hoing up a storm in a jolly tenor. We stopped to watch for a few minutes as he coaxed a shy girl of maybe eight or nine into whispering in his ear, then deftly managed a rambunctious toddler who was trying to wriggle in all directions.

"This guy's good," I said. I pulled out my camera to take a picture. Moments later, Santa got up, talked with his elves, and disappeared.

"You spooked him," Ken said. "I don't think Santa shows up on film, anyway."

"I'm pretty sure that only applies to vampires," I said, taking his hand this time as we continued to stroll.

A fair crowd was still gathered around Frank's layout. He was hoarse from retelling the story about how Craig had fallen on it. Only now Frank had taken on heroic overtones, implying that he'd saved Craig's life. Albeit temporarily.

"Poor Frank," I heard one spectator say.

"Yeah, but he did a great job fixing it. I think the UFO was brilliant."

"Are those aliens to scale?" someone in the crowd asked.

"Shape shifters," Frank said. "That's a real science fiction thing." When he noticed Ken and me, he waved us over. "I heard something hinky happened at the center last night."

"You could say that," Ken said.

"You want to hear more?" Frank reached down and picked up a model locomotive. "Remember I told you that one of my engines went missing?"

I hadn't, but I nodded anyway, just to be polite.

"Well, it's back today."

"Are you sure you didn't just misplace it yesterday?" Ken asked.

Frank looked hurt. "It'd be like missing one of your kids when you loaded up the car."

"I'm glad it turned up." Ken grabbed my arm and started moving away.

"You don't believe him?" I asked when we were out of earshot.

"It's just that in all my years as a cop I've seen families accidentally leave kids behind," he said. "Including one happy kid who got locked in a trampoline park overnight."

"That would have its ups and downs."

Ken groaned. "You're your father's daughter."

"Don't jump to conclusions." Even I winced at that one.

Cathy looked tired when we approached the toy booth, even though Miles was helping.

"Go home," I said, giving her a hug. "We can help Miles pack up."

"I like that idea," she said. She beckoned me to the back of the booth. "I didn't want to tell anybody this morning with everything going on, but I think I had a bit of morning sickness. I'm going to have to tell Parker tonight. I won't be able to hide it much longer."

"You poor thing," I said. "Parker should be closing the shop in about twenty minutes. Go get food. Enjoy your evening. And I meant what I said—he'll be ecstatic. Oh, and when we have a chance, remind me to tell you the story of the My Little Pony stuff."

She gave me a surprised look but didn't press for any more information. She just grabbed her purse and headed out before I could change my mind.

"So much for our day off," Ken said.

But Miles asked, "Are you letting all the staff go?"

"Not on your life," I said.

Miles gestured over to the comic booth. "A bit more action over there, huh?"

"Just a little," Ken said. "But it should all be over now." Only he didn't sound convinced.

The idea that somehow this outcome had been just a little too easy, a little too pat, had stuck in my mind. "Are you still worried that not reporting finding those comics will backfire?"

Ken shrugged and picked up the Kirk, Spock, and McCoy action figures sitting on our table. He batted his long eyelashes at me and asked, "Which *Star Trek* action figure do I remind you of?"

"Let's see . . ." I gave him a squinty-eyed inspection, rubbing my chin. "McCoy."

"What?" He clasped a hand to his heart, as if wounded. "Not hot enough to be Kirk?"

I sidled up next to him. "Plenty hot enough to be Kirk."

"Not smart enough to be Spock, then?" He gave me an exaggerated pouty lip.

"Plenty smart." I laughed. "But today I saw your compassionate side in what you did for Jack and Terry. That reminded me of the good doctor."

He winced. "True confession then. I didn't do it for Terry. And I didn't do it for Jack." His Adam's apple bobbed and his gaze was intense. "I did it for you."

I took the action figures and set them carefully down on our table—mint in box, remember—then took him by the hand and led him toward the curtained-off comic booth.

"I'm not seeing this," Miles said.

"What are you doing?" Ken asked. "Where are we going?"

But once the drapes were shut to the rest of the show, I kissed him.

And believe you me, he knew he'd been kissed.

# # #

I dragged myself up the steps that night. All our unsold merchandise was still in boxes stacked haphazardly in the back room. There'd be plenty of time to put it all on the shelves later.

Dad arrived shortly after me, wearing his civvies. "Didn't take long to put that place to rights," he said.

"Give your two-week notice, did you?" I pulled out a can of cat food for Othello, who was circling my ankles.

Dad collapsed into a chair at the kitchen table. "I'm done. Tomorrow I'll turn in my keys and uniform—and get those comic books out of the safe for you—and then they have to find another guy. They don't have any scheduled events until next weekend, and that's just a bridal show."

"*Just* a bridal show?" I asked. "They'd better put out a call for Chuck Norris. I heard those things can be dangerous."

"Well, I don't plan on being there." He squinted at me. "Unless you wanted to go."

"Why would I want to go to a bridal show?"

"A little bird told me that things might've heated up between you and a certain dashing police chief."

"Does that little bird have a name? Miles, maybe?"

"I never reveal my sources. I am the model of discretion."

"Not very discreet of you to practically throw me in his direction, though, was it?"

"Did it work?"

It was hard to be mad at him when he had that impish twinkle in his eye. "I know you have your preferences, and if it makes you happy, yes, things did heat up between Ken and me. But"—I paused to drive my point home—"we're miles away from talking about bridal shows. And furthermore, any future interference in my love life, real or imagined, will be met with severe sanctions."

"Is that 'real or imagined' love life? Or 'real or imagined' interference?"

I gave him my sternest warning look.

"What kind of sanctions are we talking about?" he asked.

I tapped my fingertips together in my best mad-scientist-plotting-world-domination way. "You want grandchildren privileges someday, right?"

He held his hands up in surrender. "No more interference."

# # #

As I lay awake in bed that night, Othello played tetherball with the pull strings of my blinds, and I stared up at the ceiling. When someone had configured these apartments over the store, popcorn ceilings were all the rage. This particular ceiling had been done when someone had come up with the great idea of adding a touch of glitter to that mix. While the good folks at HGTV would be aghast, I'd grown kind of fond of it. The little slivers of light that slipped into the room hit the ceiling at odd angles, occasionally bouncing around in a twinkling glimmer. I had constellations to myself that nobody else ever saw.

Stars were great for quiet contemplation. And I had a lot to think about.

Jack. In the morning, I'd get the comic books, pick up Jack and Terry, and go to the police station. Jack had walked out on me. Yes, he'd walked out on me because of my questions about his brother's whereabouts. And it turned out those questions had some merit. But he'd always remember that I questioned his brother's integrity. And I'd always remember that he'd walked out. Again. As much as I cared for Jack, and as long lasting as our friendship had been, the sad truth about an on-again-off-again relationship is that, while there's enough magnetism to keep drawing us back together, there's not enough to keep other forces from pulling us apart.

Ken. There was a definite advancement there. *If* I wanted it. Did I? Did he? That was the complicated part.

But complications. This whole murder investigation: I had thought it was going to be a complex brainteaser. But this was like opening a jigsaw puzzle, dumping a thousand pieces on the table, then finding the first twelve pieces you picked up completed a perfect rectangle. Mission accomplished. But very unsatisfying, as far as puzzles go. Although more unsatisfying for Craig, I imagined.

But what of Jenna Duncan, the woman who sold Craig the comics? What was she doing at the train and toy show? Why did someone steal the computer from the comic book store? What about Craig's comic book series? Did that work into any of this? And what about his son, the heir, whom nobody knew anything about? Were they all extraneous pieces fate just threw into the box to have a little fun?

And if the mob was after those comic books, why?

I'd started dozing when that question popped into my head with a shot of adrenaline.

Why *was* the mob after those comic books? Where did they learn about them? What connection did they have to them? How did those books end up outside where Terry found them?

There were still a boatload of questions to be answered. Maybe this puzzle wasn't finished after all.

Chapter 15

I bit a frayed cuticle as I sat in the driver's seat of my Civic, now parked out in front of Jack's house. It had taken me months to stop calling it Sy DuPont's place. Once Jack's family had managed to persuade, bribe, or intimidate Kimmie Kaminski into relinquishing the property into the family's hands, Jack had bought out the remaining heirs and moved into the spooky old place. He'd been planning a complete renovation but had yet to finalize his plans or raise a hammer. Meanwhile, he was living in a place that caused visitors to spontaneously start humming the *Addams Family* theme song. I snapped my fingers twice.

"Just take the comic books back," Dad had said. When I'd asked why I had to go, he explained that someone needed to make sure they actually got there. I'd be the most innocuous candidate.

"Innocuous?" I'd even looked up the definition. *Not likely to bother or offend anyone.*

In other words, nobody would notice I was there. Invisible.

Dad couldn't do it, and Ken certainly couldn't. Especially since Ken's story, should his name even come up, was that he never got a good look at the books in question. The books now sitting in my trunk, a pile of comic books worth more than five times the value of my car.

I'd gotten a good look. They were still sealed in plastic, of course, but I took careful cell phone shots of all of them before we'd packed them up to surrender them to the police as evidence.

Breakfast churned in my stomach as I took another sip of coffee from my travel mug. Then a sharp rap on my car window made me bobble my cup. I managed to salvage most of it, but not before a dribble of very hot coffee made its way through my pant legs.

I sucked air through my teeth and put the dripping cup into my car holder before climbing out of the car and shaking a few stray drops of coffee from my fingers.

"Sorry, dear," Lenora said. "We didn't mean to startle you." Behind her, Irene nodded.

The two eightysomething sisters, who'd lived next door to the DuPont house all of their lives, were dressed in their fall finery, including bulky oversized sweaters with leaves and pumpkins appliquéd to them.

"You ladies are up and out of the house early," I said, giving each a gentle hug.

"We were just saying the same about you," Irene said. "Coming to see our neighbor this morning?" A mischievous look crossed her face. "Or are you just leaving?"

"Irene!" Lenora said. "I'm sure that's none of our business!" But she tilted her head and waited for me to respond.

I laughed. "Sorry. Nothing juicy to report. Just picking Jack and Terry up for an errand."

Was it my imagination, or did Lenora avoid my eyes when I mentioned Terry?

"Is something wrong with Terry?" I asked.

"Oh, no, dear," Lenora said. "He's been a very cordial neighbor."

"It's more the change in Jack since Terry moved in," Irene said. "We both noticed it, didn't we, Lenora?"

Lenora nodded. "Like he's aged and all the fun's been zapped out of him."

"Well, we all do get older," I said. "And I know he's got a lot on his mind."

Irene crossed her arms in front of her. "But that's a poor excuse for growing up into a grump."

Before I could think of an answer, the creaky front door of the house swung open, and Jack headed down the long sidewalk. Maybe it was power of suggestion, but he did look at least ten years older as he forced a tight smile. "Good morning, ladies." Then he opened the passenger door and climbed in without saying another word.

Irene took my hand. "Don't you grow up too."

I squeezed it and winked at her. "Don't worry about me. Second star to the left and straight on until morning."

"That a girl," said Lenora. We said our good-byes, and I made a promise to come visit them soon and climbed into the car.

"Where's Terry?" I asked.

"Terry won't be coming today," he said tersely.

"Is he sick?"

Jack's face drew into a tight grimace. "Terry bolted last night."

About half an hour later, Jack and I—and the comic books—entered the police station. I'd stopped to call Dad, updated him about the situation, and sought his advice.

I could hear the disappointment in his voice. "It would've been so much better for Terry to have taken them in himself. Now, depending where he is and how long he stays gone, he could be in danger of forfeiting his parole."

I didn't tell Jack that part. I think he already knew.

I forced a smile to the clerk at the desk.

"Hi, Liz." She cast a confused look at Jack, then at me. "If you're here to see the chief, he's still off today."

"Oh, I know. That's not why we're here. Is . . . uh . . . Detective Reynolds around?"

"Yes and no," she said. "He's just logging some new evidence. He's been out all night, in fact. Is there anyone else who can help you?"

I tightened my grip on the box containing the comic books. "It's actually pertinent to one of his investigations," I said. "If it's all right, we can wait."

She directed us to some molded plastic seats. Jack shuffled his way through several magazines, paying no attention to the covers or contents. Unless he was speed-reading through *American Angler* and *Teen Vogue*. When he picked up *Arthritis Today*, I said, "Yes, read that one. I hear the centerfold is oo-la-la."

"What?" He did a double-take on the smiling dentured woman on the cover. He tossed the magazine down on the table. "What is taking so long?" Jack looked every bit the naughty middle schooler waiting for the principal. "I just want to get this over with." He closed his eyes. "What was he thinking? What was *I* thinking?" When I didn't answer, he drummed a rhythm on his thigh. "What am I going to tell Mom?"

I certainly had no answer. Jack's mother was a riddle wrapped in a lemon inside a porcupine. At the same time the clerk finally called my name, the outside door opened and Terry entered. The brothers looked at each other but said nothing. Out on the sidewalk, Dad waved at me without coming in.

The clerk called my name again, and we all walked to the desk in the bullpen where I'd first met Detective Reynolds.

The good detective, now looking haggard and, truth-be-told, smelling a bit ripe, gave our group a once-over. "Let's use the conference room."

What he'd called the conference room was also an inter-rogation room, but I followed them in and took an empty seat. "Are you having a good morning?" I asked innocently.

"That depends." He eyed the box in my hand.

I smiled my sweetest Candy Land smile. "We found some-thing. Or rather, Terry did. It's kind of funny, really."

I laughed. Nobody else did.

I opened the flaps of the box. "It seems that Terry here found . . . well, maybe you should tell him, Terry."

Terry, who'd been slumped in his chair, sat bolt upright. I think Jack had kicked him under the table.

"Yeah," Terry said. "I found these comic books." He nod-ded to the box that I nudged toward Detective Reynolds.

Reynolds pushed himself out of the chair to look into the box. He shut his eyes. "Are these what I think they are?"

161

"Yes, sir," I said. "I believe so. I checked them with the list of missing comics, and from the titles and condition, they appear to be the ones reported stolen."

Reynolds squinted at me, and I sent him my most innocuous smile. Maybe Dad was right.

"Terrence Wallace," Reynolds said, turning his attention in that direction, "you claim to have found these books?"

"Yeah."

More motion under the table.

"Yes, *sir*," Terry said, glaring at his brother.

"Can you tell me a little more about that?" Reynolds said.

"Nothing to tell," Terry said. "I stepped out for a smoke and there they were, on the ground by the door."

"In the box?"

"No, they were just lying there on the ground. Well, they were kind of stuck behind a planter, a little bit."

"So you picked them up," Reynolds said.

"If I didn't, someone else sure would have."

"And what were you planning on doing with the books?"

Jack clenched the arms of his chair. "Should we call a lawyer? Are you arresting him?"

"You can if you think you need to. But no, I wasn't arresting him."

"I can answer the question." Terry licked his lower lip. "I was going to read them. But I couldn't figure out how to get those plastic cases off. How's anybody supposed to check out to see if they like the books if they can't flip open a few pages?"

"Be glad you didn't remove those covers," I said. "Any damage would have devalued them."

MURDER ON THE TOY TOWN EXPRESS

"Look, I just told you I found them. I don't see what the big deal is."

"The big deal," I said, "is that you walked off with ninety grand in comic books."

Terry paled. "Ninety?" It was only with great effort that he managed to close his jaw. "I had no idea they were worth that much."

"So you were just going to read them?" Reynolds asked.

Terry nodded. "I always liked Spider-Man. When I found them, there was an old Spider-Man on top. Only I got freaked out when I heard they were looking for stolen comics, so I just shoved them under my bed when I got home."

"What an original hiding place," Reynolds said.

"But it's the truth," Terry insisted.

"And I believe you," Reynolds said. "It's plausible that the thief or thieves worried about being discovered and hid the comics outside, thinking they'd be safe until he or they had a chance to retrieve them. Maybe if we can replay the security footage from Saturday, we can figure out who that was."

"So we're good?" Terry said.

"We're good," Reynolds said. "But don't leave town."

"Got it." Terry smiled at him, then at Jack. "I guess we can go then. Back to the restaurant? Make the sauce?"

Jack clapped him on the shoulder, and they turned to leave.

"Need a ride?" I called after them.

"No, only a couple of blocks to the restaurant," Jack said, and the brothers headed out, side by side.

I whispered to Reynolds, "I thought you couldn't tell people not to leave town."

"Parolees are the exception." Reynolds let his gaze trail down the aisle where the two men had just left. "It must've taken a lot of courage to come in here voluntarily like that."

"He may have had a little persuasion."

"Uh-huh. And Miss McCall, when exactly did you find out Terrence Wallace had taken the comic books?"

"Yesterday, I think. Yes, yesterday."

Reynolds rolled his eyes. "Do I want to know when?"

"I don't exactly remember," I said. "Not the exact time, anyway."

"Please tell me it was after we arrested those other two guys for the same thing."

"Yes, it was after that." I refrained from telling him it was only moments after that. "But I overheard that you found something."

"Which is why I'm not reaming you out right now," Reynolds said.

I resummoned that innocuous smile. "A comic book?"

"Just the one we see the guy roll up and stuff in his pocket. Worth about two bucks—less since he rolled it up. But before we found that, we hit pay dirt."

I just tilted my head and smiled. "The missing computer, perhaps?"

He shook his head. "No sign of the computer, in either the hotel or their rental car. They might have ditched it somewhere. But we found this white powdery substance. Had to keep our hands off and get a whole separate search warrant for it. Looks like cocaine. Don't think it is."

"Did you taste it?"

He winced. "Someone's been watching too much television. No. I'm not quite that stupid. We'll have to get it analyzed, but it has the same physical description as scopolamine, the drug they found in Craig's system." I wondered why he was telling me all this. It occurred to me that he wasn't gossiping. He was boasting—to someone apparently people thought of as the "chief's girl."

"Nice work!" I said, at the same time feeling conflicted for taking advantage of that . . . misconception? Fact? Either way, I wanted the flow of information to continue. "You got them for the murder."

"Not quite yet, but enough that we should be able to hold them if we're smart about what charges are pressed and when. It's a game of beat the clock. The law gives us just so much time before arraignment. Before bail. For each part of the process. And we need to play it by the book, so they don't walk. But if we do our job just right, I think we might have them for the murder." His voice was electric. This was a major feather in his cap.

"Do you have any idea why those two guys wanted those comic books?"

"You said yourself they were worth over ninety grand."

"Yes, but how did they know that? How did they know Craig had them? And there's plenty of other valuable items around. Why take them from Craig, much less kill him, and in such an unusual way?"

Reynolds's lip curled ever so slightly. "I can see your dad in you all right. Right about the eyes, a little in the nose, but especially that spot right between the ears." He pointed to

165

the door. "Get out of here. Apparently I have more detecting to do."

When I stepped out of the police station, Dad was sitting in the passenger seat of my car waiting to be filled in on everything that'd happened.

"Sounds like he's doing a good job building a case," Dad said. "Is that enough to put your mind at ease that they weren't after me?"

"Maybe. I only wish we knew a little more of what the mob was doing here. And why they'd drug Craig and steal a computer. Seems kind of penny ante, don't you think?"

"So we're missing one computer and a motive for murder," he said as I waited for traffic to clear on Main.

"And a motive for theft," I said.

"You don't need a motive for theft," Dad said. "The motive is to take whatever you're stealing. Ninety grand is good motive."

"No," I said, "for why they were after those particular comic books. How did they know—"

"Relax," Dad said. "I know what you meant. I've been wondering that myself." He rubbed his knees. "Maybe the answer to that is in finding out why those books are so special. Besides the monetary value, that is."

"The original owner might know. This Jenna Duncan," I said. "But if she did know what made those comics so important they were worth killing over, then why would she sell them to Craig in the first place?"

"A very good question," Dad said. "But there's only one person who can answer it." He rubbed his hands together. "That address. Isn't that near where the mayor lives?"

"Nice neighborhood," I said.

"So the mayor's wife probably knows Mrs. Duncan, if they're neighbors."

"Probably."

"And does Lori Briggs still have all those home parties selling stuff?"

I flashed him my least innocuous smile. "I think she does."

# # #

I stared at the shop phone for several minutes, trying to figure out how I was going to best approach Lori and ask about her neighbor. And our shop phone stared back. The phone, custom painted and with wiggly eyes, was one of Dad's extravagances. Since the pull toy that it was modeled after was made right here in town, it often got residents talking and reminiscing. And getting folks reminiscing was the key ingredient to our business plan.

Finally, I picked it up and dialed.

"Morning, Liz," she said when she answered.

"Hi, Lori. I had a couple of questions I wanted to run by you. Is this a good time?"

"Well, as long as it's not too long. I'm having a Clean Queen party tonight, and I'm on the way to the store for dip."

"Oh, that sounds fun! And I've been wanting to get more of that good . . ." I removed the phone from my face and feigned a coughing spell. "Sorry about that," I said, then cleared my throat. "I don't suppose you have room for one more guest?" A little impolite to invite myself, but I doubted she'd mind as long as I bought my quota.

"Oh, sure! Cathy would probably appreciate your company."

"Cathy's going?"

Cathy heard her name and started walking toward the desk.

"Yes, Clean Queen is so good for babies and expectant mothers. Totally organic and all natural. None of those harsh chemicals. See you at seven!" And then she disconnected, on her way to acquire dip probably full of more chemicals than her cleaners.

"I'm going where?" Cathy asked.

"Lori Briggs's Clean Queen party," I said.

"Sure. She invited both of us the other day at game night. You might have been a little distracted. You were playing Power Grid with Ken and Jack. And the electricity was flying."

"Shut it, Chatty Cathy," I said, then regretted it. "Sorry, I'm a little sensitive to teasing at the moment." I filled her in on what was happening with Jack and Ken.

"Well, I'm glad you seem to be closer to a decision," she said.

"And I'm glad I don't have to keep your secret anymore."

Her eyes got big. "What do you mean?"

"Lori just told me that you were going to her Clean Queen party because the products are good for pregnant mothers and babies. So I take it the secret's out of the bag."

Cathy sucked her next breath through clenched teeth. "I guess it depends on which bag you're talking about."

"You *still* haven't told Parker?"

"He was tired from working all day, and then he went to pay the bills. Always a sore subject. You know I love working at the toyshop, but it's not the highest-paying job around. And neither is the wildlife center."

"I can try to see if I can eke out a little bit more," I said.

She shook her head. "Parker's convinced it's my spending. And maybe he's right. But when he went on about how we could cut down here and there, I didn't have the heart to tell him that we had diapers and car seats and baby clothes and outfitting a nursery in our future."

"But how did Lori find out? If *she* knows, it's going to get around town."

"I'll call her before the party and ask if she can keep it under wraps."

"You have met Lori, right? Why not just tell Parker?"

"I don't want to rush it. And the party is at seven. What made you want to come all of a sudden? I thought you hated the home parties."

"I do. If you're going to have a social event, have a party. If you want to sell people things, call it something else. I don't like mixing patronage and friendship."

"So what about your game nights? Are they parties? Or opportunities to sell games, toys, or at least candy to our friends?"

I opened my mouth to respond and realized I didn't have an answer. "You got me. I'm a hypocrite."

"And you still haven't answered my question."

"Lori has a neighbor I'm hoping to meet. I'd like to ask her a few questions about some of the things that happened this weekend."

"This neighbor have a name?"

"Jenna Duncan," I said. "Sound familiar?"

"I might have met a Jenna there. Lori's parties are very popular."

"If she's not there, maybe I could accidentally knock on her door or something. 'Excuse me, I was looking for Lori Briggs's house, and I seem to have gotten turned around. Wait! Didn't I see you at the train and toy show?'"

Cathy rolled her eyes. "Let's hope she's at the party."

Chapter 16

I had to call Cathy to help me figure out what to wear. "Casual" had different definitions depending on who says it. Jeans, T-shirt, and sneakers are how I usually defined it.

"Heavens no!" Cathy had said. Then she dictated my entire outfit from memory. When I arrived at her house, she made more adjustments, exchanging my necklace for one of hers and bemoaning the fact that there wasn't enough time to apply nail polish.

While she took a last trip to the powder room, Parker pulled me aside.

"Do you, uh, notice anything different about Cathy lately?" he asked.

"Different?" I blinked at him.

He eyed me curiously. He'd always been able to tell when I was hiding something or stretching the truth. "It's not someone else, is it?"

"What? No! What would make you think that?"

"Every time we talk, it seems like she's holding something back." He squinted at me. "You know what it is, don't you."

That was not a question. "There's something she's not telling me."

"Parker," I whispered, "just ask her. Cathy loves you. If she's keeping anything back from you, I'm sure it's not that."

Our conversation ended as Cathy bustled in. "Ready to go?" She didn't wait for an answer, so I followed her outside.

I was thankful for her fashion intervention the moment we pulled up in front of Lori Briggs's house. Other women were walking down the sidewalk or emerging from their cars looking like they were about to go yachting with the Kennedys. Casual, my foot.

Lori lived in a perfectly restored, grandiose Victorian with landscaping that must've kept a crew of twenty busy. I couldn't fault her choice in homes. Why settle for a McMansion somewhere when you can buy an "authentic" historic home that had genuine charm? Many of these had been modernized at some point along the way, losing much of their period character. Now, of course, all those modern trappings were dated, and homeowners paid top dollar to rip out all those features and replace them with modern reproductions—or even more for the real deal from wily and enterprising junk dealers who'd had the foresight to pull all that stuff out of the trash.

"Liz, Cathy, so happy to see you." Lori leaned in for an air hug. "Come in and meet everybody." And then she deserted us, leaving us to fend for ourselves.

Lori's large house was wall-to-wall women. Tall ones, short ones, fat ones, skinny ones, young ones, old ones. All impeccably dressed, flawlessly made up, and balancing drinks and small plates of appetizers with the skill of Chinese acrobats.

Lori swept in with a spray bottle and started spritzing her drapes. When a circle gathered around her, she started her pitch. "No matter how clean our house, it doesn't feel clean unless it smells clean. Am I right?"

If she'd been standing in the pulpit of any church, she would have gotten a hearty amen. But the women standing around her bobbed their heads, and a couple voiced their assent.

A familiar scent tickled my nostrils, but I couldn't quite place it.

"Doesn't it smell clean?" Lori asked.

More nodding followed.

"Like all Clean Queen products, it's plant-based and completely nontoxic." She removed the top and lifted the bottle to her mouth.

When a few women gasped, she raised her hand and added, "Not that the company recommends doing this. But when I demanded proof of its safety—you know I'd only sell you the best—the regional distributor opened up a bottle and took a big swig. That's all I needed to know. But I want *you* to know how much I believe in this product." She took a careful sip, then winked. "It's"—she cleared her throat— "actually not bad."

We meandered through the living room to the dining room, with Cathy stopping to introduce me to members of her various writing groups and literary societies. I kept looking at faces, hoping to recognize Jenna Duncan among the guests. Meanwhile, Lori started repeating her spiel to those in the dining room, airing out the drapes on the French doors. This time, she took a less hesitant sip—"Now, remember. Don't do this at home!"—and the crowd applauded.

When the demonstration concluded, conversations resumed. After what felt like three hours but was probably less than ten minutes, I excused myself from an extended conversation on rhyme schemes and left Cathy to her own devices.

I wandered into the kitchen where a somewhat flushed Lori was again demonstrating the power of Clean Queen, this time used as a degreaser. When she was done, she tossed her rag next to her now half-clean stove. "Don't clean the rest of it," she said to a nearby woman hard at work loading hot appetizers from a baking tray onto a serving plate. "I want to run that demo again later."

The woman, who I'd assumed was paid help, nodded, and I was surprised to see it was Jenna Duncan clad in an apron and stationed at the working end of the long granite-topped kitchen island. She concentrated on her work, but when she did look up, she did a double-take when she saw me.

"Jenna Duncan?" I asked.

"Yes. If you'll excuse me just a second," she said, and then she walked out with the tray.

While she was gone, I helped myself to one of the hot appetizers. I only wish I knew what it was. Some spicy filling wrapped in something. Whatever happened to mini-pizzas and nachos? When I finished that one, I helped myself to another.

Jenna certainly took her time. I thought of poking my head out of the kitchen, but that would risk being drawn into another inane conversation or worse: being forced to take in yet another Clean Queen demo, which I could hear even from the kitchen.

". . . not that they recommend you drink it."

By the time I finished nibbling my third appetizer, I was beginning to think Jenna was on the lam, and I couldn't blame her.

She returned a moment later with two empty serving plates and looking a little harried.

"Would you like a hand?" I asked.

"You're a guest here. I couldn't ask you to do that."

"Aren't you? A guest here, I mean."

"Sort of," she said. "Lori and I are hosting the party together. Which means she provides the venue . . ."

"And you end up doing all the work?"

"That's about right." She replaced the paper doily on one of the serving plates and began loading it with premade minicheesecakes.

I took the other tray and started doing the same. "Didn't I see you at the train and toy show the other day?"

Jenna bobbled one of the cheesecakes but managed to catch it before it hit the floor. When she set it on the counter, she took a deep breath and faced me.

"You and I both know you did." She wiped her hands on her white apron. "And based on where I saw you and who I saw you with, I'm going to wager that you know that I was also there to try to talk Craig into selling back some comics he practically stole from me."

"Stole?"

She forcibly crushed the empty cheesecake box and set it next to the trash for recycling. "He knew what they were worth. Well, maybe not exactly. But he took a look through the box at my garage sale and offered me fifty dollars, then acted like he was being nice when he met me halfway at seventy-five."

"You priced them at a hundred bucks?"

She winced. "I know. It's partly my fault. I had no idea they were worth anything at all. How could I? They were just sitting in a box in the attic."

"Your husband was a collector?"

"Not that I ever knew about. But he wasn't exactly here to help . . . and since I saw you with Hank McCall, I'm going to wager you know that too. And why. But I was trying to clean out the house so I could put it on the market, you see, and selling those books meant one less box to move."

"When did you find out their worth?"

"I'm still not sure of the exact amount. Only that Josh had a hissy fit when I told him I'd sold them. He went on a rampage telling me not to sell any more of his stuff and said I'd sold them to spite him. Who knows? Maybe I did. Anyway, I thought I'd be the sweet and dutiful wife and try to get the books back. Maybe offer double what Craig paid for them. But that woman at the shop said they'd mailed them somewhere. And Craig just laughed at me when I finally saw him."

"When was that?" I asked.

"At the train show," she said. "He'd never returned my calls, and I saw in the paper that his shop was going to be at the show, so I figured he'd be there too. With all those potential customers milling about, I'd hoped he'd be reasonable and make things right. If he didn't cooperate, I thought of a few ways I could make life difficult for him."

"What did you have in mind?"

"Nothing illegal. But the place would be swarming with buyers. And with a few well-timed words, I could let people know what a creep he is. Was." She let out a noise I'd qualify as a growl. "I *hate* being mad at dead people. No matter what they did to you, people don't want to hear anything but how wonderful they were."

"Trust me, I grew up with Craig. I know what a jerk he could be."

Lori burst into the kitchen and made a beeline for one of her tall pantry cupboards. "Mop. Mop. Mop. Where'd the maid put the mop?" She opened several before finally pulling out a mop and bucket. While she filled the bucket with hot water from the sink, she fanned her face with her hand. "Is it hot in here?" She undid the top button of her blouse. "I must've worked up a sweat with all this cleaning!" She winked at me. "Clean Queen is wonderful. So wonderful. Make sure you buy a case of it!"

As Lori exited the kitchen, she stumbled. She managed to catch herself but apparently didn't notice that she'd splashed a little bit of water onto the tile floor.

Jenna rolled her eyes. "I'd better get that. Last thing we need is for one of the guests to slip and sue both of us." She threw a folded paper towel onto the spill and wiped it up with her foot before bending down to retrieve the towel.

I took a piece of cheesecake from one of the trays and rearranged the rest so they were even. "So you talked to Craig that morning?" I asked, nonchalantly peeling back the paper liner.

"Yes. Not that there was any getting through to him. He was wearing that silly costume, and I think he really believed he was some kind of superhero. Anyway, he had much more important things to do than talk to me."

"Did he seem himself? I mean, was he off balance or slurring his words or anything like that? Anything odd?"

"You mean like drunk?"

"Something like that."

"I guess he could've been," Jenna said. "It'd explain him falling off the catwalk, I suppose. I honestly didn't know him well enough to say if he were acting out of the ordinary. It was hard to talk with him wearing that mask."

"Was he angry when you confronted him?"

"He mostly just blew me off. It's not like I had much of a legal ground to stand on. I was hoping to appeal to his compassionate side, but I'm not sure he had one. He actually boasted that he was going to put all that money to much better use, and if I stuck around, I'd see what it was."

"And did you? Stick around?"

She nodded. "Mostly just hoping to drive away some of his paying customers. Just plant a few seeds that he was ripping people off. And yes, I heard that some comic books went missing. If you're wondering if I stole them, not a chance. Craig would have liked nothing better than to see me pinched for shoplifting, but I think one Duncan in prison is enough, thank you very much."

"Did you tell anyone else besides your husband that Craig had those comics?"

"You're thinking someone I know tried to steal them for me? Honey, I wish I had friends that good." She carried the two plates into the dining room. I tried to remember what Dad had told me about how to tell if someone was lying, but they were mostly facial cues, and I'm pretty sure that if Jenna had "liar" written all over her face, it was erased by enough Botox to kill a cow. The growing irritation in her voice, however, was coming across quite clearly.

"There you are," Cathy said. "I just had a wonderful conversation with the library director. She's offered to let us display some of our antique toys in the glass case in the lobby. We can't put prices on them, of course, but we can put in a little sign saying they're on loan from the shop. Isn't that great?"

She picked up the crushed piece of cheesecake, examined it, shrugged, and popped it into her mouth. "What are you doing hiding in here?"

"Waiting for Jenna Duncan to come back. She's playing hostess. Or more like scullery drudge."

"Did you learn anything?"

"She admits to being at the show, but I think I just ticked her off, and I have one more question to ask."

"What is it?"

"If she'd ever traveled to Colombia."

"Why Colombia?" Cathy asked. "I thought you said they already found that drug when they searched the hotel room of those two mob guys."

"They found what looks like a drug. It hasn't been tested yet, and it's also possible Jenna's tied up in this somehow. Maybe she hired them. Maybe she supplied the drug."

"No worries. I got this."

When Jenna returned, Cathy piled on the charm. "Jenna! I just had to compliment you. Liz here said you've supplied the food. Everything is simply scrumptious!"

"I mostly just put it on the plates," she said.

"Now, don't be humble. I don't know what Lori would do without you!"

Miracle of miracles, Jenna's face actually moved. Into somewhat of a smile, no less.

"And my, you certainly don't look like you've been slaving away. You look fantastic! What a great tan. Have you been traveling? Somewhere exciting?"

"Fat chance," Jenna said. "I do have an amazing excursion planned. I'm blowing all my garage sale money and anything I earn tonight on a lavish trip to visit my mother in exotic Cleveland." She rolled her eyes. "Josh and I had been talking about going back to the Dominican Republic. Such wonderful ocean breezes. But then . . . I haven't been out of the country in so long, I'm not even sure my passport is valid."

When we left the kitchen, Cathy was waylaid by someone else she knew. I meandered through the dining room, placed an order for a nontoxic cleaner I didn't need, put my name in for a raffle, and helped myself to coffee in a cup so delicate, I was almost afraid to handle it.

Someone vacated a plush armchair next to the fireplace, and I grabbed it. This shindig was emptying out fast, and Lori had to interrupt her mopping to give out more air hugs to departing guests at the door. "Your orders should be in sometime next week," she called out after them. "Wait! I was going to do the stove again. Who wants to see the stove?"

While a few women followed Lori into the kitchen, I waited in the chair until Cathy was finished. Left alone to review what I'd learned, I almost felt sorry for Jenna. *Almost.* She wasn't exactly destitute and begging on the streets, but she deeply felt the loss of her former lifestyle. Was that enough motivation to exact revenge on Craig? He wasn't the cause of her economic downturn, but he'd most certainly exacerbated it.

But if she blamed my father for her husband's downfall, she could have been targeting him instead. Maybe she even hired Batman-man and Grandpa to do it. She could have paid off Janet to put the drug in the coffee before she handed it to me. Everyone has a price, right?

I did my best to shake off that thought. There was too much subsequent interest in Craig and those comic books for Craig to simply be collateral damage in some mob vendetta against my father.

I remembered what I'd read about the drug found in Craig's system. It made victims subject to suggestion. Too much could lead to death. So which were they after? Was someone trying to control Craig to get him to surrender those pricy comics without making a scene? Or was someone trying to kill him?

Cathy took a seat next to me on a vacant ottoman. "You look like you're ready to go," she said. "I was hoping they'd have done the raffle by now. You have to be here to win. The prize is a whole case of Clean Queen, and you saw how fabulous it is." She looked around to make sure nobody was listening before whispering, "I may have entered more than once."

"We can wait," I told her. "And if I win, you can have it. Not sure I like the smell of it."

"It's lemony," she said.

"And something else. Can't put my finger on it."

Lori strode across the living room heading in our direction. Instead, she went straight for the fireplace. "Whose bright idea was it to start a fire? Way too hot for a fire." She unbuttoned another couple of buttons of her blouse, now exposing a lace bra she probably sold at a very different home party. She took out the tongs, started to fling ashes on top of the burning wood, and ended up sending hot sparks onto her white carpet.

I got up to help stamp them out.

Lori stopped me, giggling. "I got it." She whisked out her Clean Queen bottle and sprayed it on the ashes on the carpet. It burst into flames, sending a terrible stench into the room.

"Oh, dear," Lori said. Well, maybe that's my sanitized paraphrase of her words. Red-face and sweating profusely, she seemed to have trouble standing up. She grabbed my arm.

"Liz. Help me. I don't feel well at all. I think . . . I've been drugged."

And then she passed out.

Chapter 17

The EMTs wheeled Lori away to an ambulance.

Ken stood in the middle of the living room, eying the scorched pink patch of carpet that Cathy had smartly doused with the entire contents of the punchbowl. He looked up to view the handful of ladies who remained. "So this was a party?"

Heads bobbed, but nobody answered. Maybe because parties are supposed to be fun.

"Did anyone see Lori eat or drink anything?"

"She wasn't eating," one portly woman said. "She said she was dieting. Maybe that's what got to her." A ripple of conversation erupted as guests mulled the dreaded plague of low blood sugar.

"So maybe just a combination of the heat and not eating?" Cathy said.

"But she said she'd been drugged," another woman insisted.

I wondered at that too. Lori had been quick to suspect that drugs had led to Craig's fall. I had no idea if that was a result of town gossip or if she'd overheard something. As

183

the mayor's wife, Lori was often privy to information on all aspects of the community, and since Ken reported to her husband, that often included police investigations. Perhaps she had heard about the line of investigation questioning whether Craig had been drugged, and maybe that influenced her perception on why she was feeling ill.

Or, even more chilling, might someone really have drugged her? I hazarded a glance toward Jenna Duncan, who was leaning in the doorway to the kitchen. She had access to all the food and beverages, but why would she target Lori? And would she be stupid enough to do it when she, as kitchen help, would likely be the first suspect?

"I don't feel so good either," another guest said. Power of suggestion? If we weren't careful, half the women at the party would be in the ER suffering from the effects of mass hysteria.

"I've sampled most of the appetizers," I admitted. "And I feel fine."

"Wait!" Cathy said. "Clean Queen."

"What about it?" Ken said.

"She'd been taking sips of it all evening," Cathy said.

"More than sips," another woman volunteered. "Toward the end she was chugging it."

"Clean Queen?" Ken said, picking up a bottle from a nearby table. He unscrewed the spray cap and sniffed the contents. He thought for a moment, then sniffed it again.

"It's supposed to be organic and nontoxic," Cathy said.

Ken's lips shut tight as he screwed the nozzle back on the bottle and set it on the mantel. His face looked grave, but when he wiped his mouth, I could see he was hiding a smile.

When he'd composed himself, he said, "The good news is the patient will recover. Nobody was drugged, and you're all safe. The bad news . . ."

Everyone in the room hung on his next words. "I'm afraid you're going to have to cancel all the orders. I can't allow sales of Clean Queen to continue. And I'm going to have to confiscate all the bottles present."

"But the raffle winner hasn't been chosen yet!" Cathy was indignant.

"All the bottles," he said. "I'm afraid it's illegal to sell this cleaner in this state." He couldn't stop the smirk. "At least without a valid liquor license," he added under his breath when he turned to me.

"Vodka!" I said, snapping my fingers. "I thought I recognized that smell."

"More like white lightning, but on those same lines," Ken said.

When the rest of the guests had dispersed, with Jenna promising full refunds as soon as Lori had sufficiently recovered, I apologized to Ken. "Sorry to drag you out here. But when Lori said 'drugged,' I was worried we had a serial killer on the loose."

"I'm glad you called." He looked briefly around the room. "Is there someplace you and I can talk privately?"

Jenna pointed the way down a short hallway, and Ken and I found ourselves in a dark, masculine office.

I gave him what I hoped was a flirty come-hither look. "In the mayor's private office? How naughty."

"Seriously, we need to talk. There's been a development in the case. The preliminary autopsy results are in."

"The scopolamine."

"Was in Craig's system. Yes, we know that. But that's not what killed him."

"But it weakened him, plus the injuries from the fall."

Ken was shaking his head. "Craig may have been drugged, but the cause of death was heart failure."

"So after all this, his death was from natural causes?"

Ken shook his head again. "The medical examiner isn't done yet, but he said other findings are going to make this one a clear homicide. Something about the acid levels in his blood."

"From the drug?"

"He said no, and he'll explain further in his report. But he's saying that the buildup of acid was caused by Craig not getting enough oxygen. And the lack of oxygen combined with the acid buildup led to cardiac arrest."

"Were his lungs damaged in the fall?"

"No. His doctors were sure of it because they were amazed that it was one part of him that wasn't affected. They have the X-rays to prove it."

"Then why wasn't he getting enough oxygen?"

Ken took a long breath. "The ME's not 100 percent sure. He's comparing some injuries around Craig's nose and mouth with the X-rays taken after he arrived, but he's thinking someone smothered him. It's going to be a while before he releases the body for burial."

"Someone smothered Craig *in the hospital*?" I sat down on the arm of an overstuffed burgundy leather chair. "We were on our way to visit him. A few minutes earlier and we might've walked in on the killer. We could have prevented it."

"Or escalated it," Ken said. "And gotten hurt in the process."

I swept my hair from my face and considered the ramifications. "They didn't just drug him to get something and accidentally give him too much," I said. "Someone *wanted* him dead. At least we know it was actually Craig they were after." Relief flooded me. My father's list of enemies . . . at least that line of investigation had officially dead-ended, even if it had been mostly my own paranoia keeping it alive. But I felt a stab of guilt too. Craig *had* been targeted, and this time, the killer succeeded. And apparently right under my nose.

Ken nodded and pulled me into a comforting hug. A minute later, he began to kiss my neck.

I pushed him away. "What are you doing?"

"Just thinking you were right," he said, winking at me. "It'd be a shame to waste being alone with you in the mayor's office."

# # #

Maxine showed up, bright and perky, at nine thirty the next morning, even though we didn't open until ten.

"Did the garage do a good job with your car?" I asked. "I still feel bad about that."

She waved off my concern. "Never looked better. I think they took out some of my old dings at the same time. Besides, I'm not going to complain about my new boss on the first day."

"Have you heard anything more about your job at the comic book shop?"

"I told the kid's mother that I could help them clean up and take inventory. I don't think it's good news, though. I'm thinking she'll probably want to sell it lock, stock, and barrel before next month's rent is due."

"I forgot Craig was only renting that building."

She nodded. "And there's a waiting list of people looking for Main Street frontage at the right price."

I thought about that for a second. Surely nobody would sneak into a hospital and suffocate Craig for his storefront. But it reminded me that the ties connecting the comic books to Craig's murder seemed to have melted away, and no new motives had surfaced.

"So you've met the new owners?" I asked. Follow the money, Dad had always said.

"Just briefly," Maxine said. "The kid, you could tell he kind of liked the comic books. Barely looked up from his reading the whole time I was there. His mom, though. I think she has other plans."

"Did she say more about her relationship with Craig?" I asked. "I'm sorry. That sounds so nosy. But I never heard of a Mrs. Craig. Or of a son, either."

"They were never married. I gathered it was a rather brief encounter," Maxine said. "For what it's worth, I never knew he had a kid and I worked with him every day."

"You never saw either of them before?"

"Nope," she said, and then her eyes clouded. "I don't know what I expected. The boy's not particularly sad, but then again, why would he be? I'm not sure he even knew his father. I expect the mother's trying to figure out whether Craig being dead is good or bad for her money-wise. I think he was paying child support of some kind."

"And now that's going to stop," I said, "but there's the shop, a house, and probably life insurance."

"Right," she said. "But the kid seems like a quiet boy. Well-mannered, at least, from what I saw. I hope you don't have a problem with letting me flex my hours so I can help them with the shop. I feel I owe it to Craig, and I'd hate to leave matters up in the air."

"No, not at all," I said. "In fact, I don't suppose you can introduce me to the new owners?"

"You mean, accidentally on purpose?" She smiled.

"Something like that."

"I can do that. But I want to ask you a question first."

"What's that?"

"Why the interest? I mean, it's not like I don't appreciate all you're doing, but . . ."

Dad interrupted. I hadn't even realized he'd come downstairs. "You didn't tell her why we're so interested?"

He shook Maxine's hand firmly. "Welcome aboard!" He leaned back on the stool. "I was telling Liz that I'd love to put in a comic book room. If Craig's Comics is shutting down, I'm interested in buying him out."

"Oh!" Maxine visibly relaxed. "We should be done with the inventory by the end of the week. Only I'm not so sure how early they can sell. Legally, that is. I know they want to be out of the building before the next rent check is due."

"The legal niceties can take a while," Dad said. "It'd be easier for them than trying to sell the stock to anyone else. We pretty much just have to walk them across the street. And we have an employee who already knows the inventory. Now, if only she were permanent . . ."

"I was kind of hoping the job could be more than temporary. But even if that's not possible, it gives me some cushion
to find something new."

"We can't promise anything now, Maxine," I said. "But
I've seen you work, and I'd definitely like to keep you. Give
me some time to crunch the numbers to see if I can make that
happen. There's no guarantee we'll get those comic books." I
eyed my father. I didn't know what he had up his sleeve. A
comic room? Where would we put it? I turned back to Maxine. "But even if that doesn't happen, I know my sister-in-law
who works the doll room might be looking for some time off
in the future."

"So concentrate on learning the doll room. Check."

Maxine was a quick study the rest of the morning. It only
took about ten minutes to figure out our confusing cash register. "It's not that much different from Craig's," she said, ring-
ing up a satisfied customer and sending her away with a smile.

During a lull, she asked where we kept our cleaning supplies, and when Cathy finally came in, apologizing for being
late but looking more than a little green about the gills, Maxine shadowed her in the doll room, peppering her with all
kinds of intelligent questions.

Dad quirked an eyebrow. "Who said 'Good help is hard
to find'?"

I shook my head. "I sure hope those numbers work. If we
can't afford to keep her, who is going to tell her? And where
are we going to get the money for all those comic books?
More pressing, where would we put them? A comic room?" I
looked around our packed storefront. We could probably put

a few display racks in the front, but that'd cut into our nostalgic candy and the open space we used for game tournaments.

"Trust me. I know what I'm doing," he said.

"Sorry, Dad, but the father-knows-best routine is wearing a little thin. I'm the one who pays the bills, and frankly, our creditors like it better when there's money in the accounts to cover all those checks."

"Have I ever let you down yet?" He smiled his most charming smile.

"Not exactly, but we've squeaked by pretty close a few times there."

"Yeah, well, squeaking only counts in . . . hinges. And mouse traps. And car brakes. Oh, and those slobbery little dog toys."

"Nice try. How about we add squeaking wheels and which one gets the oil—as in which creditor gets paid and which doesn't?"

He put his hands up in surrender. "I won't sign anything or make any firm verbal commitments until we have all the numbers and have gone over them together."

"Deal," I said.

"And in the meantime, you and I can try to learn a little more about Craig and who might have killed him and why."

"You don't think it was those mob guys?"

"I think they're connected in some way, but I don't see how the DA's going to press a murder charge. Yeah, so they had the scopolamine—if the toxicology proves that. But that's not what killed Craig. There's no evidence that was their intent, and no smoking gun to connect them to the suffocation."

"Someone sneaked into the hospital," I said.

"Or walked in, looking like they belonged," Dad said.

"Are there security cameras?" I asked.

"I'm sure the police already have them, as long as they didn't run out of space. The modern systems use DVRs, so they only keep so much information before it's dumped. But even if they're seen walking into the hospital, that's a far cry from placing them in the room before Craig died. And there's no case at all without a motive."

"They obviously wanted the comic books."

"Maybe, and that might've been the motive behind the whole scopolamine deal," Dad said. "But since that didn't kill him . . ."

"They must have had another reason to want him dead."

"Maybe. But until someone figures it out soon, I have a feeling that those two birds are going to fly."

"What about the forensic accountant you were telling me about. This Mark Baker guy. Might he find some connection?"

"Between Craig and the mob? You have to bet he's going to be looking."

I stared at Dad for a moment. "I hate you."

"What did I do?"

"Why is it all of a sudden my business? I feel like I should be out there doing something."

"That's my fault?"

"It has to be in the genes or something. Or in the water. From now on, I make the coffee."

"Or maybe it's in the Clean Queen."

"I was at that party, but I didn't inhale."

"So . . . who are we looking at? The two mob guys." Dad scratched his head. "You've called them Batman-man and Grandpa so often I can't even remember their names."

"Jenna Duncan isn't off my list. Craig's son or his mother."

"Anyone else?" he asked.

"I'd like to look more into Craig's new comic book venture, to see if anyone would profit from that."

"Or if he stepped on anyone's toes."

"Maybe I can just bring up the topic of Craig tonight at game night," I said, "and see what people have to say."

"Town meeting? I like it. What's on the calendar for tonight? With all that's been going on, I lost track."

"It's specialty card game night."

Dad winked. "So you might use that to find suspect number . . ."

"Uno." I grinned.

# # #

When four forty-five came around, Cathy said, "Because I came in late today, I'm going to compensate by leaving early."

"Writers group?" I asked.

"No, I'm finally going to have that certain talk with a certain someone. Wish me luck?"

I kissed her cheek. "You're not going to need it."

When she was out the door, Maxine looked after her. "I like your sister-in-law. I hope nothing's wrong that she has to take time off. She didn't look well this morning."

"Nothing to worry about. Hey, would you help me set up some tables for tonight?"

"What's tonight?"

"We host regular game nights here at the shop. Honestly, it's mostly because I'm a board-game junkie, but it drives a few customers in."

"What kinds of games?"

"It varies, but tonight is specialty card games, like Uno and Skip-Bo."

"Pit?"

"Sure, if enough people want to play. We also have some more obscure games. Like Bohnanza—which is all about trading different kinds of beans. And then there's Dutch Blitz. That's an Amish game. 'Vonderful Goot Game,' at least according to the package. I think I agree." Although it can be a bit fast-paced. We'd even had a few injuries.

"Sounds like a lot of fun. Can anyone come?"

"Of course. Off the clock, though. Sorry."

"Not a problem. I'll have to get home and check on my cat."

"We don't start until seven, anyway, so plenty of time."

"Well, then," Maxine said, reaching for her sweater, "I'll see you later!"

# # #

The first one to arrive at game night was Jack Wallace.

If he'd worn a hat, he would have been kneading it in his hands. "Hello, Liz."

"Jack, you're here early." I hadn't expected him to come at all.

He took a seat at an empty table. "Yeah. I was hoping we could talk."

Dad chose that moment to barge in from the back room whistling a song from an old musical. It took me a moment to realize it was "I'm Gonna Wash That Man Right Outta My

Hair" from *South Pacific*. So much for his pledge to stay out of my love life.

"Jack, how's it going?" he said. He had the effrontery to act surprised to see him. I suspect he'd run down the stairs after seeing Jack walk up.

Jack stood up to shake his hand. "Fine, sir. I wanted to thank you. For what you did for Terry. He told me you found him and convinced him to go to the station."

"Just a matter of knowing where to look. No sense in him getting into more trouble than he deserved."

"I appreciate it, and I wanted you to know that." He then directed his gaze at me. "And I need to apologize to Liz."

"Me?"

"You were right to not trust Terry. I should've never come down on you like that."

I shook my head. "Jack, he's your brother."

"And I'll always love him, but I also need to realize that I can't blindly stand up for him. Nor should I expect anyone else to. He needs to prove himself. He needs to regain trust, and that's going to take time, if he can manage it at all. It was unfair of me to treat you like I did."

"Enough," I said. "For what it's worth, I'm glad Terry didn't steal those comics. It wasn't something I wanted to believe."

"Liz, I just wanted you to know I was sorry. And . . ." He trailed off and looked at my father, who was still there in the room.

"I think I'll go make some coffee," Dad said.

"Thanks," Jack said. "Liz, I also wanted to make sure we could salvage our friendship."

"You know we'll always be friends."

He swallowed hard. "And if we could pick up where we left off?" If he'd looked any more sheepish, he'd be eating grass in the fields and sprouting a thick wool coat.

"I . . ." I started, but that was all I could get out.

The realization and disappointment poured over Jack's face. "That's okay. I understand," he said, his voice husky.

"Things changed."

"Ken?"

I nodded.

"He's a good man. A far better man. And not stupid enough to walk away." Jack picked up a deck of cards and rolled it on the table. "Look, I'm not up for fun and games tonight. Maybe I'd better get home."

I nodded again, not trusting my voice.

When the bell over the door signaled his departure, Dad reappeared. "You okay, kiddo?"

I looked up at Dad. He went blurry, and the next thing I knew I was blubbering all over his shirt.

"Let's get you upstairs before people start arriving, okay?"

Safe in my room, I had one last cry over Jack, thinking about all the years we'd had together, all the years we didn't. My mind rehashed every moment, from the first time he asked me out in high school, to the time he dumped me at the prom, to the recent renewal of our relationship, to the absent-minded daydreams I'd had throughout the years about what a future would be like with Jack. I loved him. I really did.

When Cathy had suggested that I needed to choose, she was right. I just didn't realize that the choice would tear me apart.

Chapter 18

"Are you feeling better, honey?" Maxine asked me when she arrived the next morning and shoved her sweater under the register.

When I'd unlocked the door, I'd ventured as far as the sidewalk. While the temperature was still unseasonably warm and the sky was clear and sunny, there was a little nip in the air. Maybe fall was just arriving fashionably late.

"What?" I asked.

"How are you feeling? Last night your father said you were under the weather. I was wondering if you caught what Cathy had."

"Oh, no, I'm fine," I said. "Did you enjoy game night?"

"It was a lot of fun," she said. "Folks just sitting around, talking, and playing games. I even rang up a few sales last night. Mostly little stuff. But I did find a buyer for that Illya Kuryakin action figure. An *NCIS* fan. Took him a minute to realize that it was the same actor who plays Ducky. Paid full price too. He was going to haggle, but I told him I was new and wasn't sure I was authorized to dicker."

"I hope you didn't feel you had to do that. Dad should have—"

"He was busy talking to the police chief and the mayor's wife. You really get the big guns in here. It's like the who's who of East Aurora. Playing games, of all things."

"They do say games are good for the mind. Einstein said that play was the highest form of research . . ." Then her words registered. "Dad was talking to the chief last night?" Probably settling the final details of my dowry. I hadn't seen him this morning. Sleeping in, I supposed. But since he'd closed up last night, I decided to let him have his late morning. "I wonder what they were talking about."

"Same thing everyone's been talking about for days. What happened to Craig. Is it true what they're saying? He was suffocated?"

"Preliminary findings," I said.

Just then Cathy pushed the door open. "Good morning, everybody."

"Someone's chipper today," I said. "Does that mean you . . ."

"Spilled the beans?" A smile erupted across her face, and I rushed to hug her.

"You were right," she said. "He was through the roof."

"Don't mind me. I'm new here," Maxine teased.

Cathy patted her hand. "I'd tell you, but I should tell Dad first. Is he upstairs?"

"Should be awake by now," I said. "Go on up."

"You can fill Maxine in. I'll be down in a minute."

As soon as Cathy was out of earshot, Maxine asked, "Pregnant?"

"It's not a secret she was likely to keep for long."

"She looks happy. That's a tough job, bringing a child into this world."

I suddenly remembered who I was talking with. Maxine was single, childless, and past an age where she would ever have children. I wasn't sure if that was something that had ever bothered her. She was also good at reading faces.

"Don't worry about me," she said. "Been there. Done that."

Her words sank in. "You have a child?"

"I did, but I was young and it was a mistake. In the end, I had to give him up."

"What happened?" But even as I asked, I could see the answer in the shape of her nose, the contours of her face, the slight cleft in an otherwise undefined chin.

I dropped the Magic 8 Ball I'd been cleaning, and it went careening across the floor. "Craig?"

Maxine's lips pinched together.

I went over to hug her. "No wonder you were so upset. He wasn't just your boss." I squeezed her tighter. "Did Craig know?"

"By the time I found him, he was just so angry. Back when I had to give him up, I'd hoped that maybe somebody good would adopt him, that he'd be off somewhere living the life of Riley in a nice house with brothers and sisters and maybe a puppy. That didn't turn out to be the case. I still planned on telling him, but I chickened out and decided to wait until after he'd gotten to know me a little better. Then there wasn't any chance."

I wasn't sure if she was into hugs, but she was about to get another one, whether she liked it or not. I rocked her two or three times when the thought hit me. "That means Craig's son . . ."

She sighed. "Is my grandson."

"Liz!" Cathy called from upstairs.

"That was quick," I said. "Is he excited?"

"He's not up there."

"What?" I ran past Maxine and up the steps leading to the apartment. The coffee and muffins I'd left for him were still sitting untouched. The door to his room, which had been shut this morning, was now wide open. Dad's bed was made. In fact, Othello was lying on it. He blinked at me but didn't move.

"This is how I found it." Cathy started. "Do you think . . . ?"

I went straight to the closet where he normally locked up his gun. The small safe was locked, but lighter than it should've been had the weapon and ammo been inside. Since his retirement, Dad had a history of going out and trying to pretend he was no longer retired.

"I thought he promised he wasn't going to do that anymore," Cathy said.

"He did. He wasn't going to sneak out anymore. He promised he'd tell me if he was going somewhere." That way, even if I couldn't talk him out of it, I could go with him. We'd joked about whether I was his sidekick or he was mine. But at least I'd know he was safe.

When I sat on Dad's bed to think, Othello climbed on my lap.

"What's this?" Cathy said.

Where Othello had been lying was a sheet of paper torn from an old steno notebook. It was crumpled and warm, with more than a few black and white hairs on it.

"'Couldn't sleep,'" I read aloud, "'so I went out to check on a lead.'"

Cathy started laughing. "You know, he actually did tell you where he was going. Sort of."

"What lead?"

I tucked the note into my pocket and went down to the shop.

"Maxine?" I called.

"Let me know if you need any help," Maxine told a customer before meeting me near the door to the back room.

"Sorry," I said. "I didn't know anyone had come in. Your first week, and we're already depending on you." I glanced over to where the customers were in full browse mode. It'd take them nearly an hour if they circled the whole store at that pace. "When my dad was talking to the chief last night, do you know what they were talking about?"

"About what happened to Craig, mostly, I think," she said. "Although I didn't hear all of it."

"Did they mention any . . . places?"

Maxine eyed me oddly.

"Dad likes to forget he's retired sometimes."

"Is he losing it? He seems so together."

"Nothing like that. He just tries to prove he can still do the job. And then he gets in over his head."

"So more like a midlife crisis kind of thing."

"Exactly," I said, but I'd never considered that possibility. "Did they talk about any places in particular that my dad might check out?"

Maxine scratched her nose with the back of her hand. "They mentioned the hospital. But the chief said he'd already gotten the security camera footage."

"That was quick," I said.

"They talked about some publishing house."

"Do you remember the name?"

"Something about Buffalo Chips. I couldn't tell if it was food or if it was like cow chips." Maxine wrinkled her nose.

"Oh, that's a local self-publisher!" Cathy said. "They charge way too much for chapbooks, though. And you have to buy like a bazillion copies. One woman in my poetry group checked."

I glanced at the clock. They'd be open now, but I wasn't sure my dad would sneak off there first thing.

"I'll look up the address for you," Cathy said.

"Thanks," I said.

"Are you sure your father's the only one who has trouble sneaking off and playing detective?" Maxine asked.

I ignored the question. It was easier than coming to terms with the answer. "Anywhere else?"

"They mentioned the comic book shop, but I don't think anyone would be there right now. The new owner was talking about coming back during the weekend when her son wasn't in school."

"That will be easy enough to check."

Cathy handed me the address of the publisher. "Shouldn't you call Ken and tell him what you're up to?"

"Let me see what I find out first," I said. I picked up the Magic 8 Ball I'd dropped earlier, shook it, and flipped it over.

"Outlook not so good," it said. Good thing I'm a skeptic.

# # #

I took a slow walk past the comic book store first. The door was locked, and I peeked in through the window. They'd made a little progress cleaning up. The comics were all off the floor and put into boxes and bins, at least. Since the store wasn't very deep, I could see all the way to the back wall. Those photographs of Craig and all those kids had been taken down.

It didn't make sense to drive to the hospital if the police already had the camera footage. But if the police already had the camera footage . . .

I took off at a brisk walk toward the police station. Even as I opened the door, I could hear Dad's jovial tones as he joked around with the guys. When one of them walked out with a half-eaten peanut stick, I knew exactly where my father had been this whole time.

"Hey, Liz!" Dad waved me back. By now the clerk knew me well enough to buzz me in as soon as my hand hit the doorknob.

"I see you got my note," he said.

"Following a lead? That could have meant you were anywhere."

"And go off investigating by myself without letting Ken know?" he said, wearing his most cherubic expression. "Since I couldn't sleep, I picked up some doughnuts for the guys and came down here to see how it was going with the footage from the hospital."

"And?"

Dad poked Ken in the arm. "Told you she'd be interested."

"Of course I'm interested," I said. "I almost walked in on the murder."

Dad's expression sobered.

Ken gestured toward the back of the station. "How about we take this discussion to my office?"

Ken's office now had several large boxes bearing the Clean Queen label stacked up against one wall.

"Shouldn't that be in evidence?" I asked.

Ken rolled his eyes. "I haven't got a clue what to do with it. I can't return it. It's contraband. I can't dump it in the creek. It's like fifty proof—all the fish would end up pickled. And I can't put it into evidence unless I want to call it a crime. Hank, do you think I have a career in this town if I arrest the mayor's wife on an old moonshining charge?"

Dad started laughing. "I'd pay good money to see you try."

Ken perched on the side of his desk and shook his head. "It'll still be sitting here fifty years from now—"

"Well-aged," Dad added.

Ken didn't answer but tried to massage the tension from his neck.

"I have a suggestion," I said. I took a quick accounting of the boxes. "And it'd probably only take you a couple of years to dispose of all of it."

Ken looked up.

"It *is* a decent cleaner," I said. "Nontoxic. Well, mostly. Organic."

Dad sent me an admiring look. "Also saves money on the cleaning budget," he offered.

"I couldn't," he said. "Could I?"

"Lock it up in the cleaning closet," Dad said. "See what happens. Better than keeping several cases of hooch in your office for the next few years."

"I'll do that." Ken grabbed a box.

Dad stood in his way. "Maybe when there are fewer people around to see it, though."

"Good idea." I watched Ken thank my father. Apparently they'd already forgotten whose idea it was.

"So what did you find?" I asked.

"Huh?" Ken said.

"On the surveillance camera," Dad said. "Not a thing."

"We looked for all our persons of interest, and we didn't see any of them going into that hospital. It's hard to cover all the entrances perfectly, though. The camera is pretty low resolution, and there are times when someone could have slipped in with the crowd that was coming and going. Lots of traffic in and out."

"Dead end," I said.

"We can still send it out and have someone run some of that new facial recognition software on it. They might come up with something that none of my men saw."

"But now that you're here, how about you come with me and track down another loose end?" Dad said.

"What's that?"

"The publishing house that was going to publish Craig's comic series. I thought maybe you and I could do a little harmless undercover work."

"They've not been cooperating," Ken said. "Not that they have to. We have nothing to connect them to anything criminal. We just asked if they'd answer a few questions, and they clammed up tight."

"Sounds suspicious," I said.

"What do you say, kiddo?" Dad asked. "Think you could play the part of an aspiring writer desperate to share her words with the world?"

"Why, I've wanted to be a writer ever since I picked up a pencil." I batted my eyelashes at him.

"Honey, I was there the first time you picked up a pencil. You stuck it up your brother's nose. Your mother was so mad, I had to smuggle you dinner."

"Everyone's a critic."

Chapter 19

Dad and I checked in at the shop, ready to apologize for being AWOL, but Cathy and Maxine seemed to be managing just fine without us. Better than fine. The shop was cleaner than normal. I changed into my glasses because I thought they might make me look just a little bit more literary, and I borrowed Cathy's notebook with her most recent poems.

"Don't you want the novel?" she asked.

I thought for a moment. She'd read portions to me during quiet mornings in the shop. I'd started having misgivings when I—or rather a character inspired by me—had heard a noise and went to investigate while wearing a sheer harem costume, complete with castanets. It did *not* get better from there. No way I was taking that. The way things were going lately, they'd end up publishing the thing.

"No, the poems are great," I said. "Just in case they want to see a sample."

"Well, if they do, you'll tell me what they say, right? It's really hard to get honest feedback."

I promised, and soon Dad and I were off to the offices of Buffalo Chips Press.

"So what exactly are we going to ask them?" I asked.

"Let's not go in there with a script," Dad said. "It's too easy to get caught that way. Always sounds phony. We play it by ear. Not too many questions, and let the natural conversation drive the interview."

"Got it."

Dad opened the door to Buffalo Chips Press, and we walked into what looked like an old newspaper office. Older than the *Superman* movies. Older than *Kolchak: The Nightstalker*, even. We were in *His Girl Friday* territory, complete with the odor of old printer's ink. Now if only Cary Grant would saunter through the door from the back room and step up to the counter. But with my luck, Lou Grant would be more likely.

Imagine my surprise when it turned out to be Lexi Wolf. Minus the whip, the swagger, the fishnet stockings, and the curls. In their place was a short, messy bob.

And khakis. Lexi Wolf—or rather Tippi Hillman—wore khakis. She sure looked a lot different from her action figure. Even different from the time she went undercover as a school teacher to penetrate the defenses of the Kohara faction. I'd underestimated Craig when I'd assumed he'd hired an imposter.

It took great effort not to squeal and go all fangirl.

"May I help you?" she asked. Also sans that awesome Aussie accent.

Dad spoke first. I'm not sure he recognized Tippi without her costume, even though he'd suffered through more than one episode, always complaining of plot holes.

"Yes," Dad said. "My daughter is a poet, you see."

I held up the notebook but was too starstruck to answer.

"And she heard in one of her writing groups that you publish poems. Since she has a birthday coming up, I thought it'd be nice to surprise her." He put his arm around me. "You can tell she's a little nervous."

"Aren't you sweet."

Lexi Wolf called me sweet!

"Why don't we step over here, and I'll tell you the kind of things we publish here. Let's see what we can do to make those dreams come true."

We followed her over to a pitted conference table where we sat while she pulled several paperbacks from a nearby bookshelf. My pulse quickened when I realized that one of them was her autobiography, *Hungry Like the Wolf*, about being a normal-sized woman pressured to lose weight during filming.

She started reviewing various options—matte versus glossy covers, different kinds of paper, various trim sizes for the books—when she stopped cold. She slammed the book down and stared straight at me.

"Yes, I am Lexi Wolf. You can stop drooling now." She slouched in her chair. "Do you even write poetry?"

"I . . . have a notebook."

Dad burst out laughing. "You got us. She has a few poems in the notebook, but we borrowed them from a friend. We saw you at the train and toy show, and my daughter is such a big fan. We just wanted to talk."

"When I was in college I wanted to be you," I said.

"Well, being Lexi Wolf wasn't as glamorous as it appeared, but it was probably more fun than calculus." She pulled out a business card. "Here. Tuck that in the notebook in case your friend the poet is interested. What would you like to know?"

All of a sudden, my vocal cords loosened, and I peppered her with questions about shooting locations, props, and costumes, while carefully avoiding the supposed plot holes that critics liked to point out. I think we were both pretty at ease when Dad started asking questions.

"So what brought you to Western New York? And to the train and toy show in particular?"

"Well, it wasn't the weather, although I do like to ski so I'm okay with a little snow. But it's the tale as old as time. There was a really nice guy. He was from Buffalo and wanted to move back, so I ended up here. Did a little local theater. Shakespeare in Delaware Park, in one of their all-female productions. That was a lot of fun, but it wasn't a career anymore. I've always been a reader, even majored in English in college before I landed the part of Lexi. This seemed like a good fit."

"The guy from Buffalo. It wasn't Craig McFadden, was it?" Dad asked.

She rolled her eyes. "I've made some mistakes in my life, but he wasn't one of them. No, Steve and I are still together and very happy. And since I agreed to move to Buffalo with him, he financed this thriving venture." She gestured around the dilapidated office. "My cleaning staff is on vacation."

"You knew Craig, though," I said.

She nodded. "He came to me with an idea for a comic book series. I told him I'd never done comics before. Mostly this place was just inserts for local newspapers—sale ads, that kind of thing—before I added trade paperbacks. I told him I'd have to hire people to do the layouts. He didn't seem fazed, so I quoted him a super high price, kind of hoping he'd just go away. He recognized me right off the bat. I think he just wanted to thank Lexi Wolf in the acknowledgments. Next thing I know, he's forking over the deposit. Said the rest of the money would be in soon."

"What happens to that series now?" I asked.

She folded her hands in front of her and studied my face. "Why are you asking?"

I looked to Dad, who did a good job of not appearing flustered.

"We heard about the series, and it sounded interesting. Just wondering if it was still going forward. Might even make for a good investment."

"You want to *invest* in Mr. Inferno?"

"Why not?" Dad said. "You must think it has potential, if you were willing to publish it."

"I was willing to print it," Tippi said. "There's a difference."

"So with Craig dead, does the project go forward?" I asked. "The circumstances created a bit of a sensation, and I'm sure that kind of thing could be spun into decent publicity."

"That depends," she said. "Craig signed over a bunch of rights in the initial contract."

"Is that typical?" I asked.

"No, but in Craig's case, I insisted on it. Adding comics required new equipment and personnel. It protects our investment. We put time and energy and money into it. And I know how easy it is for writers to get cold feet. Or run to another publisher and leave us holding the bag. Legally, we can go forward. Just not sure it makes sense yet."

"What would tip the scales?" Dad asked.

"I sent a digital galley over to a freelance comic book editor, and he said it has potential. But that doesn't mean it will find an audience and magically catch on. I popped a preliminary cover image up on Amazon to see if it generates many presales. We'll see."

"If it does take off, and with Craig gone, who'd get the royalties?" Dad asked.

"Not sure I want to answer that," she said. "Let's just say I have a very good intellectual property attorney."

"And Craig didn't," I said.

She shrugged. "He signed the contract. Now, do you want to keep grilling me, or can I get back to work?"

"One more question," I said. "Can I get a signed copy of *Hungry Like the Wolf*?"

# # #

I scored more than a free book. Heading south out of the city, we happened across a Lloyd Taco Truck. I didn't have to twist Dad's arm to convince him to stop for an early lunch, especially since Jack's place would likely be off limits for some time. At least until I got up the nerve to see him again without bursting into tears.

But as we were leaning against my Civic eating our tacos—I got the pulled pork while Dad opted for braised beef—I realized that he'd left the toyshop before Cathy had a chance to tell him the good news. The circle of people who knew about the newest McCall in town was growing, yet Dad hadn't yet learned he was going to be a grandpa. I needed to get him there quick so he could hear it from Parker or Cathy and not through the grapevine.

"What's next, kiddo?" Dad asked.

"Back to the shop. We owe it to Cathy and Maxine to at least put in an appearance."

He looked reluctant, but when we headed down Main Street, he rubbernecked the comic book store where a woman and a teenage boy were standing in front shoving a key in the lock.

"I thought they weren't coming back until the weekend," I said. "That's when Maxine said she was going to help with inventory."

Dad smiled at me. "How about we introduce ourselves to the new neighbors?"

A parking spot magically opened up right in front of the store, but even while I centered my car between the lines, I prepared Dad for news. "There's something you need to know before we go in there." I told him what I had learned about Maxine being Craig's mother—and the teen's grandmother. "Although he doesn't know it."

"That's why Maxine was so upset over Craig's death," he said. "Such a shame she never got to tell Craig before he died. Especially after spending all those months getting to know him."

"I doubt the kid is carrying the same kind of emotional baggage Craig did. So there's still hope she'll be able to build some bridges with her grandson."

Dad took my hand. "Family. We take it for granted."

This touching Hallmark moment delayed us just long enough that by the time we arrived at the front door, the woman and her son had gone inside and locked it behind them. Dad knocked, and we stood smiling on the doorstep while the mother inspected us through the glass.

"If this is how the Jehovah's Witnesses feel every time they knock on a door, remind me to be kinder next time," Dad said out of the corner of his mouth.

We must have passed muster, because the woman opened the door. "Can I help you?"

"Hi," Dad said, turning on his charm. He introduced both of us and managed to shoehorn in that he was the former chief of police. To gain her trust? Must have worked. She invited us in.

The air in the shop was stagnant, probably the time spent baking in the sun with the awning rolled up and the AC not running. It was dim, since the overhead lights were off. There's something a little spooky about a commercial building with the lights off.

"Amanda Cooper," she said by way of introduction. "And my son, Kohl."

"Hi, Kohl," I said.

Kohl looked up when his name was mentioned, but he didn't say anything and never quite made eye contact. Instead, he flipped the page of his comic book, ran his hand along the paper, and went back to reading, his head bobbing ever so slightly in a comforting rock.

"Sorry," Amanda whispered. "He's a little uncomfortable in new situations and around new people." I didn't need that explanation to guess that Kohl was somewhere on the autism spectrum. When he did finally look in my direction, I smiled at him. He quickly broke eye contact again, but I noticed that when he looked down at his comic book, he was smiling too.

Maxine apparently hadn't picked up on the child's challenges yet, since she'd only said that the boy was quiet. I doubted it would make much difference once she learned, though. Grandmas are like that.

"We wanted to welcome you to East Aurora," Dad said. "And offer our condolences. We knew Craig for a long time, but honestly, not that well."

Amanda sent up a pained look and then tipped her head toward the corner of the store. "I'd rather not have Kohl overhear too much about his father. It's kind of a sensitive subject."

We followed her to the corner, and I glanced up at the spot where the photographs of Craig with his sponsored sports teams had been.

"Yes, I took them all down," she said, catching my gaze. "Kohl just stared at them. Looked at all the faces. All the strange boys, but not one picture of his own son."

"We didn't mean to bring up a painful subject," I said.

She shook her head. "No avoiding it. It's going to come up. I'm just trying to keep it from coming up in front of Kohl. I'm not sure what part he understands. Most of it, I expect. He knew he had a father who never came to see him. But those pictures were hard to take."

"Was Craig into sports when you knew him?" I asked.

She set her jaw. A tear formed in the corner of her eye. "Not my proudest moment. I didn't know much at all about Craig. If I had, maybe things would've been different. All I knew was that my mother hated him, and that was all I needed."

"You must have been very young," I said.

"Old enough to know better. And old enough to pay the piper." She closed her eyes. "And no, my mother didn't really hate him. She could just see where it was all leading. And I was right at that place where if she'd told me to eat ice cream, I would have had a nice bowl of broccoli instead. Craig didn't have good things to say about parents. I guess it fueled my rebellion even more."

"How did you meet?"

"Detention," she said. "My first one. Late book report. I thought it was like that old movie, *The Breakfast Club*. Everyone loves a bad boy, right? We only went out a couple times. I wouldn't call it love at first sight, and I'm not exactly easy, but I was tired of being called a goody-two-shoes and a virgin. I got rid of those nicknames fast."

"So you were never married," Dad said.

"No," Amanda said. "Not even sure I could even call him my boyfriend. It was over that quick. He'd been sent back to some juvie facility when I found out I was pregnant. I just wanted to leave him out of it, but Mom tracked him down. She got a lawyer. Made him take a paternity test. He didn't send much child support at first, but it had been going up recently."

"It must have been hard for you," I said.

"Certainly changed my plans. Instead of staying up late studying for exams, I was up walking a cranky baby. Those first few weeks were tough, but then his stomach straightened out and we were doing good. He was such a sweet boy. I got my GED at night when Mom was available to watch Kohl. Poor little guy would try to stay up until I got home. He'd run out to meet me, jabbering a mile a minute." She bit her lip. "And then he started talking less. You can probably figure out the rest."

I must have looked sad.

"Oh, but it's good. Not the life I might've picked, but Kohl is doing well. We got him into a special program early enough that it really made a difference. He's doing a pretty good job managing his challenges and frustrations. Now, of course, he's a bit stressed out. But when he's feeling secure and comfortable, he's pretty much that sunshiny boy that I remember. Not many moms of teenagers can say that. Now, some people have a hard time telling."

I nodded. "I think you met Maxine the other day. She's been putting in some hours in our toyshop. She'd just mentioned that he seemed well-mannered and quiet."

Amanda smiled, then winced. "Now I feel bad about fibbing to her."

Dad pulled a bin of comic books closer and started to thumb through them. "She was under the impression that you weren't going to be working here until the weekend."

"I wasn't sure about having her around Kohl," she said.

"Maxine seems like such a nice person," I said.

"I'm sure she is very nice. She volunteered to come in and help, even though I told her I wasn't sure I'd be able to pay her. But Kohl was upset about his father, and Maxine had worked with him. I'm sure the subject would've come up, and I was just thinking it'd be awkward for all of us. Do you think it'll offend her if I don't take her up on her offer?"

I looked to Dad. I wasn't quite sure what to say. I could understand why she'd want to insulate her son from more pain, but she was unwittingly keeping him away from a grandparent.

"I think Maxine would understand," Dad said, "but the job would be a lot easier on you with her here. Comic books definitely have a learning curve, and she already has a good working knowledge of what you have in the shop. You'd probably be cutting off your nose . . ."

"To spite my face?" she said. "Apparently that's my MO."

"Would you like us to talk to her, maybe fill her in on the . . . special challenges of the situation?" I asked.

"I guess that was a snap decision on my part. I could use her expertise. See how it works out. But I meant what I said that I wasn't sure I could pay her, at least not right away. I know Kohl should get something, but that'll be down the road. Until that happens, we're stretched kind of thin."

"Have you decided what you're going to do with all the stock when you're done with the inventory?" Dad asked.

"That I'm still trying to figure out. I just want to sell it, but Kohl has it in his head that he wants to work in the store and sell comic books. I'd like to get someone to go over the accounts and see if that's a financial possibility, especially since Kohl is the actual beneficiary of all Craig's assets."

"It was good of him to remember his son," I said.

She shrugged. "Who else was he going to leave his stuff to? Right now, though, I have no idea if he was even in the black or what any of this is worth. But I guess the shop computer was stolen, and the police have the backup files."

"They should be able to copy those for you," Dad said, pulling out his notebook. "I'll ask them. I'm retired, but I help out from time to time."

I snorted. Couldn't help myself.

"That'd be wonderful," she said.

"If you decide to stay, East Aurora is a good place to live and do business," Dad said. "And for what it's worth, Craig seemed to be making a go of it. I can introduce you around to the chamber of commerce folks. There's a meeting tonight if you're interested."

Amanda glanced at her son. "I couldn't. Not tonight."

"I understand," Dad said. "You probably need time to make up your mind. But if you decide you want to sell, I wouldn't mind putting in an offer on the stock." He pulled out one of his business cards and handed it to her. "No pressure, though. It's up to you."

"Thanks. I'll keep that in mind," she said, tucking the card into her pocket.

When we climbed into the car, I turned on the ignition. "How do you think Maxine is going to take the news that her grandson has autism?"

"I'd think she'd be delighted that she has a grandson. I hope she gets up the nerve to tell Amanda. That could work out very well for all of them." But Dad didn't look all that happy.

"What's the matter?" I asked. "Bummed out about possibly losing that comic room that we have no space for anyway?"

"Perhaps that's it," he said.

"Let's get back to the shop." I expected his mood would change pretty quickly. After all, Maxine wasn't going to be the only one to learn she was a grandparent.

Chapter 20

"Where's Cathy?" I asked Maxine as Dad and I finally got back to the shop from our little errand.

"She had to go home," Maxine said. "She said to check your phone."

I glanced over at Dad, who was leaning a little bit heavier on his cane.

"I think I'm going to rest my knee before the chamber meeting tonight," he said.

"Yeah," I teased, "you want to look your best when you mingle with all those single female business owners."

"Oh, so *you're* East Aurora's most eligible bachelor?" Maxine asked. "I think I'm going to like it here."

Dad rolled his eyes. "Hardly. Marriage may only be a word, but to me it's a sentence. With no hope of time off for good behavior."

"Don't let him fool you," I said to Maxine. "He's quite the chick magnet. I have a whole file cabinet of stepmother applications."

"Yeah, the good, the bad, and the pathological," he said, then stopped to tap the frayed box of a 1950s Visible Man figure, in all its anatomical glory. "Hey, did you hear that the Invisible Man finally settled down and married the Invisible Woman?"

I pinched my eyes shut. I'd heard this one before.

"Their kids were nothing to look at either."

Maxine laughed but rubbed her head as if she were in physical pain.

"I'm going upstairs," Dad said. "I'll give Ken a call and see if I can't get the financial records for Amanda."

"Amanda?" Maxine said.

"Yeah, let me fill you in." While Dad was almost to the back room, I added in my best stage voice, "And let me get you that application."

Dad let out a groan and Maxine blushed ever so slightly.

"Sorry," I said. "Lots of teasing goes on around here. And be prepared for a barrage of puns at times. I think my dad uses them to defuse tense situations."

"I like that better than off-color humor. Sometimes there were a few things I wish Craig'd left unsaid."

"Was he inappropriate?"

"Oh, no. Not like that. Then again, I'm not sure frumpy middle-aged women were his type."

"What was his type?" I asked.

She shrugged. "I thought I knew. But then I met Amanda. She actually seems nice."

"We just met her, too."

"What's up with that? I didn't think they were going to be back until later in the week."

"I guess plans change. But she did say that she'd appreciate your help, so if you wanted to work there tomorrow, I'm sure it'd be all right."

"Oh, okay." She licked her lip. "Not that I won't be back here."

"And we'll be looking forward to having you. Only . . . one thing you should probably know about Kohl." I explained about her grandson's autism and Amanda's desire to shield him from talk of his father.

"Is he going to be all right?" she asked.

"From what I gather, they intervened pretty early on. But you can probably ask Amanda for advice on how to get to know him without making him uncomfortable. Assuming you do still want to get to know him."

She thought for a moment. "But do they want to get to know me? I think I should play it by ear."

"You mean, not tell them?"

"Cowardly, huh?"

"Family is tough, and this is uncharted territory. I certainly won't tell them. That will be up to you. For what it's worth, I think they'd want to know."

"Something to think about, anyway. Say, do you need me at the shop tonight if you and your dad are going to this big chamber of commerce do?"

"No, Miles should be coming in to work. It'll be slow, and he does our web orders at the same time."

"Have I met him yet?"

"You may have. He was working our booth at the toy show."

"Young kid?"

"He's in college. Pretty tech savvy. Handy to have around."

"You got a nice little business here. At the comic shop, it's just me and Craig . . ."

She punctuated the sentence with a sigh.

# # #

The "big chamber of commerce do," as Maxine had put it, was a special meeting to finalize plans for reviving the Toy Town parade. Without the big corporate sponsorship, the parade had been suspended a number of years earlier, but public sentiment and a desire to bring more tourism—perhaps overruling common sense—had led to a move to restore it, but in a slightly different form: as a kick-off to Small Business Saturday, the weekend after Thanksgiving.

"You don't think it's too early in the day?" someone asked.

"If we run the parade from ten to eleven, we're hoping that people will spill into the shops afterward," Glenda said. Glenda ran the local yarn shop and had just shown me a picture of her "float," a wooly lamb resembling a pull toy, made with yarn from her shop. The ladies who came to her various crochet and knitting classes had worked on it.

I wished I had a picture of our entry to show her. Parker had volunteered to make a float for Well Played and pull it with his riding mower. Apparently it was almost done and locked in his garage, but he'd let no one, not even Cathy, see it. Dad used to call him the mad scientist of the family, saying that most of his creations were brilliant, but that every now and then he'd come home to find a monster wandering around the yard and he'd have to grab his gun and shoot it before it started terrorizing the town, so I was right to be nervous.

"Besides," Glenda continued, "we've already advertised the starting time and someone even put it on the Twitter, so that's a moot point. Can we just get on to the business at hand?"

"Which is?" Dad asked. It'd been so long since we'd been on topic that I'd forgotten too.

"The train problem," she said.

"I still don't understand what the issue is," Dad said. "The folks at the train show were very kind to offer a locomotive engine for the parade. It's been fitted with a motor. It spouts smoke and makes a chugging sound, and the train wheels move, even though it actually rolls on golf cart wheels that nobody can see. They did a fantastic job. It's really spiffy."

Glenda pressed her palms together. "But is it a toy?"

"It's a model train," Dad said. "Only bigger."

"But a model train that's bigger is basically a train," she said. "So we have all these cute toys coming down Main Street, and then a train."

"Lots of kids like trains," Dad argued.

"But does it fit the theme?" Glenda said. "If it was Thomas the Train or something like that . . ."

"But it's not," I said. "It's a good reproduction of a model train, only larger." Which only proved her point.

For the next ten minutes, various members debated whether or not to cut it from the parade. Some argued they needed to keep the continuity of the theme. Others reminded them that the train show had just officially joined the chamber, signaling their commitment to remain in East Aurora, even though they hadn't sent a representative to the meeting. Would it be wise or ethical to deny their entry?

"So we're at an impasse," Glenda said, followed by groans. It was going to be another long one.

I considered making a motion to adjourn. I'd read somewhere recently that in *Robert's Rules of Order*, a motion to adjourn takes precedence and has to be dealt with, and I was dying to give it a try. I had a feeling I'd get a quick second and win the vote in a landslide, but that wouldn't solve the most immediate problem. Then another idea struck.

"Put Santa on the train at the end," I said, "like the Macy's parade."

Dad sat up straight. "Maybe some kids too, as if it's the Polar Express? Throw some candy to the crowd?"

The groans and grumbles turned into whispers and chatter.

"I . . . love it," Glenda said. She pointed to my dad and me. "Now get us a Santa." She looked at her watch. "And since it's late, I'd like a motion to adjourn."

# # #

It was quite nippy when Dad and I walked home, and our breath immediately condensed into puffy clouds in front of us. The moon was near full in the sky, and the streetlights, partially strewn with their Christmas decorations, illuminated the sidewalks almost as if it were daytime, even though all the shops, except for a few restaurants, were closed.

We were silent as we walked past Wallace's. The door opened and I glanced up, but it was only a couple of patrons. The two young women laughed and staggered a little as they descended the steps, and Dad watched them for a few moments. I'm not a mind reader, but I knew he'd continue to watch them until he was sure they weren't driving somewhere.

I sat and waited at one of the patio tables and pulled my sweater closer. Since the fall had been warmer, it had greatly extended the alfresco season, although that, too, would be over very shortly.

The restaurant door opened again, and I could hear the conversation and smell the food. "Can I help you?" Jack's longtime hostess called out, in a voice that suggested what she'd really meant to ask was, "Why is this idiot sitting out in the cold?"

"Just waiting on my dad," I said.

And when the door closed again, my heart sank in my chest.

"It's okay," Dad said. "They turned down a side street a couple of blocks down. I think they're walking."

I nodded but didn't get up.

"Jack?" Dad pulled out a chair and sat across from me. "He's probably right inside."

"That only makes it worse."

"You knew you couldn't just go on seeing two men for the rest of your life. Something had to change. And you like Ken, right?"

I nodded again, dangerously close to becoming a human bobblehead.

"Did I . . . uh . . ." He paused for a moment and rubbed his bristly chin. "Did I pressure you too much?"

"Maybe I needed a push."

"But not in the direction I was pushing."

I propped my elbows on the table and let out a long, billowy breath. "I don't know. Sometimes I feel like I made the right decision, and sometimes . . . I just miss Jack."

"Can you go back? To the way things were?"

"And see two different men for the rest of my life?" I shook my head. "Wouldn't be fair to Ken. I don't want to hurt him."

"So you do like him."

"Very much."

We sat there for another minute or so until I shivered.

"Tell you what, kiddo, let's get you home. I'll make some popcorn and hot chocolate. You can even put on *The Notebook*."

Chapter 21

Cathy came up to the apartment bright and early the next morning just as I was finishing my second cup of coffee. Since I already knew her "secret" and because I doubted I could feign surprise well enough to fool my father, I excused myself to head down to the shop.

"Liz, before you go," she said, "Thanksgiving at our house this year again?"

"Sure!" I said with more enthusiasm than I felt. "But this time, you're going to have to let me share in the cooking. Not fair for you to be saddled with all the work."

I'd been practicing that line ever since last November. I loved the time we spent together with the family and the games we played afterward. The food, however . . . Don't get me wrong: I love my sister-in-law fiercely, but Julia Child she is not.

"I was thinking," Cathy said, "maybe we ought to invite Maxine over. I don't think she has any family."

"Good idea," Dad said, followed by a quick intake of breath. "I hate to add to your work, but what would you think about also inviting Amanda and Kohl?" He went on to explain the relationship to Maxine.

"But they don't know yet," I said. "That could end up being tricky if she doesn't tell them. Or even if she does and they don't take it well."

"Just a thought," Dad said.

"It's a good one," Cathy said. "Thanksgiving is still a week away. We can give it a few days. Maybe see how they do before we decide. I'll make sure I get a big enough turkey just in case."

"Why don't you let me do that?" I said. "We have plenty of room in our refrigerator. I can even mix up Mom's old stuffing recipe that Parker likes and start cooking it here, so you don't have to mess with food so early in the morning." Appealing to her morning sickness. I'd never sunk lower. Besides, this way I could ensure that it was real turkey we'd be eating. Cathy had been known to make "creative substitutions."

"Great, Liz. Sounds like a plan," my dad said before Cathy could respond. She'd been tag-teamed. Before she could catch on to what happened, I hightailed it downstairs.

# # #

Cathy's announcement buoyed Dad's spirits, and he was in a good mood the rest of the morning. Well, most of the morning. On the fourth or fifth attempt to hire a Santa for the parade, he slammed the shop phone down and it eyed him reproachfully. "Santa's not picking up, and he's not returning my calls."

"Are you sure you got the right phone number?" When Dad and I had discussed where to hire a Santa, he'd called

Frank from the train show who'd referred us to his Santa service. "Or maybe he's working somewhere else today. Unless . . . could you be on the naughty list again?"

"I want to try the address," Dad said. "It's not far. Want to go?"

"That depends. Do you think I'll get to pet the reindeer? Should I bring carrots?"

"Seriously," Dad said, "what kind of Santa turns down business?"

"Why all the fuss? You could always play Santa. I thought you'd be champing at the bit to ride the big train."

"Yeah, but this guy was really good. And now I'm worried about him . . . and more than a little curious. I just want to swing by the place and make sure the old guy's okay."

"You want to see Santa out of costume."

"Well, there's that," he said. "I mean, I guess I understand there's such a thing as method acting, but that Santa never stepped out of character. Never took off the beard. Not once."

"Maybe it's *Miracle on 34th Street* all over again. Maybe they hired the real Santa, and he's not returning your calls because he had to rush back to the North Pole and check on toy production."

"I hope not. As you recall, that movie started out with the Santa they hired for the parade showing up plastered."

"It just freaks you out that you never saw his face."

"Or any real part of him. And no, I don't like it. I watch people. It's what I've always done. All I know is he's around five seven and has a small mole next to his right eye. And considering what's happened at this train show, I'd like to put a real face on this guy."

"Fine, let's go."

"Really?"

"You were patient with me. You actually got through twenty-seven minutes of *The Notebook* before you dozed off. New record. I can at least humor you. And we do need to hire a Santa."

"You're curious, too."

"Chip off the old block."

# # #

Leaving Cathy running the shop on a relatively quiet weekday, Dad and I headed out again, this time to a small stretch of no-frills patio homes squeezed in on an already established street. A cheery fall wreath, decorated in orange and red flowers, hung on the door overlooking a neatly swept patio, the only thing making it different from any of the other six connected houses. "A. Werth" was hand-painted on the mailbox.

Dad knocked. All my earlier teasing aside, my stomach now twisted in anticipation of what we might find. How many doors had he knocked on when he worked for the police? How many welfare checks ended up with him finding an elderly person unresponsive, locked inside his own home? I could always tell when he'd arrived too late. He'd sit quietly at the dinner table and pretend to listen to the conversation. He'd even force himself to take a few bites of his food. But we all knew he wasn't really there.

When nobody answered the door, Dad leaned back, almost imperceptibly, to try to look into the front window. I hoped he wouldn't find Santa lying with a broken hip or worse: dead from a heart attack from just a few too many Christmas cookies.

The neighbor's door opened and a woman with curly white hair stuck her head out. "I don't think she can hear you. She's out back."

"Thank you," Dad called out, and started walking down the sidewalk that led behind these units. Only one woman was out back, pulling dead plants out of a raised bed.

"Mrs. Werth?" Dad said.

When she heard his voice, I could see her back noticeably stiffen, but she spun around a moment later with a friendly smile and looked us over. "Do I know you?" She pulled off her gardening gloves.

"I might be looking for your husband," Dad said. "A. Werth? I think he played Santa over at the train and toy show."

By this time, the woman who'd met us out front was shamelessly peering out her window.

"There must be some mistake," the woman said. "I have no husband. I'm Annie Werth." She smiled at Dad, then me, then Dad again, in that same over-the-top smile actresses use in commercials when trying to convince consumers how much fun it'd be to buy their products to scrub their floors or degrease their ovens.

"That's odd," Dad said. "He gave this address."

Annie shrugged, just a little too innocently. And then I saw it. A mole next to her right eye.

"*You're* A. Werth," I said.

"I just said as much," Annie said, although she couldn't hide the growing concern.

"You mean . . ." Dad said, doing a double-take as he squinted at her face. His eyes opened wider when he saw the mole.

Annie threw her gloves down and glanced at the neighbor's window. "Perhaps we ought to talk about this inside."

# # #

Just inside the patio door was a small dinette table, warmed by the afternoon sun, and we sat down.

"Yes," she said. "I am Santa Claus."

"Have you been doing this for long?" Dad said.

She threw her head back. "No, it's not a job I've been doing for a while." She looked up. "I think you know that. One-time wonder. The woman who runs the Santa service owed me a favor, so she let me do it."

"Why the train show?" I asked.

She sat silently for a moment. "I'm not in trouble, am I? Are you police?"

I said no at the same time Dad said yes.

"Retired," he added. "But I do help out."

"Is that what you're doing here now?" she asked, her brow furrowing.

"Actually," I said, "we're here to hire a Santa Claus for the parade. You did an amazing job."

"So those were your calls on the machine," she said, leaning her elbows on the table. "I am such an idiot."

"Why were you so desperate to work the train show?" I asked.

"I have my reasons," she said.

"Did it have anything to do with Craig McFadden?" Dad asked.

"The guy who fell?" Annie snorted. "I may have met him at the shows, but I'm not sure. Comics were never my thing. Although, I have to admit his aim was pretty good." Her smile faded. "Sorry he died though."

"His aim?" Dad said, then whipped his head in my direction.

"Frank?" we both asked in stereo.

"Conductor Frank *W.*," Dad said.

"The *W* stands for Werth, doesn't it?" I added.

Her tight-lipped scowl announced that we'd nailed it. "My ex."

Chapter 22

Annie Werth was apparently not one to remain reticent for long, at least once the topic switched to her ex-husband.

"Our divorce just became final a few months ago," she said. "It shouldn't have been contentious. It'd been coming for a long time. I was used to being an engineer's wife, you see. I'd been one long before I met Frank."

"You were married before?" I asked. Given their age, I'd assumed she and Frank must have been married a long time. Never assume.

"I was married to Todd for thirty years. Pancreatic cancer took him about eight years ago."

"I'm sorry," Dad said. I nodded.

"Todd had always been a railroader too, so I was used to the shows. Either go with him or stay home and learn to knit." The tone of voice made me think this woman placed knitting right up there with thumb twiddling and watching paint dry. "We did that for years and built a collection. Some couples have kids. Others have cats. We had trains. Todd and I started the train show, long before they added toys to it."

"And then you met Frank?" I suggested.

"Swept me off my feet, that one." She rolled her eyes. "But I didn't just meet him—we'd all been friends for years. With Todd gone, Frank took over the show. I still had all Todd's notes and all Todd's trains. Frank would come over now and then to maintain them. Mostly I think he just wanted to run them around on the tracks, and we'd have coffee or dinner. I should've known that was what he was after all along."

"You think Frank married you for your trains?" I asked.

She took a long time exhaling that last breath. "Don't know," she finally said. "I accused him of as much and he denied it. But he put a lot more time and energy into maintaining those trains than he did our relationship. I was used to being a train wife, like I said, but not a train widow."

"Then why would you want to go to the train show?" Dad asked. "If it would bring up unhappy memories?"

"For one reason, Todd and I built that show from the ground up. I shouldn't have to sneak around in disguise to go just because Frank and I are on the outs."

"And the other reason?" I asked.

"Huh?"

"You said 'for one reason.' I assumed there was another."

She rubbed the corner of her eye with her knuckle. "That's where it gets a little tricky." She looked at my dad. "I won't get in any trouble, will I?"

"That depends," he said. "Did you break any laws?"

She drew in a breath and held it. "I almost did," she finally said. "Well, more than almost, but I think I fixed it. See, in our separation of property, I ended up with the house—which I had to sell because I couldn't afford the taxes on it myself, but at least I got a substantial amount of equity from the sale—and Frank ended up with the trains. All of them. My lawyer suggested I sign off on it. And financially, it was a good deal for me. But . . ."

"You wanted the trains too?"

"Not all of them!" she said. "I'm not that greedy. But a couple of them were my father's. And one of them Todd and I got on our honeymoon. The more I thought about it, the more unreasonable that seemed. I offered to buy them, but Frank was being stubborn."

"You were going to steal them?" Dad's eyebrows hit the roof.

She took a fortifying breath before continuing. "From Santa's throne, I had a good view of Frank and his layout. When he left it, I had one of the elves post a 'Back in Ten Minutes' sign, claiming I had to use the restroom. My dad's engine was sitting idle on a piece of diverted track. All I had to do was pick it up and shove it underneath the beard. I'd just managed it when that man comes flying out of nowhere and crashes right into the layout. He was only a few feet away. I know he survived the initial fall, but I could have been killed! I thought it was a warning." She looked up. "I put it back the next day."

"And you didn't make any further attempts to take the engine?" Dad asked.

She vigorously shook her head. "That was all I needed to be drawn back to the side of the angels. I didn't want my last act on earth to be so petty. Especially dressed as Saint Nicholas. After all . . ." She sighed. "It's just a train."

# # #

"You think she's telling the truth?" I asked Dad on the way to the shop.

"No reason to suspect otherwise," he said. "She had no connection to Craig and none to the mob that I know of. She didn't have to tell us half of what she did. Otherwise, I wouldn't have asked her to be our Santa."

"Ask? You practically blackmailed the woman!" I said.

"Blackmail is such a harsh word," Dad said. "It's why we went over there in the first place."

"Yes, but her willingness to volunteer? That was all due to her knowing that you know her secret. It's manipulative."

"Maybe a little. But since it's a position that could put her around children—"

"Proving my point."

Dad nodded. "Also provides the justification to do a background check."

"So you don't believe her?" I said.

"Actually, I do. But it never hurts to check. Besides, mission accomplished. Boy, did I just save the town all kinds of money."

"Do you think East Aurora is ready for a cross-dressing Santa, especially one known to hide stolen property under her beard?"

"They'll probably never know." Dad licked his lips. "Right?"

# # #

As we drove past the police station, I could see my father almost begin to salivate, so I pulled into the parking lot.

Dad sent me a confused look. "I didn't ask to stop here."

"You were thinking it."

"That's it. We're getting rid of the Amazing Kreskin game."

"The who?"

"Mind reader. Before your time."

I closed my eyes and put my hands on my temples as if I were channeling a message. "We haven't checked in on the official investigation in a while. How about we see if there's been any new developments?" I looked up. "Am I close?"

"Nailed it." He reached for the door handle. "Remind me to hide the spoons when I get home."

"What?"

"Kreskin used to bend spoons. With the power of his mind."

Dad's winning smile was enough to get us past the clerk. Ken's office was dark, but Howard Reynolds sat hunched at his desk, embroiled in paperwork. I followed Dad there.

Reynolds looked up, then stretched his neck. "Boy, am I glad to see you," he said to Dad.

"Oh?" Dad took a seat in a guest chair, and I tried to look less obvious by leaning against a nearby unoccupied desk. "And here I thought I was just here to give you more information." Dad filled him in on Annie Werth.

"Yeah, I think you're right," Reynolds said. "It's probably a dead end. But at least it's one we can rule out. I'll run her background for you, though."

"I appreciate that," he said. "And it will probably be reassuring to the chamber of commerce."

"Although I don't recommend you tell them the whole backstory," Reynolds said. "And thanks for bringing in those videotapes, by the way," Reynolds said. "They were actually more helpful than you realized. They got Millroy and Eicher talking. That and a little savvy police work."

"Really?" Dad said. It was all he needed to say.

"We played it for the suspects. Slowly."

"But you couldn't see them do anything," I said.

Reynolds wagged a finger at me. "Never underestimate the power of a guilty mind. When one of them started making excuses, we separated them. At first, they both clammed up. Then we hinted that the other was talking. Next thing you know, we got them both singing like the high school glee club, only in better harmony."

"You got them to talk? I'm impressed." Dad didn't ask what they said. And if he had, I doubted Reynolds would have told him.

"Millroy was the one you saw leaning over the cup. We may have hinted that Eicher was an older man, probably not wanting to spend the rest of his life in jail for murder. Next thing you know, Millroy's saying he *might have* put the scopolamine in the cup, but that was a far cry from murder."

"Nice," Dad said.

"Then we took that bit of confession to Eicher, hinting that he was complicit to murder. A few more back and forths, and, as best as we can work out, the two of them conspired to put the scopolamine into Craig's cup while it was sitting out at the comic booth. The whole cup switcheroo was just a simple mistake. After Craig drank it, they told him to get the comic books and meet them outside. They both claim they had no idea he was going to climb up onto those catwalks. They said Eicher was waiting for him outside. Best I can figure out, Craig must have gone out a different door, not seen anybody, and then stashed the comics behind the planter. When Eicher got tired of waiting, he went in and saw all the ruckus. They said it took them a while to figure out what had happened, but they stayed to try to find those books."

Dad's brows furrowed. "Why . . . ?" Then he stopped.

"Why those books?" Reynolds said. "Here's where they got a little quieter. Our last check with Mark Baker at the FBI picked up on a few connections between one Joshua Duncan and a few men suspected of involvement in organized crime."

"The comic books were some kind of payoff?" Dad asked.

"Not sure yet," Reynolds said. "But comic books have been used in money laundering schemes in the past. When the IRS asks where the money came from, it's easy to point to a box of comic books you say you found in the basement. Who can prove otherwise? They're next to untraceable."

"That's diabolical," I said. "That means Jenna Duncan . . ."

"Made an honest mistake with her husband's dishonest gains," Reynolds said. "I almost feel sorry for what's happening." He glanced at his watch. "Right now, in fact."

"What's happening?" I asked.

"Search and seizure," Reynolds said. "When you tick off both the FBI and the IRS, nasty things happen fast. They think they're going to find all kinds of items used to pay off Duncan for his services. They're taking the whole kit and caboodle."

"They're leaving her with nothing?"

"Joint property, joint tax returns. And rumor was she was disposing of evidence and getting ready to flee the area."

"She was having a garage sale and getting ready to visit her mother in Cleveland," I said.

"Same diff," Reynolds said. "But from what I gather, she's talking, trying to get the whole thing pinned on hubby there. It's just a matter of time before one of them is implicated in McFadden's death. I think we got this one wrapped up. Just waiting on a pretty bow."

Chapter 23

When Dad and I arrived at Well Played, Cathy was trying to pull a table out of the closet. I ran over to stop her. "Let me get that!"

"I'm pregnant, not an invalid." Then she relaxed and let me take over setting up the tables for game night. "It feels good to be able to say that out loud."

"She's right, though," Dad said. "Got to take care of the littlest McCall." He looked up. "Barbara, if it's a girl?"

"What are you talking about?" Cathy said.

"Betsy McCall's cousin," I said, rolling my eyes. "Feel free to reject any and all of Dad's name suggestions."

"I'll do that," she said, waving an accusing finger at Dad. "Parker told me that you've been calling me Chatty Cathy behind my back again."

Dad put his hands up. "See, even if you don't name your child after a doll or toy, I can probably find a doll or toy that will fit the bill." He paused for a second. "Including Bill. Pelican Bill, Bill Ding, Wild Bill, Blinky Bill . . ."

"Please tell me that's not why you seem to prefer Ken over Jack," I said.

"Not at all, sweetheart," he said. "After all, jacks are toys too. I would've been happy with either name." He pointed at the stairs. "I can start dinner, if you'd like. Unless you want to get something to go."

Since our main to-go option was Jack, I left Dad to make dinner while I focused my attention on Cathy. "So, the secret is officially out. Any limitations or are we free to tell the world?"

"Tell anyone you'd like. Oh, and I also got to meet Amanda and Kohl today. They came in when you were out."

"Were they looking for Dad or me?"

"I don't think so," Cathy said. "Amanda said she's trying to slowly introduce the town to Kohl to see what he thinks before she makes any big decisions. For what it's worth, I think he likes the toyshop too. He took a shine to a Superman figure, and I let him take it with him. I hope you don't mind."

"As long as Dad doesn't bring you up on a bribery charge, I have no objections. Kohl seems to have a fondness for superheroes."

"I did, however, hide the price tag from Amanda. And I may have had to undervalue it to get her to accept it. She was asking about the consignment shop down the street, and I dug up an old chamber of commerce coupon book for her. I guess with all of Kohl's special needs, she relied on Craig's child support payments."

"I know Dad's set on buying them out, but I hope when the dust has settled, there's enough left in Craig's estate to allow them to stay. She seems nice."

"I thought so too. Easy to talk to. She said she has a great gingersnap recipe that got her through her morning sickness. She was going to e-mail it to me once she got back home. Oh, and Maxine also stopped by while you were out. She said the inventory's going faster than expected. Said they should be done by noon tomorrow, and she was wondering if we could use her."

"I hope you told her yes," I said.

"I did, especially considering how much you and Dad have been away from the shop."

"Which is over, I think," I said. "According to Reynolds, it's just a matter of time. They figure it was either one of those two mob guys or maybe Jenna Duncan."

"And there we were, eating cheesecake and watching Lori Briggs swig drain cleaner just the other night."

"Not drain cleaner."

"It said you could use it to freshen drains. By the way, I looked up vodka as a cleaning agent, and a few of the organic websites highly recommend it. Not quite sure that's where I want to go, since I know it's a sore spot with Parker too. But speaking of cleaning drains, I'm going to head home and ignore mine. I want to put my feet up for a bit. Is it just me, or are my ankles swollen already?"

I stepped back to look. "Not that I can tell, but you probably should get some rest." I gave her a hug. "Thanks for covering for us."

She saluted, gathered her things, and left.

The tables were a little awkward to set up with only one person, but since Dad was taking care of dinner, I made short work of it, hoping nobody was watching through the window. After all the chairs were in place, I'd begun collecting games—tonight's theme was games we played in the seventies. Of course that included the old standbys: Yahtzee, Risk, Clue, and Mousetrap. Rebound was always fun but a bit noisy. I also pulled out a few nonpristine—playing, as opposed to collectible—copies of some more obscure games. Which Witch? (before it was released as a *Ghostbusters* tie-in). Sub Search—a kind of 3-D version of Battleship. And Manhunt, an oldie but goodie from Milton Bradley that featured a detective handbook and a crime "computer" and punch cards. It was just a set of spinners hooked up to a small motor powered by a D battery. It was hard to find a spinner that still worked these days, but Miles had made us an app that replicated it pretty well.

Dad came down the stairs with a tray. Nothing fancy. Grilled cheese, cut diagonally, a handful of chips, and a few gherkins.

"Oh, the seventies," he said. "Those were the days. Where men were men and women were generally in distress or looked like swimwear models. And the weapon of choice was definitely a Smith and Wesson revolver."

I did the math in my head. "You weren't a detective in the seventies."

"No, but that's when I knew I wanted to be one."

We finished our brief dinner, then Dad carried the tray upstairs. I found a retro station to pump through the speakers, and things were already seeming a little groovy when Maxine walked in.

"Wow!" she said. "That's a blast from the past."

Moments later, the whole gang started pouring in, with Lori Briggs leading the pack as she chatted with Glenda.

"They took her away," Lori said, "in chains."

Dad interrupted. "Handcuffs?"

"Well, yeah," she said. "And they're still there, trampling all over the neighborhood."

She quieted down her complaints when Ken walked in and kissed me on the cheek.

"In public?" I whispered, aware that the room had hushed at least a few decibels.

"They'd better get used to it," he said.

Fortunately that public display of affection was over by the time Jack walked in with Terry in tow.

"Are we welcome?" he asked me before he'd even let go of the door.

"Of course," I said, stepping forward for a hug but then stopping short. I was in unfamiliar territory.

There was more than a little jockeying for position tonight. Lori Briggs sat down next to the spot where Ken usually sat. But then she was joined by Jack and Terry.

Ken sat next to where I was across from Maxine. Dad had somehow slipped the Manhunt game on the table and winked before he left to play Battleship with Glenda. I could feel my face flush when I caught his meaning. Manhunt, indeed.

"I've never played this one before," Maxine said. "How does it work?"

"Well, we're all detectives," I said, "and we have to go around the board picking up clues and writing them down in our notebooks."

Ken sighed. "Do we have to? I do this all day at work."

"Afraid I'll beat you?"

"Fine. What do we have to do?"

"First, we all have to decide if we want to solve a murder, a robbery, or a swindle." Then I demonstrated the "punch cards" and probe.

The game progressed slowly, with Ken stopping every so often to question the terminology of the game board.

"Safecracking and burglaries aren't robberies. You can only rob from a person when they're present."

"Says the law," Maxine said. "Apparently Milton Bradley had other ideas."

"What's bothering you?" I asked. "You seem all out of sorts tonight. I'd have thought you'd be more relaxed since the investigation seems to be winding down."

"Sorry," he said. But there was more that he wasn't telling me and apparently didn't want to talk about, and I didn't have to be the Amazing Whatchamacallit to see that.

I turned to Maxine. "So, how's it going at the comic shop? Cathy told me you were almost done."

She nodded. "That Amanda's a real good worker. So is Kohl. He was helping out for a bit."

"Craig's kid?" Ken said. "How old is he?"

I put my hands over Ken's ears. "Ixnay on the ildchay aborlay awslay."

Maxine laughed. "He's fourteen. And he knows more about what's going on than he lets on. I'm sure of it. We had him sorting through comic books, separating the different superheroes. It made the rest of the inventory easier."

"Was anything else missing?" Ken asked.

"I don't think so," Maxine said. "Well, except for the graded comics. We eventually got all the rest of the stock from the train show, and we did sell some there, even though we weren't open very long."

Lori laughed at something one of the Wallace brothers said. It was that over-the-top flirty laugh that men seemed to adore and that reminded me of brakes squealing before impact. I glanced over there, and she had the attention of both men. Lambs to the slaughter?

"Liz?" Ken said. "Your turn."

While I considered my move, Ken turned to Maxine. "Look, Kohl can help out, but make sure he's not working too long."

She nodded. "He got tired after a little while, so he sat down and started drawing. That surprised me. He's quite good. Like his dad, almost. Except . . ."

"Except?" I said.

"He adds all kinds of details, but his people don't have eyes. The rest of it is perfect. Here." She reached into her purse and pulled out a folded paper. "I need to frame it or something, but he drew this today and gave it to me."

I looked at the picture. It was Maxine. You could clearly identify even the clothing she was wearing, all with intricate folds and shading. Where the face should have been was just a collection of dots and squiggles.

"Amanda said he usually doesn't even try to draw the faces."

"That's really good though," I said.

"Huh," Ken said. "Is he some kind of savant? Like that one guy on the news who drew the whole of New York City after a twenty-minute helicopter ride?"

Maxine shook her head. "I asked Amanda about that. She said no. Just that he took to drawing real young, and it seemed to calm him. He works hard at it. Maybe it's one good thing he inherited from Craig."

"He inherited the shop and the house too, right?" I asked.

Ken nodded. "We found his will in the search of his house while investigating the break-in there. Things were tossed around a bit, but nothing too much was broken or damaged. Needs some serious redecorating, though."

"A woman's touch," Maxine said. "I always thought so. I offered to help him, but . . ."

She trailed off, concentrating on the game. "Did I win? I think I won," she said. "How do I check it?"

That startled me back to the game. "Other side of the punch card."

"Yep," she said. "Jim Nasium." Then she groaned. "This is your father's game, isn't it?" She thumbed through the list of suspects. "Maria Net. Dora Jar. Mel O'Day."

"Hank," Lori called out, "can't I get through one game of Yahtzee without any of your puns?"

"Sorry," he said not even looking up. "No dice."

After the groaning subsided, Ken asked, "Does anybody want to try that 3-D Battleship game?"

"Sub Search?" I said. The question was a little awkward, considering it was a two-person game. "I should carry around some candy to see if I can't make enough to at least pay for the lights and electricity tonight. You two can play without me."

"Would you like me to do that?" Maxine said.

"You had a long day. Sit down and have fun."

I went to the candy counter and grabbed an armload of candy popular in the seventies: Good & Plenty, Milk Duds, Necco Wafers, Chuckles, and the ever-popular Sky Bars, which we now had to import from Canada. I also took along some of the old-fashioned cinnamon and lemon suckers made after the recipe at Crystal Beach. The old amusement park was still going strong then. It hadn't closed until 1989, after 101 years of operation. Dad says he took us once, but I have no memory of it.

I stopped at Jack's table first, trying to greet everyone with the same friendly tone. They were still playing Yahtzee, and Lori was calling out for threes as she rolled the dice. She rolled five of them.

Terry tossed down his scoring pencil. "There goes that game." But he didn't seem too upset as he watched Lori do a celebratory dance with more than a little jiggling involved. The thought struck me that Lori won an awful lot of our tournaments, and I began to wonder if some of her male opponents were throwing their games.

"Candy?" I asked.

Both Jack and Terry made purchases from what I had in stock while Lori stretched—an action that didn't go unwatched by the men present—and bought a pack of her favorite candy cigarettes.

While she was gone from the table, Jack summoned me over. "I have to talk with you. Not here." He walked to the rear of the shop, and I followed him to the area right in front of the wall featuring our bright vintage lunch boxes. He rested his hand right next to the Aladdin *Hogan's Heroes* box that we probably would've had in a sealed display case had it been in better condition.

"Jack, what is this about?"

"It's weird for me to be here, right?"

"Maybe a little, but we live in the same town. We've weathered a breakup before and remained friends. I'd like to think that can happen again."

"That's what I figured you'd say."

"I really should get back—"

"There's something else I need to tell you." He took a fortifying breath. "It's about Terry. I'd been thinking he was keeping another secret. About all that happened at the train show."

"More involvement?"

He nodded. "But not directly. Well, I guess it is directly. He kind of came clean about it this morning, and I said I'd talk to you about it."

"Why me?" But the answer hit like a rock in the pit of my stomach. "So I'd talk to Ken for you."

He shoved his hands in his pockets. "Something like that."

I winced. I hoped I wouldn't regret this, but I'd also entertained the thought that Terry was still holding something back. "What is it?"

"Terry knew Craig from school," Jack said.

"Craig was in our class, though," I said.

"But more Terry's size. I don't remember it—such a long time ago—but apparently when Craig gave any of us a hard time, Terry would step in and challenge him."

"Craig could be quite a bully," I said. "But that was decades ago. I'm sure it cooled down."

Jack paused, looking at the lunchboxes, then at the floor, before he finally met my gaze, his eyebrows pinched. "Terry was giving Craig a hard time at the show. Teasing him about that superhero suit. I'm sure he was just mouthing off."

"What exactly did he say?"

"There was this little girl with a balloon, and she lost it and started crying. So Terry decided to taunt Craig. He said something like, 'Hey, superhero-man. You can fly. Go get that kid her balloon.'"

I pressed my hand against my mouth and leaned against the display.

"I genuinely don't think he meant to do any actual harm. Terry had no idea that sculp-drug, whatever it is, was in Craig's system. How could he? Or I'm sure he wouldn't have said what he did."

"Give me a moment to process," I said.

"How bad is this?"

"I don't know."

We must have been MIA for too long, because Ken poked his head around the corner. "There you are. What's going on?"

Jack looked at me, and I nodded. He told Ken the rest of the story. "What's this going to mean for him? Will this mess up his parole? I mean, I'm sure he was only mouthing off."

Ken opened his mouth a couple of times, looking as if full sentences had formed in his brain but refused to cross his lips. Eventually he just shook his head. "I have no idea. I think your best bet is to get Terry to talk to Howard Reynolds."

"But surely you could . . ." I started.

Ken stopped me. "It's Reynolds's case. I'm not sure it'd even be good form for me to put in a word for your brother.

But if he finds any connection between Terry and those two guys we have in custody—"

"He won't," Jack said.

"I sure hope not," Ken said. "Because if he finds anything to link them, it won't be hard to pull Terry into the whole conspiracy. Someone might find it awfully convenient that, at just the moment Craig was open to suggestion, your brother suggested that Craig could fly."

"But that didn't kill Craig," I said. "Why would Terry then sneak into a hospital to finish him off? What motive would he have?"

Ken clammed up. It was Jack who answered. "To cover up what he'd done." He closed his eyes. "Like he's done all his life."

I laid what I hoped was a comforting hand on Jack's arm. Howard Reynolds had been looking for one last piece of evidence to tie up his case with a bow. I hoped Terry's admission wouldn't unravel the case . . . or the new life Jack was so hoping Terry was ready to build.

Chapter 24

Friday morning brought another day of blue skies and warm temperatures. It was Cathy's day off, so Dad and I were glued to the shop for a little while, even though he kept looking out the front windows as if waiting for something to happen.

A woman who cleans up after local estate sales brought in a couple of boxes of toys and games. It'd been a while, she reminded me, since I'd come to one of her sales instead of waiting for her to bring the leftovers to us. I apologized briefly before taking a halfhearted look into the first box.

There was a bunch of Fisher-Price, but they were common models and the condition was poor. The wood and paper showed signs of mold, and some of the paper had peeled off. I could see why any serious collector had passed them by. Still, after a good cleaning, some child might want to play with them.

The one saving grace was a pull toy featuring a bear dressed up as a drum major. An old Gong Bell model, if I had that right. And I was pretty sure I did. Even without the box, I could probably get eighty or so bucks for it, especially after

Dad worked his magic. And it might look nice in the shop window next to the parade poster. "Fifty for all of it?" I said.

"They're not in good shape, are they?"

"These all need work. The Fisher-Price collectors probably got the best stuff." I held up the bear. "They probably didn't recognize this one."

"Not Fisher-Price?"

"Predates it, actually. Older, but harder to find the right buyer. Not as many collectors."

She agreed to my price, and I handed the toys to Dad.

"Just a few years ago, these would've fetched more," Dad said.

"Can't control the market. You can only wait it out."

"If it recovers. Old collectors are dying off faster than new ones are taking their place. That's why I'd like to diversify."

"Comic books?" I could see his logic. I pulled back my hair and glanced around the shop. "What would you cut out? You take out the doll room and Cathy will never let you see your grandchildren."

"I'm not sure we have to take out anything. You know, the interesting thing about this building is that the whole thing is zoned for retail space. Including the second floor."

"The old shop had a loft," I said. "But that's our apartment. Where are we going to go?"

"That, I'm still working on. Maybe I could stay with Parker and Cathy for a bit and help take care of the baby. And I'd kind of figured that eventually you might get married and move out."

"The key words in that statement are *might* and *eventually*."

"Don't worry. I still have a few aces up my sleeve. And we don't even know yet if Amanda would be willing to part with that stock."

"Is that who you keep looking for?" I asked.

"When she and Maxine finish that inventory, I figured one of them would show up."

But Howard Reynolds was the next person to walk through the door.

I forced a smile, even though my stomach did a few flips. "Good morning, Detective. How can I help you?"

"I wish I was looking for toys," he said. "I just had a long talk with Terry Wallace."

Dad stepped out of the back room. "And?"

"And it muddies the whole investigation. Thanks"—and he pointed at both of us—"for sending him my way, though."

"Trying to help," I said. "I feel bad for Terry. Well, more for Jack. I'd like to think Terry had no idea that Craig would take him up on his suggestion."

Reynolds bobbed his head. "Ninety-nine point nine times out of a hundred, when you tell someone they can fly, they don't believe you and everything turns out fine. Unless we can connect him to Millroy and Eicher, I *think* he's going to be in the clear. And maybe a bit less mouthy next time."

"That's got to be a hard thing to live with," Dad said.

"Nothing about this case is easy," Reynolds said.

"More problems?" Dad asked, his voice just a little too innocent. As if he wasn't dying for more info.

Reynolds rested a hand on the counter, then saw the candy display. "Mallo Cups. I haven't had one in ages. May I?"

"My treat," Dad said.

BARBARA EARLY

Better him than me. Mallo Cups always seemed to me like a cruel joke played on unsuspecting peanut butter cup lovers.

But Reynolds seemed to enjoy it and was soon licking his fingers and crumpling up the wrapper. "Here's the thing," he said, pausing to slam dunk the wrapper into our trash can. "The story Millroy and Eicher are telling is amazingly consistent. We think we're getting at the truth. Only there's a few things they both insist they didn't do."

"Like what?" I asked.

"They admit to breaking into the comic book shop, but they swear up and down that they didn't take anything, including that computer."

"They're obviously just trying to avoid another charge," I said.

Dad looked uncomfortable. Like the time I switched detergents and he got a bad case of contact dermatitis from his tighty-whities. He'd gone on for weeks about my "rash" decision. "Then why admit to breaking in at all?"

Reynolds shrugged. "They could be telling the truth about that part. We didn't find the computer during the search."

"They could've dumped it anywhere," I said.

"But then why would they even bother to take it?" Dad said. "To get some information he had on it?"

"Or to suppress it," Reynolds said. "Our forensics guy is finding a few interesting things on that laptop. Someone had tried to delete a bunch of files."

"What kind of files?" Dad asked.

"E-mails," Reynolds said. "Spreadsheets."

Dad looked grim.

"I take it that means there was something compromising," I said.

"Not sure. The tech people recovered some, so they're going over the e-mails. I thought we could get that FBI forensic accountant to look over the spreadsheets." He scratched his head. "But someone wanted to get rid of those files on that laptop. And in a hurry. And now that other computer is missing."

"You're right," Dad said. "Something's not adding up."

"And those two we got now don't admit to breaking into McFadden's house at all, even though whoever did it left the same kind of mess as those two knuckleheads did at the comic book shop."

Dad's jaw tightened. "Could there be another player?"

"Thinking it might be Terry?" I asked.

"Stealing a computer and breaking into McFadden's place?" Reynolds said. "That's just the kind of thing that got him sent up the first time. Wiping a computer? Smothering Craig McFadden with a pillow?" He shrugged and walked out.

Dad looked after him. "That was a cry for help."

"He didn't ask."

"Exactly," Dad said. "But it was far from idle gossip."

"What do we do?"

Dad pulled out his stash of scratch paper we used for scoring game tournaments and chose a pen from the jar. "Here's the question. Who would want the computer? Before that, why?"

"It looked old. I doubt anyone wanted it for resale value. If they did, they didn't know what they were doing."

"Good. Let's rule that out."

"They, whoever they are, wanted access to something on it."

"What do we know was on it?"

"Financial records. Inventory. Craig's new comic series. And apparently e-mails and spreadsheets."

Dad scribbled all that down and stared at the paper. "If they were after the financial records or the inventory, it might be to hide any record of the comics Craig purchased from Jenna Duncan."

"I thought they were untraceable," I said.

"Virtually. Especially if those comics were sold one at a time. In a group like that, they might be more conspicuous. Raise a few red flags. That's probably why those guys were here. To prevent a high-profile sale and expose the connection between their bosses and Josh Duncan."

"That's another thing that's been bothering me," I said. "Maxine knew those comics were pricy but had no idea they were worth over ninety grand. And since nobody impulse buys books like that, Craig must've had a buyer already lined up. Otherwise, why risk bringing them to the show where they might be lost, stolen, or damaged? I think he was planning on meeting the buyer there. Maybe the prospective buyer is our third player."

"He might have been trying to sell them back to the mob," Dad said. "Or Jenna Duncan."

I shook my head. "Jenna Duncan had no idea what they were worth. And Millroy and Eicher had already put a different plan in place to get them back using the scopolamine."

"A missing piece," Dad said. "Very nice! Not that I like that there's another piece missing. That's frustrating as all get out. But it's a very nice catch."

I felt my face flush. "You know, there was another man at the show asking about graded comics. He came when I was working with Maxine."

"You think he might have been Craig's prospective buyer?"

"He'd be on the security footage. He wore a big bulky jacket and came right up to me."

"That possibility's probably worth taking to Reynolds." He circled it on his paper and then darkened the circle. "We don't know how desperately our mystery man wanted those comics or why. Not sure why he'd want the computer either."

"To hide his e-mails?" I said. "Or maybe he thought he could use it to track the comics?"

Dad squinted. "He might've been the one to break into Craig's house, though, if he was still looking for those books."

"So it might have been a stranger all along."

"But what motive would he have to kill Craig? Not if he wanted those books and he thought Craig knew where they were."

"So it doesn't fit," I said.

"Raises some interesting possibilities, and we should probably try to figure out who he is. I can ask Reynolds if his tech guys came across any purchase agreements from Craig's laptop or cell phone."

I nodded, then looked over Dad's shoulder at his notes. "Then there's Craig's new comic book series. It could be valuable."

"I wonder if that first book's gotten many presales yet," Dad said.

"Let me check." I pulled out my cell and searched for "Craig McFadden" on the major online booksellers. "Whoa."

"High?" Dad asked.

"The sales rank is near the top of its category."

"Word of his murder must've gotten out. Buyers love a sensational story."

I glanced again and tapped my phone. "Someone put it right in his bio!"

"I'm going to guess that someone was Tippi Hillman."

"It's motive," I said, already grieving over my growing disenchantment with my one-time hero. "Taking the computer gives her all Craig's comics, and the murder gives her complete control of them."

"I somehow doubt that clause would stand up in court," Dad said. "And if she took advantage of those clowns leaving the comic book shop unsecured and took the computer, why would she then break into Craig's house?"

"There'd be no need. She'd already have everything." I found myself completely immersed in the mental puzzle of detection. My dad had drawn me in, once again. Last time, it had been kicking and screaming, this time by mere suggestion.

Dad looked at his paper. "How about we split up after Miles gets here? I can go to the station, see if they'll let me look at those recovered files, and maybe I can figure out what Craig was up to. While I'm there, I'll try to talk them into letting me look at the security footage to find your mysterious comic book customer."

"And I stay here?"

"I was thinking you could have another talk with that Wolf woman. She knows you're a fan, so maybe you could get a few things out of her. At least look around a bit. Make her a little nervous, but not so paranoid that she bolts. And if you can sweet-talk her into giving over a copy of Craig's book, that'd be even better."

"And if she's the killer?"

"Dang. That's right. You shouldn't go by yourself."

We debated it for a couple of minutes. Ken would probably spook her. Parker was working. We'd both put Cathy off the table, although she probably would've enjoyed it more than anybody. And it didn't seem like a good idea to invite Jack.

Then Maxine walked in. "Hi, everybody. All done and ready to work!"

I looked at Dad, who quirked an eyebrow.

"Maxine," I said, "how about running a little errand with me?"

She folded her arms in front of her. "Only if I can drive."

# # #

"I feel like Alfred in the Batcave!" Maxine squealed as we headed toward Buffalo Chips.

"I'm not sure we need to get there quite so fast," I said.

Maxine checked her speed and slowed down more than a tad. "You really don't think those two hooligans killed Craig?"

"Haven't ruled them out completely, but I just don't get their motive."

"And you think Lexi Wolf might be involved?"

"Possibly. Not likely, though, since Dad suggested I go," I said just as I realized he'd probably suggested we split up so that he could go to the station, solve the case, and then gloat about it for the rest of the year. "She benefited from Craig's death, though, so she had motive. Apparently Craig's comic series is taking off, at least in presales. Was it that good?"

"I never actually saw it," she said.

"I remember you telling me he could draw."

"Yes, but he never showed me any of his new stuff. He powered down his monitor whenever I even got close to the computer. I tried to take a peek once when he was out of the shop, but he had the whole program password protected. I think he was worried I'd leak it to someone. He never did fully trust anyone."

"It must've been hard for him, being bumped from foster home to foster home like that." I winced. I was trying to relieve some of Maxine's guilt, and I inadvertently brought up yet another way she could blame herself. "Not your fault, I'm sure."

"I wish I'd been in a position to take care of him myself," she said. "When they took him away from me, I knew it wasn't going to be pretty."

I didn't answer. I was too busy thinking what it must have been like for Craig being uprooted all the time and never making any meaningful human connections. If he was just an infant when Maxine gave him up, I would've thought someone might have adopted him. Yet somehow he ended up in the system again and again. I made a mental note to ask Dad if there might be some connection there—a member of one of his foster families who bore a grudge. Maybe the timing was just coincidental and had nothing to do with comic books at all. Dad didn't like coincidences, but sometimes they did happen.

There were a couple of cars in the parking lot when we pulled up, and when Maxine and I slipped in the door, Lexi squinted at me suspiciously but continued her conversation with a man at a desk.

Since there was nobody else working at the place at the moment, I took a seat in a chair in the waiting area, and Maxine did the same. There, on the scarred coffee table, were several editions of *Mr. Inferno: Feel the Fire*, all stamped "Advance Review Copy, Not for Resale." I snatched one up quicker than I would a pancake at one of the fire department's fundraising breakfasts. And believe me, that's pretty quick. When Lexi wasn't looking, I shoved it into my purse. I wasn't sure if these copies were free to take or not, but I wasn't leaving without one.

As my ears adjusted to the quiet, I realized I could make out bits of Lexi's conversation. Or rather Tippi's. I had to stop fangirling and start remembering that she was only an actress playing a part. Especially if it turned out that she'd played a part in Craig's demise.

The man's voice carried more easily. Or maybe Tippi was trying not to be overheard. It seemed to be some kind of press interview.

"So, with the author gone, will there be more to this series?"

"I think it's safe to say that Mr. Inferno will live on as long as there are readers interested in hearing his story."

"You have more books ready to go then? How many by the original author?"

Tippi paused for a moment and seemed to choose her next words with upmost care.

"Some of those details need to wait while we confer with his immediate heirs. Much will depend on the provisions made in McFadden's will. It'd be premature to comment."

"What can you say about the artist's unusual style? Was it a nod to Japanese anime? Or some kind of statement against the exaggerated sexual characteristics we see in many super-hero comics?"

I didn't catch her full answer. Something about artistic license and expression. "Hard to say if he was on the cutting edge of something brilliant. It will be up to the readers to decide."

That woman was smart. Make the reader curious.

While they continued the interview, going over release date, price, and other details, I stood up to stretch. At least I hoped that's what it looked like. With Tippi stuck in the interview, she wouldn't have time to hide anything incriminating that might be in the open. There were several computers in the room, and I began looking for any that could've once been Craig's. He'd had those stickers plastered to the case. They'd be easy to identify if she'd taken the computer and left them on. And still probably easy if she'd tried to remove them. We'd gotten some items in with those same stickers, and they were a bear to remove. The top would come off, leaving a gummy mess behind unless you soaked them for three days, which you could not do with a computer.

Most of the computers in the room were older models, and I'd eliminated all but one in the corner. All I could see of the last one was the cords sticking out of the back. It was, however, right in front of their restroom.

"Excuse me," I said rather loudly to Maxine, but more for Tippi's benefit. "I need to use the restroom."

It's hard to look casual when you're walking, especially when you're *trying* to look casual. I expect I half-sauntered and half-sashayed to the restroom. I cast a quick glance at the computer on the way and didn't see any stickers or residue, but the angle wasn't great. Coming out, however, would be perfect.

The dingy unisex bathroom wasn't hiding any clues either, unless it was that Buffalo Chips didn't actually have a cleaning service. After a minute or so of standing in the middle of the room trying not to touch anything, I flushed the toilet with my shoe and then washed my hands, because even that limited contact gave me the willies.

Then I had an idea. I pulled out my phone, pulled up the camera app, and had it at the ready. With any luck, I'd just look like one of any number of people who can't take their eyes off their phone long enough to accomplish other business. I opened the door, took a quick picture, and then realized I'd forgotten to mute my phone. The sound of the camera click echoed through the office.

"What are you doing?" Tippi asked.

"Sorry. Accident." I got so nervous, I dropped my cell phone.

Tippi rolled her eyes. "Next time, if you want a picture of me, just ask. I'll be with you in a moment."

I picked up my phone, which had landed on the floor right next to the computer. The model was similar to the one I remembered in Craig's shop, but there was no sticker debris in sight. Maxine might be able to identify it, though.

I shoved my phone in my purse and sashayed-sauntered to my seat just as Tippi's interview ended with a handshake.

"I'll e-mail you when the article goes live," he said.

When the reporter had climbed into his car and driven away, Tippi turned to me, her expression considerably less pleasant. "What was all that about?"

"Just came back to ask you a couple of questions," I said.

"And take my picture?" she said. "I normally charge for that kind of thing. And don't think you can post it anywhere or sell it. That'd be a violation of trademark and publicity. I still enjoy some celebrity status, you know."

"I wasn't taking your picture."

"Let me see it then."

I pulled out my cell and showed her the most recent pictures. I watched her face as she saw the picture of the computer. She thumbed back through a few more pictures, but they were all toys and a couple of Othello.

"Now who's invading privacy?" I asked.

"Sorry," she said. "Just a bit touchy. Obviously you took that picture by mistake, unless you like photographs of archaic computers."

"I was curious why so many," I said. "You're the only one I've ever seen in the office."

"They came with the business," she said. "I keep thinking that maybe I'll be able to hire people to sit at those desks. Maybe with those comics . . ." She abruptly caught herself and extended her hand to Maxine. "Hello, I'm Tippi Hillman. Have we . . ."

"We've met," Maxine said, shaking Tippi's hand. "At the toy and train show. I worked for Craig. So his comics are worth something, huh?"

Tippi bobbed her head. "Be a lot better if I could get my hands on more of them." She stopped and alternated her gaze between Maxine and me. "Do you two know the family? He had a kid, right?"

"We've met," I said.

"Think they'd deal for the rest of Craig's comics? Could be some good money in it for them if presales on the first keep up."

I sucked air through my teeth. Extra cash might make things a lot easier for Amanda and Kohl. "Here's the thing," I said. "Craig's shop was broken into."

"So?"

"Someone took his computer," Maxine said. "The one he'd stored all his comics on."

"No backups?"

I shook my head. "The police haven't been able to find any. His house was broken into as well."

Tippi's eyes grew wide as her face froze. "So some penny-ante thief is out there walking around with a potential fortune in comics and may not even know it?"

Maxine paled. "I knew Craig could draw, but . . ."

"It's not just the drawing," Tippi said. "It's the hype going right now. And such a concept. And it feeds right into a lot of popular campaigns. Normal body types and not sexualizing children."

"What are you talking about?" I asked.

"Haven't you seen them?" She flipped open one of the advanced copies. I scooted forward to look. All of his characters, male and female, adults and kids, were proportioned like young boys.

"I've seen anime a little like this," I said. "Chibi?" But even in Japanese manga, the females were identifiable, even though not as exaggerated as in many American comics. But Craig had taken sexuality completely out of the equation. I'd also figured out why Craig was so interested in youth sports and had taken so many pictures. He'd used the action shots from the games as models for his youthful superheroes in action.

"We'll call it something different," Tippi said. "He's empowered children. And I think that's going to reach his audience. Not sure if it's a gimmick or a trend. But as long as people pay to read, I'll take either." Tippi paused to study Maxine. "Of course, the original investors should get a cut. I imagine the lawyers will have to get involved too."

"Original investors?" I asked, wondering why Tippi seemed to be addressing Maxine.

"Craig's original deposit came in checks made out to cash." Tippi put an hand on Maxine's arm. "You are one of the investors, right?"

Maxine swallowed hard. "I may have loaned him a little money. To get him started."

"Tippi," I said, "do you have a list of these investors?"

Chapter 25

Maxine was silent on the way home. She stared morosely into the twilight, and I regretted asking her to come along. It was going to take time to get over losing a son, even one she didn't know very well.

But the closer we got back to town, the more unease I felt. "You never mentioned that you invested in Craig's new comic series." I stared down at the list of Craig's investors—all women. Coincidence? One other was from the region, but a few more had addresses around the country.

"No, I suppose I didn't," she said.

"Do you know who these other women are?"

"I can't say. I've never met any of them."

We'd driven another block before I realized that Maxine hadn't really answered my question.

"But you know how Craig knew them." It was a guess.

She sniffled but didn't answer, keeping her eyes on the road.

"Maxine?"

"Look, Liz, from what I know, Craig found most of his . . . investors . . . online. Now let me drive so we don't end up in another pie stand."

It was meant to end the conversation, but it just made my brain start spinning. The slight pause before "investors." If these women weren't investors, why did they give Craig money?

Also niggling in the back of my brain was the fact that someone had stolen Craig's computer and wiped the shop's laptop. Or tried to anyway. Was it to hide the record of these . . . online investors?

"Maxine, did *you* wipe the laptop?"

"What?" she mumbled.

Another nonanswer.

If Maxine had wiped the laptop, had she also taken the computer to suppress some kind of information on it? And if she'd taken that, might she have also broken into his home too?

"Maxine, who are those other women?"

She drew a breath through clenched teeth. "For someone who considered himself so smart, Craig could be an idiot." She kept on driving, pausing to flip on the headlights. "They're all . . . we're all . . . women he bilked. At least I got that much from the laptop before . . ."

"Before you wiped it. I get that. You're his mother. It's not hard to understand that you'd want to protect him."

Maxine snorted.

Okay, not to protect him. "To protect *them*?" I glanced up at Maxine. The occasional oncoming headlights reflected across streams of tears running down her face. She reached to wipe some of it away.

"Pull over," I suggested. "You shouldn't drive when you're this upset."

"You'd like that, wouldn't you?"

"What?"

"I'm not stopping this car until I figure out what to do."

If I'd suspected before, *now* I knew. Maxine's involvement went far beyond wiping the laptop.

"I can help you do that," I said. "I can help you figure this out. Why don't you talk to me?"

While she was considering that, I put a finger around the handle of my purse that I'd set on the floor by my feet and started inching it up. If I could get to my cell phone inside . . .

But as soon as I'd maneuvered the purse into my lap, Maxine grabbed it. I tugged back, and we struggled over the bag, the car swerving into oncoming traffic that warned her with loud horns. She managed to regain her lane while tossing my purse into the back seat.

I lunged for it.

"If you do that again, I will crash this car. Sit down!"

I eased down into my seat. Except for the context, the words could've been said by any harried mother in the country. Only hers were not a warning but a threat.

I struggled to keep my voice calm. "Maxine, I don't understand what you're doing."

"You know enough to be a problem."

"Just that you wiped the laptop. And you probably also took the computer."

She sniffed again. "It was all right there in front of me the whole time. The multiple accounts. The fake names. He kept all the e-mails."

"The evidence that proved he defrauded his investors?"

If she'd snorted before, she cackled at this.

"Defrauded. That's a kind word. Want to know what he did?"

"Yes. Please tell me." I'd decided my best bet was to try to calm her down and keep her talking. I think that's what Dad said to do when negotiating a hostage situation, which my alarmed brain just realized this was becoming. I hoped the same tactics still worked when you were the hostage.

"I found Craig on a message board designed to reunite adopted kids with their birth parents. Well, it turns out, he'd registered for it under seven different e-mail addresses."

"Why would he . . . ?"

"Because he'd surf the stories of mothers looking for sons his age."

"And pretend to be those sons?"

"Basically, yes. He was a little smart about it, in that he wouldn't answer their posts. He'd just copy those details and make his own post in the section for sons looking for their mothers. Then he'd wait for them to come to him, like a spider luring flies into his web."

"So you might not even be his mother." Although I somehow doubted it. The resemblance was still striking.

She shrugged. "No idea. He didn't use a fake name to set up the account I found. That's how I traced him here."

"Aren't names and contact information on those sites private?"

"You young people. Just because I have a little age on me, doesn't mean I can't still hack a computer. You could say I have over thirty years of experience. Not only did I find those e-mails, but spreadsheets he used to keep all the details about these aliases. And others he used to track his . . . income. Some women just wanted to help him. Others didn't want it known that they'd had a son, so he blackmailed them for even more. It's where he got the money to open the shop."

"So you discovered all this on the laptop and then wiped it." I struggled to come up with a reason. "Because if police found it, it would give you a motive?" I didn't wait for an answer. "But I know you didn't stage the break-in at the comic shop," I continued. "Those two mob guys already confessed to that. Besides, you wouldn't have had to break in. You had a key."

"And if I'd used my key, everybody would have known I took the computer. I wasn't sure what to do. I figured investigators would check it out eventually. But then the security service called me about the alarm."

"It didn't go to the police?"

She shook her head. "Craig had disconnected the part that called the police directly. We'd had too many false alarms, and the company threatened to start charging us. They normally called Craig, and he went to check things out. Since Craig obviously wasn't answering, I guess I was next on the list. When I went over there, the door was jimmied and the place was a mess. I figured if I took the computer, the police would just blame whoever broke in." She blew out a breath. "I shoved it in this little shed off the alley. We never used it for anything but rock salt and our snow shovels. Nobody ever thought to check there."

"But you also broke into Craig's house?"

"If he was stupid enough to leave evidence all over his computer . . ."

"What did you find?"

"Dirty laundry. A messy bathroom. Dishes in the sink. Typical guy place. Oh, why? *Why* did he have to be so secretive?"

"Maxine. All those things. The computer. The break-in. They're minor. The big thing is the murder. And I know you didn't kill Craig. You were with me."

Tears continued to stream down her face as she forged ahead, her driving growing increasingly erratic.

How could she have killed Craig? We'd arrived at his room at the same time. Unless . . .

"You didn't want to ride together because you wanted to get there before me. Did you even go home to feed your cat?"

"This was before I hacked his laptop. When I still thought we might have . . . some kind of relationship. The fall threw me, you know? Like it was a reminder that I might not have forever to get around to telling him I was his mother."

"So I went a little early. I called the hospital and got his room number. Just in case you were already waiting in the lobby, I went in the back way by the cafeteria. He was chatty and talkative when I got there, just propped up in the bed."

"So you told him you were his mother?"

"I started to. But you know how I beat around the bush. I had just gotten to the topic of mothers, and he began yammering. He told me all about how he'd bilked all these stupid women. He was bragging. You don't want to know the words he used or the names he called them. It's like he had no filter at all."

"That was the drug," I said. "It acts like a truth serum."

"So he really meant what he said." A hitch in her voice had softened the last part. "I had to know for sure. 'What about your real mother?' I asked him.

"He laughed. 'Why would I want a mother?' he said. 'What's she going to do, bake me cookies?' Then he just swore and said he wished I was dead. Or wished his mother was dead. I never got to tell him."

"But he was alive when you left."

"I didn't leave. I just sat in the chair, dumbfounded." She bit her lower lip and negotiated the car through a last-minute turn, screeching the tires. "I don't know if it was what the hospital gave him, or if that drug was still in his system, but in five minutes, he was sleeping.

"He looked so peaceful. So much like he did when he was a baby. I knew then it was time to finish what I should have done in the first place."

"*Should have done*? Maxine, you tried to kill him before?"

"A few weeks after he was born. He was a mistake, you know. His father wasn't in the picture, and my parents pretty much showed me the door. He was doomed from the very beginning. What kind of life did I have to offer him? He wouldn't stop crying and I had no sleep. I'd held a pillow over him then too, until he was still. When I lifted the pillow, he looked so peaceful. Only then I chickened out." She shook her head. "They took him away from me. Oh, I got counseling. They blamed it on chemicals in my brain, you see. Postpartum depression. But it turns out I was right. Not only Craig, but a lot of people would have been better off if I finished the job."

We were coming up on a police car parked on the side of the road. We had to be going over the speed limit, and I waved frantically as we passed. The same young officer who had been following me the day I crashed into the pie vendor at the flea market was sitting behind the wheel. He'd recognized the car. And he . . . waved back.

"He knows what side his bread is buttered on." Maxine snorted. "He's not going to pull over his boss's girlfriend."

Not unless I could get his attention. I lunged for the steering wheel just as she was making a turn.

We struggled for control, the car jerking to the left and then to the right, even as Maxine pushed down on the accelerator and the car gained speed.

As we hit the curb, my head struck the roof, and every bone in my body jolted. The car went airborne and started to spin. Next thing I knew, glass and splinters flew everywhere. The car came to a sudden stop, and the air bags pushed me back even as momentum threw me forward against my seat belt. Water poured in. Before I could figure out where the water was coming from, I knew we were stopped. I reached for the door handle, but it didn't budge.

I could hear screaming, but I just wanted to—had to—get out of that car. I found the seat belt and unbuckled myself and started to climb out of the window.

Arms reached in to help me. Someone told me to stay where I was, but I ignored the voice. "Call the police," I croaked. Once outside, I looked back at the car. Maxine was drenched and slumped against the steering wheel and deflated air bag. The windshield was gone. And several large lobsters flopped around sluggishly on the hood of the car.

We'd crashed into the new seafood restaurant—and directly into that spiffy three-hundred-gallon lobster tank.

Chapter 26

Dad, Ken, and Howard Reynolds arrived at the same time.

The emergency room staff still had me hooked up to a couple of monitors, and for some reason, they'd decided I needed an IV, even though it was only a glucose solution. A few cuts, probably from the aquarium glass—which broke into shards instead of blunt little nuggets like the windshield had—had been cleaned and bandaged. They were concerned about my head and neck, and I was immobilized pretty well until they could get me in to "take some pictures," as they called it. But they were taking their own sweet time about it, so I doubted they believed they'd find anything serious. I had a feeling I was about to discover how good that health insurance Dad had bought for all of us in the shop actually was when these deductibles started adding up.

Dad rushed in like he wanted to hug me but wasn't sure how to navigate all the medical equipment or the braces they'd used to stabilize my head and neck. He reached over to kiss my cheek, then grabbed my hand instead. "You look awful."

"Just what every woman wants to hear."

Dad hovered in closer. "Have they looked at your nose yet?"

"Everything else."

"It's swollen, but it looks straight. Maybe it'll be okay if they ice it. I think you have a couple of black eyes starting, though."

"He's right, Liz," Ken said. "You look . . ."

"Don't say it," I warned him. "All told, I don't feel too bad."

"Sorry, Lizzie, but you will," Dad said.

"I'll be back to get a statement," Reynolds said. "I want to check on the other patient."

His voice trailed off as he escaped the confines of my curtained-off area, but then I lost track of him. I knew that Maxine had been taken somewhere else after our arrival, but where she went and how she was doing wasn't shared with me.

Ken ducked out too. A moment later, he returned with a chair for my dad.

Dad sank down into it and rested his cane on the floor. "I'm so sorry. I had no idea I was . . ."

"Sending the killer along to protect me?" I said. "How could you?"

"How did you figure it out?" Dad asked.

"She was that missing factor we were talking about. Someone who had motive to wipe the laptop, steal the computer, and break into Craig's house. She knew that if police found those files, it wouldn't be long before they'd be looking at her as a suspect. And I have to think she also wanted to protect his memory a little by hiding those things she thought shamed him."

"But this was after she killed him?" Ken said.

"I think there's a lot more to that story," I said. "I'm not sure she ever got over the grief of losing her son." I had to stop for a moment. She'd loved him, tried to kill him, yet still somehow wanted him in her life. I suspect the image of the distraught young woman she had been, alone with a crying baby and a pillow, would haunt me far longer than any demon-eyed Santa. "She didn't give Craig up voluntarily."

Dad squeezed my hand tighter.

"I liked her," I said. "I really did."

"I did too." Dad stood up to grab some tissues from the nightstand and dabbed my eyes. "Trust me, Lizzie, you don't want to cry with a broken nose."

I sniffed, although it didn't help. Nothing was going in or out of my nostrils, and I had a sinking suspicion Dad was right about the nose. "What is this going to mean for Amanda and Kohl?"

"Probably not all that much," Dad said. "They didn't know of her relationship to Craig, and even if that comes out, they weren't that close to Craig in the first place."

"Will it have to come out?" I asked.

"That Kohl's grandma was a looney who killed his dad? It's going to be hard to keep under wraps," Dad said. "It depends on what happens with Maxine."

"What do you mean?" I asked.

Dad looked at Ken, then at me. "She hasn't regained consciousness yet. You know what that can mean."

I did. Long hours of waiting. Of not knowing.

"Ken?" a voice called from the hallway.

Ken pulled open the curtain. "Back here."

BARBARA EARLY

And soon an unfamiliar face popped into view. Only not totally unfamiliar. "You," I said. "You were the one asking about graded comics."

I looked to Ken for answers.

"Liz, I'd like you to meet Mark Baker, FBI accountant extraordinaire." Ken turned back to Mark. "That's Liz McCall. Usually she's a lot prettier."

"I know," he said. "We've met. At that fiasco of a train show." He elbowed Ken. "And you make it sound like I audit the FBI. I'm really a forensic accountant. I follow the money."

"Is that what you were doing at the train show?" I asked. "Following the money?"

"When I pulled up the video footage at the station, I recognized Mark right away," Dad said. "Ken phoned him, and he agreed to meet us to talk. He'd just arrived when the call came."

Baker nodded. "McFadden posted those comic books on Craigslist. They popped up on our radar because those same books, similar condition, were reported stolen two years ago. One or two of the same titles might have been coincidence. But five or more rare comics? I had to check it out. I called McFadden, and he said he'd bring those issues to the show."

"Only when you got there . . ."

"I didn't hear McFadden had died until later that night. I just figured that someone else got them before I did or that somehow Craig was onto me."

"We have the books," Ken said.

"I'll be needing them as part of my investigation."

Ken crossed his arms and glared. "When we're done with them as part of *our* investigation." Then he burst out laughing.

"Sorry, I've always wanted to say that. Since they're unrelated to the murder, I don't think that will be a problem. Talk to Reynolds, though. He's got a couple of men in custody you might be interested in."

Dad pushed out of his chair. "Reynolds is down the hall checking on a suspect. If you'd like, I can walk you down."

With promises to return, Dad led Baker away, and Ken sat in the vacated chair.

After several minutes of silence, I asked, "Do I look that bad?"

Ken nodded absentmindedly, then caught himself. "Sorry. Still processing. Liz . . ." He took my hand. "If I'd have known that your involvement in this case would lead to that horrific accident, I would never have let you get involved."

"*Let* me?"

"That didn't come out right. It's different for your father. He's a trained professional."

"He's a *retired* trained professional. And if you recall, I was on record for you not involving him in cases from the beginning. I just tagged along to make sure he came home at night."

"But that's not what you were doing, was it? You were off on your own investigation."

"Not entirely on my own . . ."

"Liz, the fact that you took the killer along with you to question a witness may not be your best defense right now."

"I can't believe we're having this conversation. What is it that you're trying to say that can't wait until I get out of the hospital?"

He rested his forearms on the bed rail. "Liz, my job is stressful enough. I don't know if I can do it if I have to worry about whether I'm going to get a call that you've been in a terrible accident while off on your own . . . or even not on your own," he said before I could object again, "chasing some some criminal. I guess I'm looking for assurances that this was some kind of aberration."

"Huh," I said as I rested against the pillow. Ken's concerns had mirrored my own reservations about being involved with a cop. Could I give him those assurances? Crime wasn't something I sought out. My only involvement had been to keep Dad safe. And yes, it was true that I'd discovered some latent talent. And if I admitted the truth, some satisfaction in working out the puzzle of the case. I wasn't so sure that if Dad stepped into something else, I wouldn't follow him right into the thick of things again. Just to keep Dad safe, of course. But that last bit rang false, even without being said.

"Where does that leave us?" I asked.

He squeezed my hand and leaned in for a gentle, perhaps friendly, kiss on the cheek. "I think we ought to take it slow. Besides, when you're feeling better, there are a few things we need to talk about."

# # #

By the time Thanksgiving rolled around, I was just starting to feel like myself.

Dad had been right, of course. My "I don't feel too bad" declaration in the hospital was followed by days of aches and pains from injuries I hadn't originally felt and from sore muscles and joints complaining about the jolt of the accident. Probably better than Maxine, though. Even though she'd awakened after a day in ICU, she still had quite a road to recovery.

Dad managed to acquire a frozen turkey early enough to defrost. I had let it brine overnight, and Thanksgiving morning found me up early in our cozy little apartment, where I decided to sit and chop vegetables for the dressing at the table rather than stand at the counter.

"Let me get that," he said as I was about to pick up the large roaster to place in the preheated oven.

I took my hands off the roaster and let him. Dad's insistence on doing the heavy lifting reminded me again of my care for him following his release from the hospital, although his recovery had been much more extensive. I hadn't even been admitted, although it was morning before I'd been able to go home. And either the painkillers were making me forget or I'd blocked out trying to climb the stairs to the apartment.

With the turkey now roasting, I poured myself another cup of coffee and sat down next to Dad, who was reading his paper. "Dad?"

"Hmm," he said without looking up.

"I want to talk about Ken."

He folded up his paper. "Is Ken coming today? I'd hoped you'd invited him."

"I didn't invite him. He's actually working today so some of his guys can celebrate with their families. We decided to take things slow."

"What does that mean?"

"I haven't the foggiest," I said. "I'd like to think it's just a speed bump that we'll get over, but I'm not quite sure it's that simple. It seems we're too alike in the wrong way. Both of us are afraid of committing to someone who'll make us worry about . . . disturbing phone calls."

"There's a way to block those," Dad said.

"I'm not talking about telemarketers. And I think you know that."

He scrubbed his face with his hands. "I know exactly what he means. Thanks to what happened"—he picked up the wrist brace I'd set aside to do my chopping—"I now know what you mean when you remind me I'm retired and tell me to stay at home."

"*Ask* you to stay at home."

"That's not how it sounds to me," he said. "And I unfortunately now know what your mother meant, early on, when she tried to tell me the same thing. Before I shut her out and ruined her life."

"Dad . . ." I put a hand on his forearm. "If anyone ruined Mom's life, it was Mom."

He nodded but remained grim. "I like Ken. But if either of you have any doubts, don't make the same mistake I did."

"If you didn't involve yourself in any more investigations . . ."

"I've promised that a million and a half times. Both to myself and to you." He shook his head. "I can't keep that promise."

"What about the toyshop? It was always your dream."

"You know dreams. They have a tendency to fade come morning."

I must have looked alarmed. "I'm not giving up the shop," he said. "But aside from your injuries, I do feel good that Craig's killer is behind bars. Or will be. I hear they're probably going to release her from the hospital tomorrow."

"To jail?" I said.

"Psych exam first, then we'll see. She didn't pop up on anybody's radar because she had no criminal record."

"She tried to kill her own baby once."

"Yeah, but charges were never filed. She'd been under a doctor's care for the postpartum problems—I don't know much more about that. Records are sealed. But I gather the doctors all thought she'd recovered quite well, considering. Not sure if they'll try an insanity defense, but you have to admit, she had a pretty loco motive. Locomotive. Huh?"

I winced. "I should've seen that one coming. How many train puns do you know, anyway?"

"No idea. I've lost track."

"It's still a little sad that Craig never got to know his mother," I said. "Or Kohl, his grandmother. Do we know how she found Craig without him suspecting?"

"One of the forensics tech guys found some cookies on Craig's computer?" He shrugged as if this made no sense. "I'm an Oreo man, myself, unless I can score some homemade chocolate chips." He looked up hopefully.

"If I have the ingredients."

"As for Kohl, he might be better not knowing. Think about it. If Maxine hadn't been caught, what if someday she decided that Kohl looked peaceful when he was asleep?"

I shuddered. "As horrifying as that car ride was, if it means Kohl is safe, I'd do it all again."

"See. You get it."

I sighed. I couldn't promise to "stay out of trouble" any more than Dad could.

# # #

"Did you bring the turkey?" Parker asked, peering in the back seat of the Civic. But the only things there were two cat carriers. Despite our best attempts to get Maxine's cat and Othello to bond, they still hissed at each other. Parker had volunteered to play cat whisperer and told us to bring both of them along to see if he couldn't get them to play nice.

"In the trunk," I said, "along with the dressing, gravy, mashed potatoes, and some chocolate chip cookies."

He hugged me. "Love you, sis." When I popped the trunk, he lifted the lid on the large roaster pan. "Aw, you've already carved it. Now I don't get to demonstrate my awesome knife skills."

Dad nudged him. "We were worried you'd attempt surgery and try to bring it back to life."

Parker snagged a piece of thigh meat. "The poor fellow hasn't died in vain."

Dad grabbed the carriers, and we climbed the steps. The most amazing smells greeted us when I opened the door. Cinnamon and apple and maple and pumpkin and a touch of nutmeg.

"Are we in the right house?" Dad whispered.

"What are you cooking?" I asked Cathy, then lifted the latch to let Othello out. He went immediately over to the other closed carrier and started sniffing the door. A hiss came from inside.

"It smells wonderful in here."

"Yankee Candle, actually." She winced. "I'm sorry, but due to circumstances beyond our control, there'll be no green bean casserole this year."

When she returned to the kitchen, Parker stepped in the door with another load of food. "We were this close to calling the fire department," he whispered, then craned his neck to make sure Cathy couldn't overhear. "Just about everything should be safe, but if you value your life, skip the coleslaw."

Cathy's dining room was lovely, even if the scented candles were a little overwhelming.

Dad blinked twice, apparently feeling the same sting I was, then announced loudly, "Look at that. I think it's warm enough to open the windows this year." He opened the slider.

"Look who I found wandering out front," Parker said, ushering in Amanda and Kohl.

Amanda was carrying a large divided tray.

Cathy poked her head out of the kitchen to say hello. "You didn't have to bring anything."

"Just something Kohl and I do every year. He wanted to bring it."

Kohl smiled that shy smile of his, and Cathy lifted the lid. The divided tray held popcorn, pretzels, jelly beans, and toast.

Cathy looked a little confused, but Dad chuckled. "What a great idea," he said. "Kohl, we like Snoopy too."

"Wonderful," Cathy said. "How about we keep it for game time after dinner?"

By this time, a full growl was coming, not from any stomachs, but from the cat carrier.

Parker lifted it up and sent a stern glare to Maxine's black cat, who quieted down instantly. "Let me see what I can do with these two." He glanced up at me. "Have you figured out her name yet?"

I shook my head. "Maxine never called her anything but kitty, so I guess we're free to name her anything we want. Just haven't figured it out yet."

"Poor nameless kitty," he crooned into the carrier and was rewarded with a purr. He headed toward the back bedroom. "Come on, Othello," he said, and Othello followed obediently.

I shook my head as the door closed. "Cathy, your husband is amazing."

"Don't I know it," she said, then winked. "I hear he comes from good stock."

Amanda got Kohl settled in the family room where Dad turned on the game, then she joined Cathy and me in the kitchen.

"How are you feeling?" Amanda pointed to my wrist brace. "I heard about your accident."

"On the mend," I said. "I feel bad about recommending Maxine. I never would have if I'd known." I hadn't even considered her a suspect, perhaps because she was standing with me in the hallway outside of Craig's hospital room when the medical personnel were running in. That puzzled investigators too, until the ME explained to Ken that while Craig's fatal heart attack was brought on by his suffocation, that effect wasn't necessarily immediate.

"It still doesn't make any sense," Amanda said. "What did she have to gain from killing Craig?" I caught Cathy's eye, but neither of us volunteered any more information. All the sordid details would eventually come out, but they didn't have to come out on a holiday.

Dinner was very edible this year, and after we ate—but before dessert—we squeezed in two rounds of Pictionary.

Kohl was a force to be reckoned with. Whichever team he was on won, but at the end of the second game, it was clear he was becoming overwhelmed with the stimulation.

"Why don't you go draw in the family room?" Amanda said.

Kohl didn't meet her gaze but carried his bag to the coffee table next to the sofa where the two cats were sleeping. They weren't quite cuddling up together, but definitely coexisting.

Cathy stood at the white board we'd set up for the game. "I hate to erase this," she said, pointing to Kohl's last drawing. "He is really good, you know."

"That's exactly what Tippi Hillman told me yesterday," Amanda said.

"So you met Tippi?" I asked. "I thought she might come looking for you."

"She was keen on getting her hands on the rest of Craig's comic books," Amanda said. "I told her I didn't have access to them yet."

"I take it the police still have Craig's computer," I said.

She nodded. "Which will be returned to me eventually. Tippi was willing to wait."

"You didn't sign anything, did you?"

"Not until I find a good property rights attorney. She did tell me that she wanted to continue Craig's series, and she brought along one of Craig's comic books. While she was giving me her spiel, Kohl started copying some of the pictures and drawing them into his notebook. She got all excited. Kohl got excited. She asked him if he wanted to draw comics like his father."

"What did he say?" I asked.

Amanda smirked. "He frowned, and I was about to tell him that he didn't have to draw anything he didn't want to. But then he said he didn't want to draw *like* his father. He wanted to draw *better*."

Parker wet his finger and gave Kohl a point on an imaginary scoreboard.

"So if Craig's series sells, Tippi was going to see if she could find someone to continue to write the stories and have Kohl illustrate them." She took a breath. "I have reservations. I don't want to capitalize on Craig's misfortune, or even on Kohl's challenges, but if it's what he's good at and what he wants to do, I could hardly stand in his way, either. But I'd also like to find a teacher who'd help him develop his own style, not just copy."

"If you're planning on staying," Dad said, "there are classes at the art store, and the Albright-Knox Art Gallery in Buffalo has a program for teens as well."

"I'll have to look into that." She smiled. "And yes, we've decided to stay. I can't move into the house until all the paperwork is done, but I saw it and just fell in love with it—or rather what it could be with a little work. And the whole community has impressed me. The schools look good. Even Kohl said he wants to stay, and I have a hard time even getting him to change his socks sometimes."

"Does that mean you'll keep the comic book store open?" I asked.

"I was hoping we could talk about that today." She cast Dad a hopeful look. "I just don't think I'm the entrepreneurial type, especially since I don't know enough about comic books to make a go of it. Is that offer to buy the stock still good?"

Dad gave me his best "what do you think?" look.

I sent back my "where will we put them?" raising of the eyebrows.

Dad responded with his best "get ready because I'm doing it anyway" expression. Too bad we hadn't played charades tonight. We would have cleaned up.

"Yes," he said to Amanda.

"Only I need to be out of the shop by Monday," she hedged.

"How about Dad and I stop by tomorrow and finalize the details?" I said.

"Sold," she said, shaking our hands. "Now all I have to do is find a job."

"What do you do?" Dad asked.

"Mostly just worked retail," she said.

Dad looked at me. I looked at him. This time we agreed. "You know, we've been looking for some help . . ." I said.

Chapter 27

Parker waved from his lawnmower as he pulled our float past my spot on the toyshop stoop. He'd constructed a giant toy box. Every so often, the classic toys inside would rise up a little, like they were growing out of the box. I started laughing when I noticed that a large box with a cellophane front didn't contain a life-sized doll, but a real-life Cathy posing as a doll. The audience packing the sidewalks must have liked it too; they cheered as it went past.

The hopes and predictions of the chamber of commerce were met or exceeded. The street was mobbed, and hopefully all these folks would soon spill into the shops—in particular, ours. They wouldn't find comic books, though, at least not yet, even though we spent most of yesterday rolling them across the street on Craig's cart—Amanda had thrown that into the deal along with the store fixtures. It was all still sitting upstairs, packing our living room, and the only thing Dad would say was that he was almost sure he could make it work.

To give credit where it was due, Maxine had done such a good job cleaning the comic book shop—before she almost killed me, that is—that Amanda's landlord had given her Craig's security deposit back. I expected the cash was more than welcome to help cover their transitional costs until Craig's estate could be fully settled. The next tenant would have to do very little except refurnish it for his business.

"Oh, what's moving in?" I'd asked.

"A private investigator," the landlord said. I was considering whether a quiet community like ours could support a full-time PI, but I figured even a bedroom community such as ours must have its share of infidelity investigations. With all those bedrooms, someone somewhere was probably in the wrong one.

"Former cop," he added. "Gave you as a character reference, in fact," he said, gesturing to my dad, "which was good enough for me. Name of Lionel Kelley . . ."

A brisk breeze drew my attention from my daydreams and back to the parade. Some of the Irish dancers looked a little frozen, and the sky was a bit more overcast than it had been of late, but it didn't rain. Another gust blew away a few balloons, and I found myself thinking of Craig even as they rose in the sky and disappeared.

I was still a bit distracted, watching one rise, swirling in the air currents, when Ken pushed his way through the crowd and climbed onto the stoop. "Liz, we've got to talk."

I'd been avoiding this. I still didn't know how to make our relationship work. "If it's about what we talked about . . ."

"No, this is something different, and I kind of need you to know something before it comes out. It's better if you hear it from me." He looked around uneasily. "Can we go inside?"

"But the parade . . ."

He grabbed my arm. "Please, Liz. It's important."

"There you are!" a husky voice said, and a willowy blonde climbed onto the stoop and took Ken's arm. Dad had to step back so there'd be room.

Ken looked as happy to see her as a middle schooler whose mother had signed up as class chaperone. She stuck out a hand. "Nice to meet you. I am Marya Young," she said in a slight Russian accent.

"Liz McCall," I said, shaking her hand. "Relative?" I asked Ken.

Ken blanched, swallowed, and then said, "Liz, I'd like you to meet . . . my wife."

I don't recall how I responded. But not long after, we were all standing on the stoop together, silently watching the rest of the parade.

My cheeks flared hot, even in the cooling temperatures, while my thoughts cycled back and forth from *How could he?* to *How could I not know?*

I missed much of the parade. It just passed. Bands, floats, dancers, even the clowns driving the little cars. They just all melted together like chalk art in a rainstorm.

Then the music switched to "Here Comes Santa Claus," and the Santa train came into view.

Annie Werth had made good on her promise to play Santa, and she was ho-ho-hoing up a storm. I hadn't known—but from Dad's sly smile when I looked up at him, I think he did—that Frank was riding the engine too, fully decked out in his engineer's hat and costume. Both waved to the crowd.

Then the wind picked up. Annie made a grab for her Santa hat, but the wind carried it away, along with the white wig.

The crowd gasped, and several mothers covered their children's eyes.

At first Frank didn't know the reason for the crowd reaction, but when he spun around, he got a good look at Santa. He tugged off her beard, just to be sure. Frank must have let go of the controls at the same time, because the train came to a halt in front of the toyshop.

Dad tapped Ken on the shoulder. "If that gets ugly, you might have to . . ."

But after a couple of looks and brief words, Frank leaned down to hug Annie, followed by the longest, most passionate kiss ever witnessed between a train conductor and Santa Claus. A few people applauded, and one fellow nearby shouted, "Get a room, Santa!" A few wolf calls followed.

Dad squeezed my hand. "At least I'm still batting five hundred."

Acknowledgments

The hardest part about writing acknowledgments is trying to mentally replay all those moments where so many people helped in any part of the process so you don't leave anyone out. The second hardest part is getting the names spelled correctly.

First, I'd like to thank my husband, Rob, who really makes my writing possible. My words tend to come in spurts, fueled by inspiration and looming deadlines. When those long days occur, it helps to have someone who'll do things like toss in a load of laundry, read over a passage I'm struggling with, or whisk me off to dinner when he knows I need a break.

And then there are my local writing friends. Thanks to my regular critique partners: Lynne Wallace-Lee, Aric Gaughan, Nonna Gerikh, Katie Murdock, and Ken Swiatek. And to my fellow Sisters in Crime: Alice Loweecey (who often shares rides to events, more than one of which evolved into brainstorming sessions) and Lissa Redmond (who painstakingly answers my police procedure questions—any mistakes are because I didn't think to ask the right questions). Also to Janice Cline, who reads all my earliest efforts.

Of course, to the good folk of East Aurora—and yes, it's a real place—thanks for providing such a cozy town for inspiration. And for patiently putting up with me when I either get it wrong or have to play havoc with the geography to suit a story. So sorry for the crime wave!

Many thanks, as always, to my superagent, Kim Lionetti, and to all the staff at Crooked Lane.

And thanks to you, the reader. There are many books on the shelves, and you picked this one. I hope you've enjoyed the time we've spent together!

Acknowledgments

I am indebted to numerous individuals and organizations for their help in researching and writing this story.

My critique partner, Penny Linsenmayer, who first showed me an old newspaper article online and asked, "Did you know that women cut down trees during the war?" Penny and I can talk WWII for hours on end, and she seems happy to keep me company at ridiculous hours in Starbucks and Barnes and Noble cafés while we write our books.

My friend Kenneth Taylor, who has worked in the Scottish forests his entire career and who introduced me to the real Mrs. McRobbie, a lady who fell in love as a teenager with the woods and with a woodsman. I was so sorry she left us before she had a chance to read Maisie's story.

James McDougall of Forestry Commission Scotland, who worked so hard to make the Lumberjills Memorial a reality, sixty years after their contribution should have been marked, and who introduced me to my very own lumberjill.

Mrs. Christina Forrester, who was a lumberjill from 1942

to 1945, and who was so kind and generous with her memories and enthusiastic support. She can have no idea how moved I was to sit with her at the feet of the Lumberjill Memorial this summer, hoping that I have done a little bit to contribute toward a wider recognition of her war service and that of her WTC colleagues. Thanks, too, to her daughters, Irene and Christine, for joining us.

Mairi Stewart, whose fabulous book *Voices of the Forest: A Social History of Scottish Forestry in the Twentieth Century* (Edinburgh: Birlinn, 2016) gave me so much written and photographic information. Mairi herself then filled in numerous gaps in my manuscript.

The late Affleck Gray, who worked with the lumberjills throughout the war and who knew it was important to record their stories. His collection of their memories, *Timber!: Memories of Life in the Scottish Women's Timber Corps, 1942–46*, Flashbacks series (Edinburgh: Tuckwell Press, 1998) gave me enough to fill five lumberjill novels.

David Gilhen, who runs a Facebook page in memory of the men of the Halifax 100, and who kindly shared with me his time and extensive knowledge to make sure I got that part of John's story right.

Dr. John Prescott of Guelph University for his advice about the estate of John McCrae.

Everyone on the Facebook group Inverness Then and Now, who had such fun arguing with each other when I asked about which dance hall John would have taken Maisie to.

Our two sensitivity readers, who were asked to read my

manuscript with particular regard to my representation of an amputee and of someone dealing with post-traumatic stress disorder. Both readers gave me great insight into these experiences, both internal emotions and outward perceptions, and I hope that I have used their advice respectfully to strengthen John's storyline even further. They both made me understand that the experience of living as an amputee and with a prosthesis, or with PTSD, is very different for each person, and it is therefore impossible for any author to claim to represent the entirety of either one of these conditions through a single character. However, I have tried to offer this portrayal of John, his experiences and his injuries, with the utmost respect to all those who have dealt with, and continue to deal with, these issues.

All my bookish friends—readers and writers—who kept telling me I'm doing okay, especially the 2017 Debuts, the SCBWI members in Houston and Austin, everyone at Inprint, Writers in the Schools, Brazos Bookstore, Blue Willow Bookshop, and my wonderful critique group, Andrea White, Chris Cander, Tobey Forney, Mimi Vance, and Penny Linsenmayer. It is your support, your passion, and your ability to challenge all my preconceptions about life that keep me writing.

To Jordan Hamessley, my literary agent at New Leaf Literary & Media, who represents me and my stories, and who seems happy to talk me down off the ceiling every so often. Thanks too must go to Joanna Volpe and Devin Ross for all their support.

To Alice Jerman, my wonderful editor at HarperTeen,

who took a chance on me and my debut, *Wait for Me*, and who loves Maisie, John, and the lumberjills just as much as I do. Knowing that I was writing this book just for Alice—to appeal to her interest in history, her great sense of humor, and her love of kissing scenes—made it all so much easier this time round. And also to the rest of the team at HarperTeen, and at Harper Collins Children's Books in the UK—including, Alison Klapthor, Renée Cafiero, Sabrina Abballe, Michael D'Angelo, Gina Rizzo, and Jean McGinley—and particularly to Aurora Parlagreco, who yet again designed for me a beautiful jacket cover which so perfectly tells you about the story inside.

All these people have generously shared so much of their knowledge and wisdom with me, and for that I am so grateful. However, please know that the responsibility is entirely mine for all the places I've stretched the facts for my own ends, or where I've just got something wrong.

Finally, I would also have been unable to write this book without the unswerving support of my parents, James and Shirley Sibbald, who lived through World War II and who have shared their memories with me throughout my life, and my sister, Jane Andrew, who loves me even though I make her roll her eyes on a regular basis.

And finally, for the support, the care, the fun, and the constant love they give me every day, this book is dedicated to my husband, Perryn, and my amazing children, Jemma, Kirsty, and Rory. I would be nothing without all four of you.